THE ILLUSTRATED
Faerie Queene

Edmund Spenser

THE ILLUSTRATED

Faerie Queene

A MODERN PROSE ADAPTATION
BY DOUGLAS HILL

Newsweek Books
NEW YORK · LONDON

FRONTISPIECE:
Queen Elizabeth going in procession to Blackfriars in 1600. Such processions were elaborately stagemanaged and designed to provide splendid demonstrations of the power of the monarchy.

First published in the United States of America in 1980 by Newsweek Books, New York

First published in the United Kingdom in 1980 by Newsweek Books, London

This book was designed and produced by
Russel Sharp Limited
66 Woodbridge Road
Guildford, Surrey GU1 4RD

Designed: Trevor Vincent
Picture researcher: Anne-Marie Ehrlich

Text set by SX Composing Ltd, England
Printed in Hong Kong by Dai Nippon Printing Co. (HK) Ltd.

Library of Congress Cataloging in Publication Date
Hill Douglas Arthur 135
The Illustrated Faerie Queene includes index
Summary: Follows the adventures of Twelve Knights each an
        example of a different virtue as they undertake
        difficult quests for their queen
1 Spenser Edmund 15527–1599 adaptions
2 Knights and Knighthood—fiction 1 Spenser
Edmund 1552–1599 Faerie Queene 11 Title
PZ4H64521 (PR9199.3.H477) 813.54 (FIC)

ISBN 0-88225-297.6 80-392

CONTENTS

For Sheila Watson
adviser, confidant, friend

'Ne wanted ought, to shew her bounteous or wise'
[FQ I.x.ll.]

Introduction

All the beauty, grandeur, and drama of *The Faerie Queene* were inspired by the reign of Queen Elizabeth I. When she came to the throne in 1558, England was torn by national and international crises; but during her forty-five-year rule Elizabeth brought the nation out of that chaos, leading it into a period of unprecedented prosperity and power and also to a glorious cultural renaissance. Edmund Spenser was a small child when the young Elizabeth became queen, and he grew to manhood in the exhilarating first two decades of England's revival. It was that achievement, the greatness to which Elizabeth led the nation, that Spenser set out to celebrate and honour in his masterpiece, *The Faerie Queene*.

Certainly Elizabeth had needed all her qualities of courage, character and will to face the challenges that awaited her accession. In the 1550s England was in serious decline—nearly bankrupt, falling far behind her rivals in Europe, fighting a debilitating war with France while living in fear of the mighty Spain. Religious and political strife had been weakening the country ever since Henry VIII, Elizabeth's father, had broken from the Roman Catholic Church. And these upheavals had worsened during the reign of Elizabeth's half-sister, Mary Tudor (1553–58), who briefly restored Catholicism to England. With the Protestant Elizabeth's accession civil war became an alarming possibility—especially with the threat to the young queen's position that was offered by the Catholic adherents of Mary Stuart, Queen of Scots.

But Elizabeth had a genius for the mechanisms of power. With the aid of wise and wily statesmen like Lord Burghley (or Burleigh) and Sir Francis Walsingham, she quickly made peace with France while keeping pace with Spain. She reformed the currency and put the economy on its feet by encouraging English seafarers, like Francis Drake and John Hawkins, to explore, colonize, and open new avenues of trade. And she urged through Parliament a religious "settlement" that eased the dangerous divisions in the nation. The queen insisted on a spirit of tolerance; during her reign religious persecution almost vanished, even if prejudice did not.

Perhaps most important, she carefully built up a special relationship with the English people. She used every available device, from propaganda to pageantry, to transform herself into an almost mythical figure. Her court teemed with glittering heroes, like Sir Walter Raleigh, the Earl of Leicester, and Sir Philip Sidney, whose successes and fame magnified her own. She became the Virgin Queen, wedded, in her own words, solely to her people. And they responded not only with loyalty and devotion but with fervent love, seeing her as both the source and the symbol of a new national identity and pride, a new spirit of excitement, energy and expansion. That spirit was particularly expressed in the new literature of the time. Its greatest flowering was not to come until the later years of Elizabeth's reign, but there were some early blooms, full of promise, such as the prose of John Lyly, the early verse of Raleigh, and the first major work of Edmund Spenser.

Spenser was born about 1552, the son of a Lancashire clothmaker who lived in London. In 1576 he emerged from Cambridge University with a master's degree, and a burning literary ambition. But most recognized poets of the time were members of the leisured nobility. No one who lacked private means could hope to live as poet without a patron, someone of wealth and influence who could offer financial support and an entry into the only circles that mattered, those in and around the court of Elizabeth.

Luckily for Spenser, he had met Sidney and the Earl of Leicester. And he proved himself worthy of their help when he produced his *Shepheardes Calender* (published in 1579), a sequence of pastoral poems that showed his ability to combine a wealth of material— philosophy, love lyrics, natural description, and social commentary and perfectly expressed the new, vital, Elizabethan spirit.

Thereafter Spenser's future should have been assured, but events went against him. The Earl of Leicester fell from the queen's favour and somehow, perhaps through comments in the *Calender*, Spenser had annoyed Lord Burghley, Elizabeth's premier statesman. Thus the recognition Spenser had won led to only minor "advancement": in 1580 he was appointed private secretary to Lord Grey de Wilton, who was being sent by the queen to deal with a new rebellion in Ireland, which was then in an almost permanent state of insurrection against English rule.

Grey soon crushed the rebellion of 1580, though his near-genocidal methods led to his recall and disgrace. Spenser remained in Ireland as a fairly prosperous civil servant for most of the next twenty years. He visited London several times.

These were the years when England emerged, after destroying the

Spanish Armada in 1588, a newly dominant world power. The economy was booming and an empire of trade and colonization was in the making. These events had their cultural equivalents in the explosive birth of the Elizabethan drama, the first plays of Christopher Marlowe and Thomas Kyd, and the early poems of young William Shakespeare.

All this achievement inspired an unprecedented patriotic fervour. And Spenser, who had in the 1570s decided that a heroic age needed a heroic national poem was spending his years in Ireland writing it.

Like every educated European of his time, Spenser was steeped in the literature of ancient Greece and Rome. But he did not want to model his own poem too closely on Homer's *Iliad* and *Odyssey* or Virgil's *Aeneid*. He sought a contemporary form, and found it in a kind of poem that had emerged from the European renaissance—a blend of the classical epic with the medieval chivalric romance, such as the popular *Roman de la Rose*. The finest example of this "heroic romance" had come from the Italian poet Ariosto in his *Orlando Furioso* (1532), a rich and sprawling poem about Roland, the legendary knight of Charlemagne.

Spenser borrowed freely from Ariosto in nearly everything but approach and tone. Ariosto was sprightly and witty; Spenser was more serious. His work is more like Camoes' *Lusiad* (1572), the "national poem" of Portugal, or the Italian poet Tasso's *Gerusalemme Liberata* (1575). These were the poems that Spenser wanted to emulate—and surpass. They were more in keeping with the Elizabethan belief that great poetry must have a strong moral purpose, that it must contain at least as much educative "moral philosophy" as aesthetic delights.

Naturally, writing a poem that extolled the greatness of England meant writing about the queen, who embodied that greatness. So Elizabeth became Queen Gloriana of Faeryland, her realm peopled by chivalrous knights and lovely ladies, monsters and giants, sorcerers and witches—all the colourful figures of high romance. Gloriana herself does not appear directly in the poem, but her presence is felt throughout, providing a central theme that united Spenser's enormous canvas. More unity and more emphasis on English patriotism is derived from the presence throughout the poem of the legendary Arthur, who as a young prince travelled to Faeryland in search of its magical queen. Otherwise, Spenser planned his poem as twelve more or less separate adventures, each undertaken by a particular knight from Gloriana's court.

Some of these knights were admiring representations of great men of Elizabeth's court. But each knight also explicitly symbolizes one of the essential virtues, as Spenser saw them, that would be found in the ideal chivalric hero and Renaissance man. He had intended to base his choice of virtues on those singled out by Aristotle in his *Ethics*, but in the end he took only Temperance and Justice from that source. For his other central themes he made use of accepted Elizabethan ideas of human excellence.

Spenser's educative moral purpose led him to write his poem in the form of allegory. Behind every character, every relationship, every sumptuous descriptive passage or dramatically violent battle, there lies an instructive meaning, which may be religious, ethical, political, social, or several of these at once. The hero of each book, during his quest, does battle with enemies who represent the vices, temptations, and sins that threaten virtuousness. If he loses one of these battles, he must go through a process of refining and strengthening his principal quality—often with the help of Prince Arthur, who represents all twelve virtues in their perfectly realized and invincible form. In the end virtue triumphs when the knight confronts and overcomes his greatest enemy, and completes his appointed quest.

Though Spenser called his allegory a "dark conceit", the disguises are fairly easy to penetrate. For instance, Elizabethans would not miss the allusions to Catholicism in the enemies of the knight of Holiness, or the image of Ireland in the quest of the knight of Justice. Nor would they be puzzled by the meaning of the knight of Temperence's encounter with Mammon. The very names of most characters, like Duessa, Furor, Medina—reveal what aspect of good or evil they represent, while many minor characters quite plainly bear the names of the abstractions they personify—Despair, Lust, Excess and so on.

Spenser sought to further emphasize his purpose by weaving together elements that enhance the colour and drama of the various stories as well as clarifying their allegorical meaning. For example, evil dwells in atmospheric caves or forests. He brings in classical myth as freely and abundantly as Elizabethan reality. He makes use of symbolism from a huge range of sources—the Bible, classical philosophy, astrology, numerology, colour symbolism, and much more. And he uses his own profound sensitivity to the lives, labours, and loves of ordinary people whether it be the pathos of a lost baby, the misery of a rejected lover, or the broad comedy of a boastful coward.

All these elements are woven together into a pattern whose structure is as beautiful and intricate as that of a great symphony. And they are expressed in poetry that is unsurpassed in its wealth of imagery, its melodic line, its flexible stanzas.

When the first three books of *The Faerie Queene* appeared in 1590 its quality was acclaimed at once. On a visit to London in that year he was presented by Sir Walter Raleigh to the queen, who granted him a small annual pension. After two years in London he returned to Ireland to resume his duties, and to finish his masterpiece. In 1594 he married a well-born Irish woman, Elizabeth Boyle, and the next year furthered his reputation with new poems, including the lovely sonnets of *Amoretti*. The next three books of *The Faerie Queene* were published in 1596, firmly establishing its place as the finest poetic expression of the Elizabethan age.

Then in 1598 rebellion blazed up once again in Ireland. As the violence increased late in that year, Spenser travelled to London. There he fell suddenly ill, and died in January 1599, with his great poem incomplete.

The nation mourned him, and he was buried with every honour in Westminster Abbey, near the resting place of Geoffrey Chaucer. It was an appropriate tribute to his stature, and to the fact that *The Faerie Queene* was indeed the supreme national poem of Elizabethan England, and the greatest achievement in English poetry since Chaucer's *Canterbury Tales*.

Times change, however, as do language, style, and taste. Even in Spenser's own time the dramatist Ben Jonson had worried that Spenser's intentionally archaic, quasi-medieval diction could be a barrier to readers. And it proved to be even more so in later centuries, by which time other stumbling-blocks emerged. Direct, explicit allegory went out of fashion, and fewer readers seemed willing to undertake the task of unravelling the poem's intricate patterns or discovering its historical allusions. And so today, four hundred years later, *The Faerie Queene* has become almost exclusively the concern of scholars and specialists, unfortunately called the least-read great poem in the English language.

It deserves far better. Spenser's poetic language is certainly less remote from us than Chaucer's, his moral purpose less overpowering than Milton's. No one need be a scholar to recognize most of the historical references or grasp the basic, universal truths expressed in the allegory. Nor does one need be a specialist to enjoy the multitude of characters, the exciting action, the magical creatures, the sheer sweep and gorgeousness of the imaginative creation.

And that is the principle behind this abridged "re-telling": to get around the barriers of diction and density, and show modern readers the essence of *The Faerie Queene*—the stories, the settings, the allegorical meanings—enhanced and clarified with illustrations that capture much of the Elizabethan splendour of the original. Necessarily, then, this adaptation carries with it the hope that it will became an introduction and a guide, leading readers to the glory and greatness of the poem itself.

Douglas Hill   London, 1980

BOOK ONE

The Legend of the Knight of the Red Cross, or Holiness

The hero of the book of Holiness, the Red Cross Knight (who is not named until late in the book, though few Anglo-Saxon readers will fail to recognize him), is a young and untried champion sent by Queen Gloriana on a quest of high importance. He is to accompany the lady Una (representing religious Truth, indeed the One Truth) to her own land, and free it from oppression by a frightful dragon. But Una's land is the Garden of Eden, and the dragon is the allegorical figure of Evil itself.

On his way the Red Cross Knight is diverted into various lesser adventures, against some of the forces that oppose holiness, and at first he acquits himself well. But then more deadly enemies—especially the sorcerer Archimago, a figure of Guile and Fraud, and his associate, the *femme fatale* Duessa—gather against the knight. His inner strength proves insufficient: he strays from the true path, and at last is brought down by an evil giant who stands for the sin of Pride.

But the knight is rescued by Una and Prince Arthur, whose own virtuousness is invincible. In the "heavenly" House of Celia the Red Cross Knight is purified and instructed—and then, properly armed now with true holiness, goes into his epic battle against the dragon.

Of course the holiness being presented in this book is in the form that would meet with the approval of Elizabethan English Protestantism. The Red Cross Knight's enemies might include those obvious unholy threats like Pride and Despair; but many of them, from the monster Error at the beginning to the sinister Archimago and Duessa, also reflect what Spenser's world saw as the deadly dangers of Roman Catholicism. So Archimago, for instance, is not merely a representation of Guile. He would also make many Elizabethan readers think of the Pope; and indeed the giant Orgoglio is similarly not only Pride but also one of the personifications of Philip II of Spain, the premier Catholic power and Protestant England's most bitter enemy.

Knight in full armour— seeming as youthful and untried as Spenser's Knight of the Red Cross—painted by Vittore Carpaccio (c.1450–1523).

Across the plain rode a noble knight, in full armour, bearing a silver shield. A surcoat over his armour displayed the emblem of a blood-red cross, and the same design was emblazoned on his shield—displaying to all that the knight was a servant of the Lord who died upon the holy Cross of Calvary.

The knight rode steadily, his solemn face showing the fearless determination of one who lived for knightly combat and heroic deeds. His armour and shield also seemed to bear witness to many fierce encounters, with their several gashes and dents. Yet the knight of the Red Cross had never borne those arms in battle, nor any other. He was riding out towards his first adventure.

Beside him rode a lovely lady, on a palfrey whose hide was a perfect snowy white, yet would have seemed blemished by comparison with the lady's complexion, if she had not kept her face veiled behind her wimple. Over her head, as well, she wore a long black stole, as if she were in mourning, and her posture too hinted at some deep sadness. By her side she led a pet lamb, milk-white, the image of innocence—just as the lady herself was the embodiment of purity and true virtue.

Her name was Una, and she was a princess descended from a line of ancient kings and queens who had, long before, ruled over a vast realm from the eastern to the western sea. But their rule had ended when a monstrous and terrible dragon had come into their kingdom.

It had laid waste the lands with the flame that gushed from its mouth, and had driven the lady's royal parents to take refuge in their sturdy castle, where they remained, besieged by the hellish beast. But Una had fled, and had ridden far to seek a champion who would destroy the dragon.

She had come at last to the court of Gloriana, great queen of Faeryland. And the queen had named the knight of the Red Cross to perform the deed. So they had ridden forth together, the young knight burning with eagerness to confront his foe, to earn honour and to win the queen's approval, which he craved above all else on earth.

The lady Una, who is Truth in Spenser's allegory, leads a pet lamb that symbolizes purity—as does this holy maiden in a detail from Bernardo Martorell's painting (1430) of St. George and the dragon (see p. 45).

As they crossed the plain—with the lady's servant, a dwarf, lagging as always far behind—dark clouds began to gather, and soon they were in a drenching downpour of rain. But ahead they had seen a broad expanse of forest, and they spurred towards it for shelter.

The spread of leaves excluded every drop of rain, but also shut out much of the daylight. Entering the dimness, the lady and the knight saw before them a myriad of paths leading into the forest depths. Idly they began to wander the paths, marvelling at the huge variety of trees that grew on every side.

But when the storm died away, and they sought to retrace their steps, they found that they could not. The paths had become a maze: each one that they chose twisted back upon itself, taking them farther into the forest.

Finally the knight decided to follow the broadest and most worn path, sure that it would bring them at some point to the forest's edge. So they rode on through the labyrinthine ways, the trees ever more dense around them, until in the heart of the forest the path brought them to the black mouth of a cave.

Curious, the knight dismounted, giving his lance into the care of the dwarf. But the lady Una demurred.

"Take care," she said, "that you do not rashly stir up some lurking evil. Hold back, sir knight, till you have made sure of the way ahead."

"It would be shameful, lady," replied the knight, "to be constrained by fear. Honour and virtue must be my light among these shadows."

"I would not ask you to disgrace yourself," said Una. "But I know this place, and the peril that it holds. This forest is called the Wandering Wood, and this cave is the lair of a creature known as Error, hateful to both God and man."

"Come, let us flee," put in the dwarf nervously. "This is no place for living men."

But the knight, youthfully hungry for every chance to prove his worth, brushed aside the warnings and stepped forward to peer into the cave. From his glittering armour a ghostly light reached in to the cave's blackness. And it revealed a huge, deformed shape.

It was a loathsome creature whose upper body was shaped like a woman but its lower half like an enormous serpent, spread in tangled coils over the cave's filthy floor, and bearing at the tip of the tail a scorpion-like sting. Around and over the monster crawled a thousand smaller creatures that were her young—all of different shapes, all of them hideous—whom she suckled with the poison that was their food.

When the glimmering light from the knight's armour penetrated the darkness, these small horrors crept fearfully into their mother's mouth and vanished from sight. Then the mother rose in fury, lifting her tail with the murderous sting, and rushed to the cave mouth.

She saw the waiting knight, and instantly turned to flee, afraid of his shining armour, for she hated light above all things. But the knight drew his sword and leaped into her path. Then her fear turned back to rage: roaring, she again curved up her venomous sting and advanced threateningly.

The knight swung his sword in a mighty blow, the blade glancing from her head to bite deep into her shoulder. Pain lifted the monster's fury even higher, and she sprang upon the knight, winding her serpentine tail around his body. The knight could move neither hand nor foot within the crushing coils of Error.

"Sir knight, be not faint-hearted!" Una cried. "Call upon your faith as well as your strength—strangle the monster before she can strangle you!"

Hearing her words, the knight overcame his moment of weakness. He fought to free one hand, then grasped the monster's throat with such strength that she was forced to relax her coils, to seek her escape.

As she did so she spewed from her mouth a reeking torrent of black vomit, full of half-digested gobbets of flesh, mingled with books and papers and foul eyeless creatures that wriggled or crawled away into the darkness. The poisonous flood sent the knight reeling back, and when the monster saw him falter, she opened her mouth again and belched forth all the small misshapen horrors that were her offspring. They swarmed over the knight, their slimy bodies seeking to entangle him and trip him up.

Then anger and resolution filled the knight, and he struck furiously at the monster with his sword. The blade sliced cleanly through the neck, and noxious black blood gushed forth as the headless corpse of Error toppled to the ground.

The creature's offspring flocked round her gaping wound, sucking at the blood that fountained from it. And their greed betrayed them. Swollen with the gruesome feast, their bellies burst, until all of them lay dead.

The lady Una hurried to the knight. "You have proved well worthy of the arms you bear," she cried. "I pray that you succeed so well in every adventure to come."

They remounted, and again followed the most clearly marked pathway, until at last they emerged from the Wandering Wood and resumed their journey.

Late in the day they came upon an aged, grey-bearded hermit, barefoot and black-robed, seeming most humble and pious. Greeting the old man respectfully, the knight inquired if there was honourable adventure to be sought nearby.

The hermit claimed to know little of such matters, living in his lonely retreat devoted to prayer and religious duty. "Yet there is a wicked one," he added, "dwelling in a wilderness near here, who has been ravaging the countryside."

The young knight was eager at once to pursue the evildoer. But the lady reminded him that night was falling, and that he had already fought one wearying battle that day—at which the hermit agreeably invited them to take their rest in his home.

The hermitage was small and poor, but the knight and the lady spent the evening pleasantly, enjoying the old man's talk of holy men and godly matters. When at last they retired to their beds, the hermit turned studiously to his books.

But they were not books of piety and devotion. They were volumes of dark magic and baleful enchantment. For beneath his hermit's guise the old man was an evil sorcerer of great power, a master of guile and deceit whose name was Archimago.

With spells from his books the magician summoned a host of evil spirits, who swirled around him like flies. He chose two of them for his purposes, and sent one away, bearing a message.

It sped deep into the bowels of the earth, through the twin gates of ivory and silver that led to the home of the god of slumber, Morpheus. Awakening the god, the spirit requested, on Archimago's behalf, the use of a false dream that could delude sleepers. Morpheus complied willingly, producing what the sorcerer wanted out of his dark store of dreams.

Archimago may represent Catholicism, indeed the Pope himself, in Spenser's poem. But he also appears as a generalized figure of Deceit, much like this character from a moral treatise by Henry Peacham, Minerva Britannia *(1612).*

When the spirit bore the dream back to Archimago, the magician had altered the other spirit into the exact semblance of Una. Immediately he sent the false dream into the mind of the sleeping knight, and sent the false Una in its wake.

It was a dream of fleshly pleasure and wanton play, in which Venus herself seemed to bring the lady Una willingly to his bed. And when the knight started awake, appalled by such lewd images, he found that indeed the lady lay beside him, blushing, offering her lips. He sprang up, dismayed at her shamelessness. And she began to weep, begging him to understand her plight—for, she said, she had fallen in love with him, and was sleepless with the fear that he would reject her if he knew.

The knight innocently comforted her. "Lady, your love is as dear to me as life itself, and binds me to you all the more. You need fear no hurt from me: return to your rest, and be no longer troubled."

The false Una, for all her wiles, then had no choice but to withdraw. And the knight lay musing sadly on the apparent immodesty of the lady to whom his service was pledged.

*   *   *

Enraged by the spirit's failure to seduce the Red Cross Knight, Archimago cast a spell on the messenger spirit, transforming it into the shape of a lusty young squire. He placed the two, the squire and the false Una, together in a night-shrouded bed, then—still in his guise of a pious hermit—hastened to the knight, calling him to witness how his lady was dishonouring herself.

The knight sprang up, sword in hand, and followed the old man. When he found the false couple in their passionate embrace, he might have slain them in his rage had not the hermit restrained him. Storming away, he roused the dwarf to prepare their mounts, and rode forth as dawn glimmered in the sky.

The true Una arose soon after sunrise, and was stricken to find herself deserted. Yet she readied her own mount and followed, determined to search for the knight without pause or rest. And Archimago watched gleefully, for he hated Una's purity above all else. He too followed—but first garbed himself with armour and shield exactly like those of the Red Cross Knight.

The true knight had been wandering far away, indifferent in his misery to his path, until he saw an armed warrior approaching. The other was a pagan knight, a Saracen, who bore the words "Sansfoy" on his shield. With him rode a glamorous woman, clad in scarlet and richly bejewelled.

Unhesitatingly the two knights challenged each other, and spurred towards combat, lances couched. Both spears struck at once, so fiercely that the horses were flung back upon their haunches, the lances shattered, and both knights reeled in their saddles.

But they recovered quickly and drew their swords. Stroke for stroke they exchanged, neither yielding a step, while fire sparked and flashed from their shields and blood streamed from their wounds.

"Curse that cross!" roared the Saracen. "You would have been dead long since had you not borne that charm!" As he spoke he slashed mightily at the knight's head. The blow sheared away one side of the knight's helmet, glancing off to notch his shield.

But the Red Cross Knight held firm and replied with a blow of even greater power. The sweeping blade hewed irresistibly into the Saracen's helmet and split his skull, tumbling him dead on to the reddening earth.

Seeing her champion fall, the woman shrieked and fled. The knight ordered the dwarf to bring the Saracen's shield, as was his conqueror's due, and rode in pursuit, calling to the woman that she had nothing to fear from him. She halted, begging him for mercy while he soothed her terror. Reassured at last, she told him her story.

Fidessa was her name, she said, the daughter of an emperor of a western land, and once the betrothed of a fair young prince. But before their wedding the prince had been slain by a cruel enemy, and his corpse spirited away. And ever since she had been mournfully searching for the body of her love. On her travels she had met the Saracen, Sansfoy—eldest of three brothers, the other two named Sansloy and Sansjoy. The Saracen had taken her with him, and had sought often to dishonour her, though she had resisted him.

Much moved by the tearful account, the knight assured her that she had now lost an enemy and gained a friend. He invited her to travel with him, for protection, and she shyly agreed.

As they rode away together, the sun grew hot, and when they came upon two wide-spreading trees they sought the welcome shade. Fidessa was now wholly cheerful and sprightly—and the knight, charmed by her lively prettiness, plucked a leafy twig from one tree, to make a garland for her brow.

But drops of red blood oozed from the broken twig, and a ghastly, hollow voice from the tree itself brought the knight to his feet, hair standing on end with horror.

"Do not tear at the body imprisoned within this bark," said the voice, "but flee this accursed place before evil afflicts you as it did me."

"What ghost fills my ears with these warnings?" said the knight.

"No ghost," groaned the voice, "but one who was once a man, Fradubio by name—a weak-willed man, now with my beloved altered to the form of a tree by an evil witch."

Urged by the knight, Fradubio went on to explain. He had been a knight, travelling with his lady love, when he had met another knight also accompanied by a beautiful woman, who was in fact a cruel sorceress named Duessa. The two knights had fought, and Fradubio had defeated the other, whereupon Duessa had given herself to him as a victor's prize.

But then she had worked her deadly magic, casting a spell that made him see his own lady as deformed and loathsome. Revolted, Fradubio had ridden off with Duessa, not knowing that the witch had then transformed his true love into a tree.

For a time he had journeyed happily with Duessa, taking his pleasure in her sensual beauty, until one day he had accidentally come upon her bathing herself in herbal essences. And then he saw her in her true form—a filthy, misshapen, hideous hag. Duessa, realizing that she had been discovered, overcame him with a spell and brought him back to that very spot, changing him too into a tree to stand beside his lady.

Deeply saddened by the tale, the knight made what amends he could by covering with clay the wound where he had torn away the twig. Behind him the lady Fidessa watched, unmoving. She, even more, had reason to know the truth of Fradubio's tale. For her scarlet-gowned beauty was a disguise, as much as her name. She was the sorceress herself, Duessa.

The evil Duessa's seductive advances to the Red Cross Knight have parallels in the temptations of St. Anthony, confronted by a demure maiden whose bat-wings betray her demonic origin, in a painting (c.1430) by Sassetta.

As the knight turned to her, she pretended to crumple at his feet as if fainting with horror. He lifted her, trying to awaken her with kisses and caresses. Then he placed her on her steed, and they rode on.

*   *   *

Far behind them, the lady Una wandered still, through wilderness and wasteland, in search of her knight. Her arduous way led her into the depths of a forest, where she dismounted to rest in a hidden glade, loosening her stole so that the beauty of her uncovered face seemed to light up the gloomy thickets. But as she rested, out of the woods sprang a giant hunting lion, charging at her, roaring, with gaping fangs.

But before it reached her the lion halted, her unblemished beauty and purity reaching out to quell its savagery. It fawned at her feet, licking her hands, and Una stroked it with affection, tears in her eyes at the thought that she could awaken love in a ferocious beast while her own knight had forsaken her.

Lions tamed by virgins and becoming their protectors formed a common theme in medieval and later folklore. Here, from the Arthurian tales called the Vulgate Cycle *(c.1300), Sir Lancelot crosses a stream to confront lions guarding a royal lady.*

From then on the lion accompanied Una, a steadfast protector. They wandered through the wild lands, meeting no living person, until the day they came to the foot of a mountain and met a country girl bearing a pot of water. Una spoke to her sweetly, but the girl could neither hear nor speak, and fled in terror of the great lion.

She rushed to her home, nearby, a small cottage where her mother also lived. The mother was an ancient crone, totally blind, who spent every waking hour in an excess of religious devotion, wearing sackcloth and ashes, fasting, tirelessly mumbling over her beads.

Una followed the girl, and courteously requested shelter for the night that was drawing in. But the girl and the old woman shrank away in fear to the far corner of the cottage. So the impatient lion simply swept the door aside, and Una, in her weariness, entered in to seek some rest.

In the deepest night, a man approached the cottage, with a heavy burden on his back. He was a thief, who robbed churches of their ornaments and artefacts, and his name was Kirkrapine. Some of his loot he would bring to the deaf-and-dumb girl, so as to use her for his lustful pleasures. But this night, as he entered the cottage, the lion sprang protectively up and the huge claws tore the thief to bloody shreds.

The two women wept and tore their hair in crazed anguish, the old mother shrieking at Una and heaping curses upon her. Una left the cottage at once, with the lion, and the women followed her, the crone still screaming with fury. But as dawn lightened the sky they turned back to their home, and met on their way an armoured knight, with a red cross on his breast.

It was the sorcerer Archimago, still in the Red Cross guise. Hearing the old woman's story, and so knowing he was close behind Una, he spurred ahead. When he came upon the lady he paused, for fear of the lion—but Una rode quickly to him.

"My lord," she said tearfully, "where have you been? I feared that I had displeased you, and caused you to shun my company."

"Dear lady, I would no more forsake you," Archimago replied with all his guileful charm, "than nature would forbear to bring forth the fruits of the earth. I merely rode aside to confront the wicked man of whom the hermit spoke, and who will work his wickedness no more."

Delighted, Una accepted the explanation, and they rode away together, while she recounted all that had befallen her. They had not ridden far when they saw a knight galloping towards them—a Saracen, with "Sansloy" inscribed upon his shield.

The Saracen readied himself to fight. And Archimago, in his disguise, could not avoid the conflict while Una was watching. So he responded with couched lance, but the powerful Saracen's charge ended with his spear plunging through shield and armour, and Archimago crashed wounded to the ground.

The Saracen sprang down, sword in hand. "Now," he cried, "the one who slew my brother Sansfoy shall himself be slain!" Ignoring Una's pleas for mercy, he wrenched the helmet away from the fallen knight—and stared in amazement. He recognized Archimago, and knew the old man to be a sorcerer, not one who fought in knightly combat. Nor could Archimago explain the puzzle, for he lay unconscious with the shadow of death across his eyes.

Una, too, sat dazed with astonishment at the magician's deception, until Sansloy rose and plucked her roughly from her saddle, inflamed by her beauty. The faithful lion sprang to her defence, but the Saracen blocked its charge with his shield and thrust his sword deep into the mighty heart. Then Sansloy swung Una up on to his charger and carried her away, indifferent to her pleadings. And far behind, her white palfrey trotted dutifully after them, seeming to be the only thing in the world still faithful to the lady Una.

*   *   *

The true Red Cross Knight, still with the witch Duessa whom he believed to be a virtuous lady, had come to a wide path beaten flat by hordes of travellers, all making their way to a stately palace that stood nearby. The knight, at Duessa's urging, joined the crowd, impressed by the height of the palace's towers and the gleaming gold of its walls.

In fact the gold was only foil, spread over brick that was laid without mortar. Behind the bright facade much of the building was old and in disrepair, and the whole edifice, which was called the House of Pride, stood upon foundations of sand.

But the knight, as he entered, saw only the sumptuous decoration, the costly furnishings—all outshone by a high throne glittering sun-bright with gold and diamonds. There sat a beautiful young queen, as splendidly gowned as her palace was ornate, with a mirror in her hand. When she was not gazing into the glass, she raised her eyes upwards, disdaining in her pride to look at anything lowly. Lucifera

The procession of the Seven Deadly Sins, as Spenser depicts them— Wrath and Lechery, Envy and Gluttony, Sloth and Avarice, all on their symbolic mounts, with Pride (Lucifera) in the ornate coach, and Satan himself as coachman. Engraving from an English 18th-century edition of the Faerie Queene.

Prides Procession with Idleness, Gluttony, Lechery, Avarice, Envy & Wrath, drove by Satan.

was her name, most proud of queens, though in truth she was a usurper to the throne she held.

A page named Vanity brought the knight and Duessa to the throne, where they knelt low in deference. Then they joined the throng of brilliantly garbed courtiers, who made Duessa welcome, for they well knew who and what she was. At length the queen rose and made her regal way out of the throne room, and the entire crowd followed her as she moved to a glistening golden coach, so richly arrayed as almost to compete with Juno's sky-travelling chariot.

But Lucifera's coach was drawn by six ill-matched beasts on which rode six strange beings, the close counsellors of the proud queen.

First of these, riding a slow-moving ass, was Idleness, sometimes called Sloth, thin, sickly and half asleep. By his side was the bloated enormity of Gluttony, on a filth-streaked swine, cramming food between his fat lips as he rode.

Then came the rough and hairy form of Lechery, mounted on a goat and carrying a heart that contained all the falseness of the seducer's art. Avarice rode beside him, on a camel laden with treasure, though the rider was thin and ill-fed, his garments threadbare.

Next came Envy, riding a snarling wolf, with a venomous toad in his mouth and a viper at his breast, staring with hatred at the splendour around him. And beside him on a roaring lion rode Wrath, a torch in one hand reflected in his maddened eyes, a dagger in his other hand, his clothing torn and bloody from his berserk rages.

Behind the frightful six rode the coachman—Satan himself, striking out with his whip. And all the company followed the coach out of the palace to take their pleasure in the open air, travelling on a roadway made from the bones of men who had fallen victim to that place. But the Red Cross Knight turned aside from the grisly procession, though he had seen that the lady he knew as Fidessa had been placed within the coach, next to Lucifera herself.

At length the queen and her followers, tiring of their revelry, returned to the palace. But on the way they met a fierce knight, another Saracen, with "Sansjoy" written on his shield. The newcomer saw, at the saddle of the Red Cross Knight, the shield of his brother Sansfoy, which the Christian knight had taken as his prize.

Bellowing his vengeful challenge, Sansjoy drew his sword. But Lucifera silenced him, ordering that if either knight had claim to the shield of Sansfoy, they could fight for it the next day, in a knightly tournament. Both warriors agreed, and returned with the others to the palace. There the night was spent in riotous feasting, with Gluttony as steward, until Sloth came to call them to their beds.

When the palace was silent and all were sleeping, Duessa rose and crept to the chamber of Sansjoy. Treacherously she told the pagan knight of her love for his dead brother, and her hatred for the Christian knight. And she promised Sansjoy to use her evil arts on his behalf, if he would afterwards become her protector.

*　　　　*　　　　*

The following morning the courtiers gathered, with music and feasting, to watch the joust. Beneath a canopy on the greensward outside the palace, Lucifera sat in proud splendour. Nearby, Duessa sat alone, with the blood-smeared shield of Sansfoy hung from a tree beside her.

A blaring trumpet summoned the two knights to battle, on foot, with shields and swords. The pagan Sansjoy was powerful and vengeful, and his sword rained hammer-blows on the Red Cross Knight.

Medieval manuscript illustration of a formal joust, where the knights have broken their lances and have drawn swords, while the ladies look on.

But the Christian warrior returned stroke for stroke, thunderous blows from which sparks flew like streaks of lightning.

Soon the armour of each man showed huge gouges and dents, with riven gashes through which the red blood flowed. Yet they fought on, neither gaining the advantage, until the pagan glimpsed his dead brother's shield, swaying where it hung, and vengeance was renewed within him.

"Go, villainous Christian," he roared, "take a message to the ghost of my brother—that his shield is regained and his honour restored, by your death!"

His sword crashed brutally down upon the crest of the Red Cross helmet. The metal withstood the blow, but the knight staggered, his senses half leaving him. And Duessa cried to Sansjoy, "Yours is the shield, and myself as well!"

Her voice cut through the daze gripping the Red Cross Knight. Believing that she had called to *him*, he rallied his valour, and struck a retaliatory blow, so powerful that Sansjoy had to fling himself back to avoid being cleft in two.

The movement unbalanced the pagan, and he fell heavily. And the Red Cross Knight cried, "Go you instead, Saracen, carry your own message to your brother!"—and swung his sword up for the final stroke that would end the battle.

But Duessa raised a hand, and a dark mist shrouded the fallen Sansjoy, so that the Christian knight could not discern his enemy. Then Duessa ran to him, calling, "Stay your wrath, sir knight, for demonic powers have claimed the pagan, and have carried him to hell! You are the victor: the shield, and I, and the glory, all are yours!"

The knight's fighting fury abated as he stared, amazed, at the cloud that hid his foe. But the trumpets sounded, and heralds proclaimed him the victor; and after making his obeisance to the proud queen, he returned to the palace where his wounds were tended, while Duessa wept false tears at the sight of such injuries.

But later, when darkness had fallen, Duessa again crept from her bed and hurried to the field where the magic mist still wrapped Sansjoy. The Saracen lay in a swoon, half-dead from his own wounds— and hurriedly Duessa fled to seek aid.

Her dark magic carried her to the far eastern horizon, to the dwelling of one of the most ancient and powerful beings of all: black Night herself, older than Jove, a stooping withered crone mantled in gloom and shadow. The witch told Night of the three pagan brothers— who were of Night's own dark race—and how one was dead and another near death. The crone, who had been taken aback by the brightly adorned beauty of her visitor, demanded to know who it was dared trouble her with such tales.

"I am kin to you as well," said the witch. "Beneath this guise, I am Duessa."

"Duessa, daughter of Deceit and Shame?" asked Night. And she greeted the witch with cackling joy, and agreed to aid her. In Night's black, iron-wheeled chariot they sped to the place where Sansjoy lay, and took him up.

From there they hastened to Avernus, the smoking, sulphurous pit where Pluto's fiends and the tormented souls of the dead shrieked and wailed as they passed, where the monstrous three-headed dog Cerberus rose snarling until the power of Night calmed him. They passed the place where Sisyphus eternally rolled a mighty boulder up a hill, failing always to reach the top; where Tantalus stood, aflame with thirst, neck-deep in water that he could not drink; where the immortal healer Aesculapius sought forever, but in vain, to close the wounds of Hippolytus, slain by the sea-god Poseidon.

To Aesculapius Night took Sansjoy, ordering him with all her awesome power to use his arts to heal the pagan knight. Then she returned to her dwelling, and Duessa to the palace of Lucifera.

But there she found that the Red Cross Knight, though still weak from his own injuries, had left in haste. The knight's other companion, the fearful dwarf, had been secretly exploring the palace—and had found horrors of such dimension that he had rushed to his master, imploring him to flee the dreadful place.

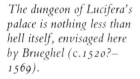

The dungeon of Lucifera's palace is nothing less than hell itself, envisaged here by Brueghel (c.1520?–1569).

The dwarf had come upon a deep dungeon holding vast numbers of wretched, wailing captives: all those who had fallen victim to the queen of Pride and her six fearsome counsellors. Among them were mighty rulers of the past, no less in thrall to evil than lesser folk—the proud king of Babylon who had proclaimed himself the only god; Croesus, who had craved ever more riches; the terrible warrior Nimrod; all the great Romans from Romulus down to Caesar and Mark Antony; even Cleopatra, among many other proud and vain women in that prison.

The knight had been unable to find Duessa, but was unwilling to remain longer in that evil place. With the dwarf, he had escaped out of the palace by an unguarded door, shuddering with horror to find along the way thousands of heaped corpses, further victims of the deathly house of Pride.

Earlier, far away, the knight's true lady had been in no less deadly danger. The fierce Sansloy, who had carried Una off, took her to a wild wood and there sought to seduce her with all his charm and guile. But when her purity remained steadfast, the Saracen grew enraged. Tearing away her veil and wimple, he determined to force his lust upon her. She struggled, screaming, and her cries reached the ears of a troop of fauns and satyrs merrily playing in a nearby glade.

The shaggy, goat-footed beings hurried to seek the cause of such screams—and when Sansloy saw them, he sprang to his steed and rode away in terror. Then the wood folk gathered round Una, staring with amazement at her beauty, smiling to reassure her, bowing before her and kissing her feet. Her fear abated and she returned their smiles, and they led her away with songs and dancing and pipes sounding merrily, through the forest to their glade.

There the old forest god himself, Sylvanus, rose to greet her, although the woodnymphs and hamadryads turned jealously away. And the satyrs prostrated themselves before her, in crude and savage worship—and Una stayed with them a while, resting after her travels, trying to teach them a different worship, not of herself but of the One Truth that she held so dear.

While she remained there, a noble knight entered the forest, an honorable warrior of high fame, seeking his kinsfolk, the wild demigods from whom he took his name, Satyrane. He was the son of a fair lady who had been ravished by a satyr, and his savage father had raised him in the wilds, teaching him all the forest ways, including how to tame and dominate the fiercest wild beasts. But when he had reached manhood Satyrane had ridden forth to seek adventure.

Above, a painting by Peter Paul Rubens (1577–1640) of sportive nymphs and satyrs. Sir Satyrane is an example of the "hero as wild man" whose nobility and virtue are natural, inborn. Myth and legend offer many such heroes, especially Hercules, shown here with club and lion-skin fighting the Hydra, a many-headed monster, in a 17th-century French engraving.

INDEFESSA GERENS REDIVIVIS BELLA COLVBRIS ARGOLIS AD LERNÆ, TVNDITVR HIDRA VADVA

Now, coming upon Una in his native woods teaching sacred truth to the worshipful satyrs, he was deeply affected by her wisdom and beauty. From then on he stayed near her, listening as she spoke of her true faith, and saddened by her own unhappiness as she continued to mourn the loss of her true knight of the Red Cross.

Satyrane vowed to help her, but he knew that the satyrs would not readily let her leave. So one day when the wood folk had roamed far in their revelries, the two stole carefully away. And soon their flight brought them out of the woods on to the expanses of a plain.

There they came upon a pilgrim, simply clothed and leaning on a staff. But when Una asked if the pilgrim had seen or heard anything of the Red Cross Knight, the man looked mournful. "Sad I am to tell you," he said, "that these eyes have seen the knight living, and have seen him dead."

Stony horror struck Una senseless from her saddle, into the arms of Satyrane. When the knight had roused and comforted her, the pilgrim explained that he had seen the Red Cross Knight that very day, in battle with a Saracen. And the pagan had slain the Christian. The victor, added the pilgrim, was even then close by, cleansing his wounds in a stream.

Satyrane galloped away, vengeful on Una's behalf, while the lady followed as swiftly as her small palfrey could carry her. But she had fallen behind when Satyrane confronted his foe, who was Sansloy, the same pagan who had earlier sought to ravish Una.

"Arise, villain," thundered Satyrane, "for you have cast shame upon knighthood by the slaying of the Red Cross Knight."

"I did not do so," Sansloy sneered, gathering up his weapons, "but I would have done had I encountered him—just as I shall now slay you for your slanders."

They flung themselves at one another, swords clashing, and soon their armour ran red with drenching blood. When Una arrived at the scene, she recognized Sansloy at once, and fled in terror. The pagan might have pursued her, but Satyrane blocked his way, and Sansloy had to protect himself from the redoubled fury of the other knight.

So the terrible combat continued—watched, in secret, by the pilgrim whose words had begun it. For he was in reality Archimago, the deceitful sorcerer. And soon he turned his back on the battle, and hurried in pursuit of Una.

*   *   *

Meanwhile Duessa had left the House of Pride in search of the Red Cross Knight, and soon found him far afield, divested of his armour,

Spenser took the idea of the enfeebling pool from the Greek myth of Hermaphroditus, with whom the nymph Salmacis fell in love. When the youth resisted her, she called upon the gods, who united them in one body, both male and female. Thereafter the nymph's pool weakened all who drank from it. Painting (c.1581) of Hermaphroditus and Salmacis by Bartholomeus Spranger.

resting beside a crystalline stream. She reproached him for leaving her behind, but did so in tones of coy sweetness that charmed him all the more. Then she joined him on the shady grass, watching wordlessly while he sipped from the clear stream.

Yet she knew that the stream had been cursed by the goddess Diana, so that all who drank from it would become weak and enfeebled. The knight, at peace with his "Fidessa", did not at first notice its effects. But when the stillness was rent by a monstrous bellowing, which seemed to shake the very ground, the knight leaped up and reached for his weapons only to find himself faint, his hands trembling.

As he strove to don his armour, into sight strode a hideous giant, three times taller than the tallest man. His name was Orgoglio, born of the Earth herself, arrogant and terrible, wielding a huge oak tree that was his club. Furiously he advanced upon the knight, who could scarcely lift his sword in his weakened hands.

The enormous oaken club thundered down, and had the knight not stumbled aside he would have been crushed to powder. Even the wind from that gigantic blow was enough to fling him to the ground, where he lay half-stunned—while the giant raised his club for another crushing blow.

But Duessa cried, "Orgoglio, do not kill him! Keep him as a bond-slave, and I will gladly become yours!"

The giant halted, agreeing, and Duessa went readily into his arms. Then Orgoglio took up the unconscious knight and returned with Duessa to his castle, where he flung the knight into the depths of a dungeon.

To Duessa he gave all honour, clothing her in rich garments, placing a jewelled crown on her head, presenting her finally with a frightful beast. Seven heads it had, and a tail that reached to the heavens—with a breast of iron, a back of scaly brass, and eyes that glowed red as blood. And it became Duessa's mount, to strike terror into human hearts.

But when the Red Cross Knight had fallen, the loyal dwarf had been watching from hiding. Afterwards the dwarf had gathered up the knight's armour and weapons and had mournfully wandered away. But he had not gone far when the lady Una appeared, still flying from the sight of the hated Saracen.

When she saw what the dwarf was carrying, her breath stopped, and she fell to the ground as if her heart had burst within her. The frightened dwarf chafed her wrists and temples, and three times she awoke, only to fall again each time into a swoon of grief. But at last she rallied her strength, and listened dolefully while the dwarf told her all that had befallen the Red Cross Knight since last she had seen him.

Misery and horror poured fiery agony through Una as she heard the tale, for no lady had ever loved more truly than she had come to love her knight. But she gathered her resolve, and set out once again to seek her love, not knowing whether he was alive or dead.

As she followed the path that the dwarf had indicated, she saw riding towards her a strange knight, young and fair, garbed in brilliant armour, with a sturdy squire riding behind him. The knight's helmet and crest were golden, and gold was the hilt of his sword, while across his chest he wore a wide belt glittering with precious stones, the largest shaped like a lady's head and shining brighter than any star.

Facing page: a 14th-century German altarpiece showing the seven-headed Beast described in the New Testament book of Revelation. By placing Duessa on a similar beast, Spenser is identifying her (as part of his anti-Catholic fervour) with the Whore of Babylon, who rides the Beast.

Yet the young knight's shield was covered, and so he always kept it, unless he had need to overcome dire monsters or unequal hosts of enemies. For from the shield, when uncovered, would shine a light that would dim the sun itself, a light that was proof against all magic, that could reveal the truth behind all deception, that could turn evil men to stones, and stones to dust.

That invincible shield, and all his other vestments and arms, had been made for the knight by the greatest master of enchantment, the magician Merlin—for the knight was in truth the young Prince Arthur, riding in pursuit of a private quest.

The prince greeted Una courteously, but her reply showed him that some deep sorrow weighed upon her heart. Gently he inquired after the cause of her pain, offering his aid. And his kindly concern encouraged her to pour out her story.

"Madam," said the prince when she had done, "you have endured much that might have broken the stoutest heart. But fear no longer, for I will not forsake you till I have freed your knight and restored him to you." And so he rode with her, comforting her, while the dwarf guided them to their goal.

*   *   *

Bronze statue of Arthur (c.1480) at Innsbruck, Austria. Arthur has many special roles within the allegories of Spenser's six books, but overall he appears as the embodiment of perfect—and invulnerable—knightly virtue.

When they reached the high castle of the giant, Arthur dismounted, leaving Una in safety, and with his squire approached the gate. The squire raised a small horn, of twisted gold—a legendary horn whose sound could open any door—and blew a blast. The huge castle trembled, and the gate flew open.

Through it rushed the giant, glaring round to see what had made such an awesome sound. Behind him rode Duessa on her seven-headed beast. When Orgoglio saw the prince confronting him with sword and shield, he bellowed with rage, and lashed out murderously with his oaken club.

Arthur sprang aside from the blow, and so powerful was it that the club buried itself three yards deep in the groaning earth. As the giant struggled to free the club, Arthur leaped forward, and his flashing sword struck off Orgoglio's left arm.

The giant howled inhumanly with pain and fear, and Duessa urged her grisly steed forward to the attack. The brave squire tried to block its way with his sword—until the witch flung a baleful potion upon him. The squire fell, beneath the claws of the beast.

But Arthur sprang to his aid, and his sword cleaved one of the monster's heads, splitting it down to the teeth. Blood burst from the wound, ankle-deep on the ground, and the beast screamed and threshed its tail so that Duessa was nearly unseated. But then the giant, strength renewed with towering rage, flung himself at Arthur again. The vast club thundered down, and Arthur took the full force of it on his shield.

The impact battered him to the ground, half-unconscious, and then the giant might have crushed him like an insect. But the blow had torn away the covering of the enchanted shield—and its blazing light lanced out, unendurable to any eye.

The giant staggered back, blinded, and the seven-headed beast fell stunned to the ground. Duessa screamed in terror, but to no avail, for the prince regained his feet, and his sword struck off the giant's right leg at the knee, felling him like some mighty tree.

Then the prince leaped upon his fallen enemy, and beheaded him with one sweeping stroke. And as the lifeblood gushed from Orgoglio's wounds, his body seemed to deflate, until nothing was left but a shapeless mass like an airless balloon.

The terrified Duessa tried to flee, but the squire, now recovered, dragged her back and held her captive. And Una rushed to Arthur, breathless with praise and gratitude for his heroism.

But the prince's task was not yet complete. He entered the castle, where he found an aged, white-bearded man, feeble and blind, whose head was uncannily turned round on his bent neck. This was Ignaro, keeper of the castle, bearer of the keys to its doors. Yet when the prince asked the whereabouts of the Red Cross Knight, the old man in senile ignorance replied that he could not tell.

So the prince simply took the keys, and searched. He found rooms filled with vast hoards of treasure; but he also found floors awash with the blood of innocents, and an altar where the bodies of true Christians had been tortured and sacrificed. Finally he came to an iron door for which there was no key. He called through a narrow grille, and from within came a hollow, plaintive voice that spoke of death as if it would be welcome.

Pity and anger swelled within Arthur, and he battered down the door, stepping into a dungeon of hellish darkness and appalling filth. There lay the Red Cross Knight, starved, withered, half-dead.

Arthur bore him out of the castle, and Una wept bitterly at the sight of the wasted form. "From all the wrongs you have suffered," she cried, "surely only good must now follow!"

"The only good to come from pain," said Arthur, "is to gain wisdom, so that evil can be avoided hereafter. But take heart, sir knight—there is the foul giant, slain, and there is the witch, the cause of all your suffering. You shall decide if she is to live or die."

"No, it would be evil to slay her," Una protested. "Merely remove her deceits from her, and let her go."

So they stripped Duessa of her scarlet robe and rich adornments,

The evils of Orgoglio's castle, with its gruesome altars and dungeons, allude to the grim activities of the Spanish Inquisition—a tribunal set up to discover and punish heresy—here shown burning "heretical" books in a 15th-century painting by Pedro Berruguete.

and stripped her also of the fraudulent beauty that her magic gave her. Naked, she was revealed as she truly was.

They saw a repulsive, wrinkled hag, toothless and bald, with skin scabbed like the bark of a tree. A fox's tail hung down behind her, smeared with filth—and one of her feet was taloned like that of a bird of prey, while the other was heavy and furred like the paw of a bear.

36

Then they released her, and swiftly she fled to hide her ugliness and shame within dark caves in a wilderness far from human sight.

*   *   *

While the Red Cross Knight rested, until he had gained strength enough to travel, Una begged Prince Arthur to tell them of his parentage and origins. But the prince could not do so.

"My lineage, even the name of my father, are unknown to me," he said. "As a babe I was given to be raised by an old knight, Timon, once the most skilled warrior on earth. And my tutor in all other matters was the wise sage Merlin, who would tell me only that I was the son of a king, and that in time I would know more."

Una asked what high adventure had brought him into Faeryland, and the prince replied, "I am here because of a deep yearning within me, painful as a wound."

He told them how one day, after a long and wearying ride, he had fallen asleep in a meadow—and there had come to him, in a vision or a dream, the fairest and most royal maiden that could ever live. The prince had fallen deeply in love with her, and she, as they talked together, seemed to return his love. And before she vanished she told him that she was the Queen of Faery.

Arthur's vision of Gloriana is one of the many tributes paid to Queen Elizabeth in Spenser's poem. Equal devotion appears in this painting from 1569 by Hans Eworth: Elizabeth confronts the goddesses Juno, Minerva, and Venus, showing herself their superior in their own qualities of majesty, wisdom, and beauty.

When he awoke, Arthur vowed to seek her, never to rest till he had found her. And he had been searching since that day.

Soon it became time for him to resume his search, and for Una and the knight to continue their journey. But first Arthur and the Red Cross Knight pledged loyalty and friendship to one another, sealing it with gifts. The knight gave the prince a book of the Holy Testament, written in letters of gold. And Arthur gave a box carved of diamond, which held a few drops of a wonderful liquid that could heal any wound.

Then they parted. Una and the knight travelled slowly, for the knight remained desperately weak. So they had not gone far when they saw a knight galloping towards them, as if in blind terror. He wore no helmet, and oddly had a length of rope knotted round his neck. The Red Cross Knight stopped him, asking what it was that he was fleeing. And the stranger, eyes bulging with fear, told them of a being who had led him to the edge of horror.

The knight's name was Trevisan, he said, and lately he had been riding with another knight, named Terwin. They had encountered a man whose name was Despair—a man seeming friendly but deeply dangerous and evil. His insidious talk, of gloom and grief, misery and loss, could oppress the stoutest heart with the feeling that life was not bearable. Despair had encouraged the two knights to suicide, and had given a knife to Terwin and a rope to Trevisan. Terwin had then died by his own hand; but Trevisan had found scraps of courage enough to flee, and was fleeing still.

The Red Cross Knight, weakened as he was, determined to confront the villain. He followed Trevisan's directions to the house of Despair—a dreary, bleak cavern at the foot of a lowering cliff. Around it stood the dark forms of dead trees, from whose bare limbs dangled the corpses of many men who had hanged themselves, while more bodies were scattered on the ground where others had flung themselves off the cliff.

Within the cave the knight found Despair, clothed in rags, skeletally thin, with tangled, greasy hair through which his hollow eyes stared dully. At his feet lay the body of a young knight, a rusty knife plunged into his breast.

"Murderer," cried the Red Cross Knight, "I bring you justice— your life for the life of this man!"

"I did not kill him," said Despair. "He died because he wished no longer to live. You speak of justice; but is it not just to let a man die who comes to loathe his life? Now he is at peace, enjoying eternal rest. Is that not what we all should seek—the quiet grave after life's bitterness and pain? Death comes like sleep after toil, port after a stormy sea, rest after battle."

The Red Cross Knight's encounter with Despair, the godly man's ultimate enemy, is as baleful as that portrayed in this etching, The Knight, Death, and the Devil, *by Albrecht Dürer (1471–1528).*

"But a man's life has its own term," the knight replied, "which he may not shorten or prolong."

"Yet death is the proper end of all," said the sly voice of Despair. "What does life bring, that it should be so desirable? Fear, sickness, pain, sorrow, loss, age—and sin, all the more sin as life goes on. A shorter life means less woe, less sin to be punished on the day of wrath. What of yourself, wretched man? Why should you seek to continue your life? Is it not enough that you have betrayed your lady, proved yourself false and faithless, defiled yourself? Does not the Almighty say, let all sinners die? Come, let death put an end to all your suffering and iniquity."

The words struck deep into the knight's conscience. Through his

mind paraded a vision of all his sins and failures, so ugly a sight that he felt himself growing faint. Then Despair showed him another vision, of wailing ghosts steeped in the fiery agony of eternal damnation. And so Despair took hold entirely of the knight's mind and will, until at last when the skeletal hand proffered a dagger, the knight took it up, trembling, convinced that he did not deserve to live.

But Una had entered the cavern. Striking the knife from his hand, she said sternly, "For shame, faint-hearted knight! Where is the courage and honour now that were yours when you rode out to seek the dragon? Why should you let Despair bewitch you, when you well know of Heaven's mercy? Come away from this cursed place!"

With her help, the knight arose and left the cavern. And Despair, cheated of a new victim, took a noose and hanged himself—yet did not die, just as he had tried and failed to take his life a thousand times before.

*   *   *

Una realized that all the pain and privation that the Red Cross Knight had suffered had left him far too weak to confront an enemy as terrible as the dragon. So she turned aside from their route and brought him to an ancient house, renowned as a place of goodness and purity, where lived a wise and holy woman devoted to godliness and to aiding the wretched and the poor. Celia was this woman's name, and she was the mother of three beautiful daughters, Fidelia, Speranza, and Charissa.

They were admitted to the house by an aged, stooping porter, Humilita, who led them through a narrow and straight passage into a courtyard. There a steward greeted them with courteous gladness. His name was Zeal, while the gentle and soft-spoken squire who came to join them was named Reverence. The squire conducted them to Dame Celia, who embraced Una with warmth and joy, for she was well acquainted with the princess and her royal parents. But she greeted the knight with curiosity.

"It is strange to see a knight errant in this house," she said. "There are so few who seek the narrow path, for most prefer to stray on broader paths of pleasure, even though they lead to destruction."

Fidelia and Speranza, who aid the purification of the Red Cross Knight, are of course the virtues of Faith and Hope, here depicted in frescoes by Giotto (1266?–1337).

As Una began to explain, they were joined by two of Celia's daughters, graceful, modest and demure young women. Fidelia, clad dazzlingly in white, bore a golden cup filled with wine mixed with water. A serpent coiled within that liquid, yet the maiden was in no way troubled by its presence. In her other hand she carried a book, sealed with blood, filled with writings of hidden lore. Her sister Speranza, all in blue, carried a curved silver support on which she leaned, and her eyes were ever raised up towards heaven.

Dame Celia told Una that their sister Charissa, the only one of the three so far married, had lately given birth to a son and was still recovering. And so they talked together, and partook of Celia's hospitality, while Una explained that she had brought the knight to be restored and strengthened by holy teachings.

Celia consented, and when the knight was rested their work began. At first he was attended by Fidelia, who opened her secret book and instructed him in all its lore, speaking of justice and mercy, of God's grace and the discipline of holiness. The power of Fidelia, conferred by God, was vast: she could part the seas, move mountains, turn the sun backwards in its path, even raise the dead. And as the knight learned from her, he was filled with guilt and self-loathing for the sins of his past; yet Speranza comforted him, allowing him to lean upon her silver support, to take heart that he need not languish in sin forever.

Una was distressed at her knight's misery, but Celia explained that the sins within him were like a deadly illness, a festering corruption that must be cleansed and purged away. So she sent physicians to the knight: Patience, with salves and medicines to make the anguish more endurable, Amendment with instruments of fire to cut away the corruption within. And the knight was further purged by visits from Penance, with his iron whip—Remorse, who brought blood from the very heart—and lastly Repentance, who bathed the knight's tormented being in the cleansing pain of salt water.

At last sin and evil were driven from the knight, and he was brought by Repentance to Una, who wept for the agonies he had suffered but kissed him with joy for his recovery. Then she took him to Celia's third daughter, Charissa.

They found her to be a beautiful young woman surrounded by the happy throng of her children. She sat on an ivory chair, clad in yellow with a golden crown, and bare-breasted in order more easily to feed her youngest. And from Charissa the knight learned of God's love, and the joys of righteousness.

Then he was given into the care of an aged matron whose name was Mercy. She led him out on to a narrow path, strewn with thorns and other obstacles, which led to a hospice where seven godly men tended the poor, the needy and the ill. Charissa was the founder of the hospice, and Mercy the patron; and there the knight rested a while, and learned more of the work of holy charity.

From there Mercy guided him to a small chapel, up a steep and dangerous hillside, where they met an immensely old man named Contemplation. Mercy asked him, on behalf of the mighty Fidelia,

Sister to Faith and Hope is the "greatest" virtue of Charity (Christian love), seen here by Lucas Cranach the Elder (1472–1553) to be as generous and maternal as Spenser's Charissa.

to reveal to the knight the ultimate goal of all his pains and strivings. And the old man, whose spirit was quick and powerful for all his seeming frailty, led the knight on an even more tortuous climb—to the summit of the highest mountain, high as the one on which Moses received the commandments of God.

There the knight saw, in the distance, an immense and lofty city, whose walls and spires were formed of pearl and precious stones in a manner beyond human skill to describe. Amazed and overcome, he asked the aged man what city it was. And he was told that it was the city of God, the new Jerusalem, where those who had been redeemed of sin by the son of God now lived as saints within God's loving embrace.

"I had thought," murmured the knight, "that Cleopolis, city of the Faery Queen, was the most glorious city, with its bright crystal tower, Panthea. Yet this city surpasses it by far."

"So it does," replied the holy man, "yet Cleopolis is the most glorious of earthly cities, taking its glory from its queen, who is herself heaven-born. And you do well, fair knight, to serve her in this world. But a time will come when you will set aside knightly duties, and seek this path again, to dwell yourself in the new Jerusalem. For you too will be a saint, and the patron of your country—Saint George of merry England you will be named, forever."

The knight pondered as they retraced their steps, then asked, "Father, why do you name me as a knight of England, when all know that I am of the race of Faeryland?"

"Your true heritage has been unknown to you," said the holy man, "but I know that you are descended from the Saxon kings of Britain. You were brought to Faeryland by an elf who stole you as a babe and left a changeling in your place—so you believed yourself to be of Faery race."

Bemused, the knight then took his leave of the holy man and made his way back to the house of Celia to rejoin Una. And soon, fully restored and prepared, he and his lady bade farewell to Celia and her daughters and rode out on their adventure.

*   *   *

As their journey brought them into Una's native land, where her parents had languished for so long as captives of the dragon, the lady's heart grew heavy. "Now, dearest knight," she said, "though you have endured so many sorrows for my sake, you are approaching the greatest peril of all. You will need all your courage and valour if you are to overcome the fiend."

While she spoke they were approaching a tall castle, dominated by a tower of brass, within which Una's royal parents were besieged by the dragon that had despoiled all their lands. They rode towards it, when from the distance they heard a monstrous, hideous roar, which trembled the ground and filled the air with terror. And then they saw the dragon—stretched on a nearby hillside, itself like a huge hill.

The towers of the New Jerusalem, the City of God—to which, visibly, not all travellers attain—from a medieval French illustrated manuscript.

*Facing page:
Bernardo Martorell dramatic painting (1430) of St. George and the dragon.*

The dragon saw the gleam of the knight's armour and sprang up, charging upon them. And the knight, sending Una a safe distance away, spurred fearlessly to meet the monster. Its mountainous size overshadowed the land, and its spread wings were like the mainsails of a man-o'-war. The vast body was covered with scales of brass, which clashed and clattered as it charged; the scaly tail, three furlongs in length, bore steel-sharp spikes upon its tip, as deadly as the cruel claws upon each foot. Within the hellish jaws were three rows of iron fangs, still bloodstained from its last grisly feast; and sulphurous smoke trailed from its nostrils and throat in a stinking, choking cloud.

As the knight defiantly couched his lance at the advancing horror, the dragon glided to one side on spread wings and lashed out with its tail. Knight and horse were flung crushingly to the ground—but were up at once, charging again, lance driving fiercely against the creature's breast. The brazen scales turned the thrust aside, yet wrath rose more furiously within the dragon, for while it had fought and defeated many a brave knight, it had never suffered such a blow.

Raging, it leaped into the air on spread wings, sweeping down like a bird of prey and snatching up both horse and rider in its talons. But the knight fought mightily, and his struggles forced the dragon down, forced the claws to open and release him.

44

A third time then the knight charged, his lance hurtling with the strength of three men. Its point glanced off the armoured neck, but stabbed deep into the left wing, close to the huge body. The dragon's roars of pain rose like the bellowing of a winter storm at sea, and black blood streamed in rivers from the wound. Furious flame gushed from the beast's nostrils, and its tail lashed out again, winding round the legs of the knight's charger, dragging it and its rider to the ground.

But the knight rose to his feet, sword in hand, and struck thunderously at his enemy. The blade did not penetrate the armoured hide, but the awesome power of the blows staggered the beast. Screaming, it sought to escape in flight, but its wounded wing failed.

Then its breath burst forth in a gout of flame, enveloping the knight, searing his body within the armour that had become red-hot. The knight stumbled, half-overcome—and the dragon slashed again with its spiked tail, and felled him.

He pitched backwards into a pool of water to whose edge the furious combat had brought them. And there he lay, unmoving, while the monster roared its victory cry and Una, watching from afar, wept strickenly at the fall of her hero.

But it was no ordinary pool into which the knight had fallen. Its waters had rested in that land from earliest times, and its virtues had resisted even the dragon's foul presence. It was called the Well of Life, and had the power to cure the sick, to cleanse the sinful, to rejuvenate the aged, even to revive the dead.

So, after a night of mourning and prayer, Una was stunned with joy to see her champion arise from the pool just as the sun rose to brighten the land. The knight seemed as if he had been reborn and baptized anew—his armour and weapons shining, his strength restored and enhanced.

The dragon rose at once to renew the attack, and the knight met its charge unflinchingly. With furious strength he brought his sword down on to the creature's crested head. And perhaps the waters of the pool had lent a magical sharpness to the blade, for it cleaved through the brazen armour of the skin and gashed a deep wound in the dragon's skull.

Once again the demonic beast screamed in pain, a sound like the roaring of a hundred lions. Once again its deadly tail lashed round, so savagely that the spikes on its tip drove through the knight's shield and through his armour, plunging deep into the flesh of his shoulder.

But honour and courage came to the knight's aid. Despite the terrible wound, he swung his sword with undaunted strength—and the bright blade slashed through the dragon's tail.

Now the beast's pain and fury burst forth more volcanically than ever, blotting out sun and sky with belching smoke and fire. The dragon sprang at the knight, two of its taloned paws clamping on to his shield, its vast weight bearing him to the ground.

The knight fought to free his shield from that grip, striking and striking again with his fierce sword, until the dragon had to remove one paw from the shield to defend itself against the blows. And as it did so the knight swept his sword across and hewed off the other paw, dragging his shield away and regaining his feet.

Once more a diabolical flood of fire from the screaming dragon's mouth engulfed him. And again the knight staggered, and was hurled back by the inferno. Again he fell, overwhelmed by the flame and by the anguish of his wounded shoulder.

But the dragon did not complete its victory. The knight had fallen next to a wondrous tree, which like the pool had been in that land from earliest times, placed there by God Himself and so protected from the dragon's wrath. A wealth of rosy apples grew on the tree, which could grant everlasting life, and so it was called the Tree of Life. Next to it grew an equally fruit-rich tree, whose apples conferred the knowledge of good and evil, the knowledge that led in the beginning to the fall of man from perfect innocence and grace.

From the first tree there flowed a stream of magical balm, which had the power to heal all wounds and restore life to the dying. And into that stream the knight had fallen—to lie unmoving while night fell, with Una as before weeping where she watched and prayed.

At sunrise, once again, the knight rose restored, healed of all his wounds, ready again for battle. The dragon held back a moment, as if for the first time feeling dismay and fear. Then it charged with all its monstrous ferocity, flame storming from its mouth, fanged jaws stretching wide as if to swallow the knight whole.

But the knight did not flinch in the face of the monster's rush. And upwards, into the cavern of those terrible jaws, he thrust his sword with all his power, piercing fatally deep.

It was the dragon's life-blood that gushed forth as the knight dragged his sword free. And down it fell, dying, like some huge rocky cliff that has been undermined by the eroding sea. Down it fell, thunderously, to lie like a heaped mountain, dead at the knight's feet.

*   *   *

From the distant tower, at the sight of the dragon's fall, trumpets sounded—a triumphant blare of joy and release. The great brass gate was flung wide, and through it came the king and queen, Una's parents, with all their ministers and courtiers, and a throng of ordinary folk who also had been penned within the walls. The procession advanced swiftly, with music and laughter and glad songs, as the people rejoiced at their liberation. The aged royals bowed low before the knight, their deliverer, while the people spread laurel boughs at their feet, and maidens twined a garland crown round Una's head.

Then the throng bore Una and the knight back to the castle, though many people remained to marvel at the fallen monstrosity of the dragon. At the castle the king and queen embraced their daughter and her champion, bestowing rich gifts upon the knight, and making preparations for a celebratory feast.

The celebration held nothing of pride or ostentation, for that was not the manner of Una's land. But they dined well, while Una related to the old king and queen all that had befallen her and her knight on their travels.

"My children, you have borne great evils," said the king, "so that I know not whether to praise you or pity you. But now you are safe, in this land of Eden, and here you may remain."

The wedding of the Red Cross Knight and Una is one of the most joyous happy endings in Spenser's poem. Painting of an English marriage feast by Joris Hoefnagel (c.1542–1600).

"I fear not, my lord," said the knight, "for as your daughter knows I must return to the Faery Queen, in whose service I must remain for six more years, to aid her against her enemies."

The king was saddened—but he assured the knight that, before he should leave, he would have the finest gift that was in the royal power

to bestow. He turned to his daughter, who had thrown away her veil and her dark stole of mourning, and shone forth, clad all in white, with the dazzling radiance of the morning star. And the king proclaimed there the betrothal of Una and the Red Cross Knight, and named the knight heir apparent to all the kingdom.

Una and the knight bowed low, accepting with love and gladness the king's command. But at that moment a distraught messenger rushed in, prostrating himself before the king and then hastily reading from the paper he bore.

The message warned the king against giving his daughter in marriage to the knight—for, it said, he was already pledged to another. And though the knight had proved false and perjuring, the message went on, those earlier pledges still should hold true. The message begged the king to see that justice was done, and it was signed "Fidessa".

The court stood silent, stunned, as the king turned gravely to the knight and asked what the message meant, with its wild charges of broken pledges and dishonour.

"My king," said the knight, "during my wanderings I encountered the woman who calls herself Fidessa. But she is in truth the sorceress Duessa, mistress of all false deceit, who with her wicked arts led me in my weakness to stray awhile from the true path."

And Una confirmed his words. "The witch brought this gentle knight into such wretchedness," she said, "that death threatened him daily. And she did so with the aid of a magician named Archimago— who, I do not doubt, is hiding his wickedness in the guise of this very messenger, seeking again to bring woe to myself and my love."

The king angrily called guards to take charge of the messenger. And indeed he was exposed as the guileful Archimago, who was then bound hand and foot in chains and flung into the castle's deepest dungeon. Then the king proclaimed that the wedding should take place at once, and himself performed the holy service that united the knight and his lady in marriage.

Afterwards throughout the land there was rejoicing and festivity. Music and song filled all the halls of the king's castle, often accompanied by a heavenly sound as if angels themselves were joining in the songs of praise. And for a long time the knight and his lady remained together in blissful harmony and love, and nothing marred their perfect contentment.

But the day came at last when the knight had to remember the vow he had sworn, to return to the service of the Faery Queen for six more years. And so he readied himself and rode away, leaving the lady Una to mourn his absence and to await his return.

BOOK TWO

The Legend of Sir Guyon, or Temperance

Sir Guyon embodies the virtue of Temperance in the sixteenth-century sense of the word—not "abstinence", as it is loosely used today, but the stricter meaning of the classical Greek maxim, "Nothing to excess". The point is made explicit early in the book when Guyon and his adviser-companion visit the house of Medina, whose name echoes the ideal of the ethical "golden mean", the controlled middle way between all the unharmonious extremes that threaten the human temperament.

Guyon's quest, on which he too has been sent by Queen Gloriana, is to take him to a place where extremes of every sort (but especially fleshly ones) hold total sway. It is called the Bower of Bliss, and Guyon is charged with its destruction, and with ending the corrupting activities of its mistress, Acrasia.

As in the first book, the knight is sidetracked into other adventures, which shed more light on his central virtue and its enemies. Again he is tempted and tested—most seriously by the wealth-obsessed figure of Mammon—and requires Prince Arthur's aid. Guyon then is restored and strengthened in the House of Alma, a representation of the human body and mind, where he learns how order, balance, and temperance are maintained when the soul (Alma) is in command. From there he moves swiftly to destroy the Bower of Bliss and capture Acrasia.

To us, the destruction of the Bower might seem an excessively stern, dour, and cruel act. But Spenser wants his readers to see that the apparent beauty, pleasure, and freedom of the Bower is illusory, and debilitating. Guyon (like Spenser) is no grim Puritan opposed to beauty and pleasure. It is *excess* that he opposes; indeed, the personification of Excess sits at the very gate of the Bower. So we are to see that even true beauty and pleasure, taken to intemperate excess, can enfeeble and destroy a man, and make him no better than a beast.

A Renaissance miniature of a Garden of Love, beautifully landscaped and complete with fountain and naked damsels—as is the dangerous Bower of Bliss that the knight of Temperance must overthrow.

When the Red Cross Knight had left the land of Eden, the sorcerer Archimago knew he could safely make his escape from the dungeon where he was chained. His black arts freed him from his chains, and his vengeful malice sent him in pursuit of the knight—knowing he could no longer harm Una, safe in her own land.

As he travelled, he came upon a fully armed knight, whose shield displayed no heraldic device but a portrait of Gloriana, Queen of Faeryland. The knight was accompanied by an elderly, black-robed Palmer, sage and sober, who walked with his staff in front of the knight's charger, leading the way and maintaining for both an un-varying pace.

Archimago, assuming a guise of a humble squire, begged the knight to stop, and told him how he had seen, only lately, a maiden most brutally ravished by a treacherous knight. The newcomer, whose name was Sir Guyon, angrily undertook to find and punish the one who could so stain the name of knighthood.

Following Archimago, Guyon came upon the maiden, weeping and disheveled. She sought at first to hide herself, in her shame, but Guyon reassured her, promising to right the wrong that had been done. And she revealed that the knight who had despoiled her had borne a silver shield quartered with a blood-red cross.

Guyon was mystified, for he knew that the Red Cross Knight was a man of truth and honour who had lately won great glory. None-theless, Guyon rode in search of him, on the maiden's behalf—not guessing that she was in truth the witch Duessa, whom Archimago had reclaimed from the wilderness and had magically readorned with false youth and beauty.

The sorcerer's directions led Guyon at last to a glade where the Red Cross Knight was resting. Then Guyon charged, lance readied for battle. Seeing him, the Red Cross Knight leaped to his own saddle and spurred forward, his own lance couched. But at the last moment Guyon raised his lance and pulled up his charger.

"Sir knight," he said, "I cannot address my spear against the sacred emblem that you bear. Nor can I believe that such a one as you is guilty of a dire crime."

The Red Cross Knight also reined back his steed. "No more could I, Sir Guyon, do violence against the image of that heavenly queen which you bear. But why did you seek at first to challenge me?"

Guyon told him of the squire, and the maiden who had apparently been ravished. But when the Red Cross Knight sought to confront his accusers, he and Guyon found that the two had fled, and so were proved false.

By then the aged Palmer had come up, and greeted the Red Cross Knight courteously, praising the high fame and glory that he had so recently achieved. So they conversed together awhile, the two knights pledging anew their friendship. Then the Red Cross Knight took his leave of them, and Guyon and the Palmer resumed their journey, the Palmer as ever leading the way and instructing the knight in the proper path of temperance and reason.

Their travels, long and arduous, brought them one hot day to seek the shade of a forest. But as they entered, they heard a woman's voice, raised in a cry filled with grief and sorrow. Guyon dismounted and

Pilgrims paying toll on their travels, from a 15th-century Flemish manuscript. Some devout travellers returned from pilgrimages to the Holy Land carrying palm leaves to display their achievement—so many godly travellers came to be called "palmers", like Guyon's companion.

hurried into the thicket from which the cry had come. He found a lovely lady lying beside a bubbling spring, a dagger jutting from her breast. On her lap a baby lay, dabbling its hands with playful innocence in the blood that streamed from her dreadful wound. And beside the lady lay the body of a handsome knight.

Guyon, deeply pained by the scene, saw that the lady herself was near death. Quickly he plucked out the knife and staunched the blood—until at last her eyelids fluttered open. Guyon gently lifted her up, imploring her to tell him how the tragic circumstance had happened.

Falteringly, the lady told her story. Her name was Amavia, she said, and the dead knight was her husband, Sir Mordant. Some time

before he had ridden forth to seek knightly adventure, leaving his wife behind, and pregnant. But Mordant had fallen into the power of a dangerous enchantress, named Acrasia.

The enchantress bound men to her with chains of fleshy pleasure that they could not resist. They became her slaves, drunk and crazed with lustful delight, on the wandering island where the enchantress had her home, called the Bower of Bliss.

The lady, hearing of her husband's fall, had gone forth in search of him, and on that dangerous journey had given birth to the boy-child that now lay on her lap. When she had found Mordant, she had fought to break Acrasia's enchantments and had at last won her husband away—but not to safety. Acrasia had put a final spell upon him, so that when he paused to drink at the spring, he fell dead.

Then the lady had sought to take her own life; and even as she spoke her terrible wound took its toll, and death claimed her.

"Here is an image of human nature," Guyon mused sorrowfully to the Palmer. "Passion taking advantage of the weak flesh, and overcoming reason. The strong become victims of pleasure, the weak of pain."

"So a middle way must always be found," replied the Palmer, "between the heat of pleasure and the cold grip of suffering."

*　　　　*　　　　*

After they had prepared graves for Mordant and his lady, Guyon took the baby to the crystal spring, to wash away the blood that so gruesomely covered the little hands. But to his amazement, the washing had no effect: the stains would not be removed.

The Palmer told him that it was due to the virtue of the pool itself. Once, long ago, he said, one of Diana's nymphs had been pursued by Faunus, lustful god of the wilderness. And when the nymph had called upon the goddess to protect her and preserve her chastity, Diana had transformed her into a stone, from which welled the water that formed the spring. To this day, said the Palmer, the water remains pure: nothing can defile it.

Guyon then gave the babe into the Palmer's care. But when he returned to the place where he had left his charger, he found to his deep anger that the horse was not there—that it, and his lance as well, had been stolen.

Proceeding on foot, he and the Palmer came at last to a castle, rising from a rock on the edge of the sea. There lived three sisters, two of whom—the eldest and the youngest—were in constant strife against the third. It was the middle sister who greeted Guyon and the Palmer: a gracious and modest young woman named Medina.

54

News of the arrival of guests soon came to her sisters, who were dallying with their knightly lovers. The eldest sister, Elissa, was the lady of Sir Hudibras, a knight much given to rash foolhardiness; while the youngest, Perissa, was the beloved of a pagan knight, Sansloy, the same Saracen who had once sought to force himself on Una, the lady of the Red Cross Knight.

Both these warriors arose to seek Guyon and try his mettle. But, on their way, because they were always in deadly rivalry, they fell to arguing, and then to fighting, so that the house shook with the fury of their swordplay. Guyon, sword drawn, rushed to part them and quell their wrath—but the two left their own quarrel and turned on him. Like a ship cleaving between two threatening waves, Guyon responded fiercely, plying sword and shield with all his prowess so that both knights fell back before the onslaught.

Then Medina ran to them, begging them to cease. And though her sisters tried to urge their lovers into further discord, Medina's words made them see the foolishness of their angry combat. So peace was made, and all three knights returned with the sisters to divest themselves of their armour and to sit down to dinner.

The eldest sister, Elissa, made much play of being annoyed, as if the food and the company were unsuitable; and the youngest, Perissa, indulged to excess in food and drink and in wanton flirtation with her knight. But the fair Medina kept control of the dinner with her reason and moderation, and at the end courteously requested Guyon to tell the company of himself, and what adventure was the cause of his present journey.

Guyon began by speaking of his undying allegiance to the wondrous Queen of Faeryland, Gloriana. To her court one day, he went on, had come an elderly Palmer, who spoke of grievous wrongs being done in the realm by a wicked enchantress. The queen had chosen Guyon to accompany the Palmer and redress those wrongs, by putting an end to the enchantress's wickedness.

He then told of his encounter with the dying Amavia, and how he had taken possession of that lady's infant—all of which had enhanced his determination to rid the world of Acrasia and her evil ways.

In the morning Guyon and the Palmer took their leave of Medina. But first Guyon placed the bloodstained baby into her care, and asked that the infant be named Ruddymane, so that always he would remember how his parents had died, and would avoid the evil that had been their downfall.

Meanwhile his steed, and his lance, were far away, in the possession of a scoundrel named Braggadochio. He was a foolish, vain and empty-headed wastrel, with nothing in him of chivalry or honour, who had been passing through the forest when he had seen Guyon's charger. So he had stolen it and the lance away—and thereby came to feel puffed up with self-importance at the brave show that he was sure he made, on that gallant steed.

As he proceeded, Braggadochio saw a man idling in the sun, dressed in clothes as gaudy as a peacock. The would-be knight rode nearer, threatening the other man with the lance; but the brightly dressed one threw himself to the ground in terror. "Spare me, lord," he cried, "and I will become your vassal, pledging you loyal service while I live!"

Braggadochio grandly agreed, and so the other, whose name was Trompart, became his servant. Nor was it long before the sly Trompart learned what kind of man his master was, and just how to flatter Braggadochio to his own advantage.

As this well-suited pair travelled together, they came upon the magician Archimago, wandering alone with his plots for vengeance upon his enemies. The sorcerer greeted them, and in their conversation began spinning a web of lies about evils that had been done to him and others by two knights, one named Sir Guyon and the other bearing a Red Cross.

Braggadochio swelled up with seeming fury, and shook his lance. "Show me where these villains lurk," he roared, "and I will wreak vengeance upon them!"

"I will, my lord," replied Archimago, "but first you should obtain a sword—for these are two knights of great prowess."

"Do not be so foolish," snorted Braggadochio, "as to measure a man's worth by his weapons." And he related a fanciful tale of how he had once slain seven knights at once with his sword, and vowed thereafter never to wear a sword again unless it was that of the noblest knight on earth.

"By your leave, sir knight," said the magician, "that I can provide. For the noblest knight now living is certainly Prince Arthur, who is presently in this land. By tomorrow I will bring his sword."

Braggadochio grew uneasy at this offer—and then turned pale and fled with terror, Trompart at his heels, for Archimago had summoned the power of the north wind, which swept him up and carried him away at his behest.

The frightened pair fled to a nearby forest, where they hid, hair standing on end at the rustle of every leaf. Their fear grew greater when through the forest came the silvery blare of a hunting horn, followed by the sound of someone moving swiftly through the undergrowth. Braggadochio, in terror, crept away to hide in a deep thicket, but Trompart remained behind, peering nervously out to see who was approaching.

It was a lady of unsurpassed grace and beauty, golden-haired, dressed like a hunter in a tunic of white silk and high boots of the finest leather. She carried a boar-spear in one hand, and at her back were slung a bow and a quiver of arrows. And she moved through the forest with light-footed agility and speed as if she were the goddess Diana herself.

Trompart did not know whether to hide or flee, and before he could decide the huntress had seen him. She called out pleasantly, asking if he had seen a deer that had fled after one of her arrows had wounded it.

"Forgive me, goddess, if that is what you are," the servant babbled, "but I have not seen it."

Before the lady could reply, her eye caught a movement in the bushes where Braggadochio had hidden himself. Dropping her spear, she drew and nocked an arrow—but Trompart hurriedly leaped forward.

"Stay your hand, lady, for that is no beast!" he cried. "That is my master, a famous warrior!"

As the huntress lowered her bow, Braggadochio crept out, yawning and stretching as if he had been sleeping rather than hiding. He stared lecherously at the lovely woman, yet kept his distance for fear of the weapons that she handled so expertly.

"Good day, sir knight," said the lady courteously, "I trust good fortune attends you in your knightly adventurings."

"So it has done," boomed Braggadochio, "in all my warlike deeds, which have written my name high among the most famed and glorious knights. But tell me, lady, why does one as beautiful as yourself hide away in this dark wood, when you belong among the joys and pleasures of the court?"

"Such vain delights are easily found," said the lady, whose name was Belphoebe, "but worthless. I seek the value and the honour that comes with toil, and peril, and care."

She might have continued, but Braggadochio had been gazing rather than listening. He moved suddenly towards her, lust kindling in his eyes. Belphoebe sprang back, her spear levelled at him menacingly. As he halted, she turned and sped away into the forest depths.

The false knight made no effort to pursue her, too fearful of her arrows. "How dare she so insult me," he blustered, "with her disdain?"

"Let her go," said Trompart, "for I fear she may be a spirit, or some heavenly power."

"I thought the same," said Braggadochio quickly, "which is why

I hid, for nothing on this earth can make *me* afraid, save supernatural power, whether of hell or heaven."

So they left the forest, though the false knight was finding great difficulty in managing the fierce and noble charger of Guyon, which resented the clumsy, untrained hands upon its reins.

*   *   *

At that time Guyon was still journeying, on foot, with the steadfast Palmer beside him, when they caught sight of a tumult in the distance. Drawing near, they found what seemed to be a madman, dragging a handsome youth along the ground by his hair, often turning and beating him till his tormented flesh bled. Behind them hobbled a wrinkled and white-haired hag, screaming with hate-filled venom, urging the madman to ever more furious violence.

Guyon at once took hold of the madman, to drag him away from his victim. But the madman rounded on him in a foaming, demonic fury, striking, kicking, biting, tearing, scratching. Guyon, trained for knightly combat, was taken aback by such a crudely wild assault—and the madman's strength was great, though uncontrolled. As they lurched to and fro, grappling, Guyon stumbled and fell, with the madman upon him, beating at his face, and the hag screeching murderous encouragement.

Guyon gathered his strength and flung the madman away, drawing his sword angrily as he rose. But the Palmer interposed.

"Hold, Sir Guyon," he called. "This creature cannot be overcome by strength or steel. His name is Furor, one of knighthood's worst enemies. To defeat him you must first quell the hag, his mother, whose name is Occasion, the source of all wrath."

Guyon turned then to the hag, grasping her by the hair and flinging her to the ground. Yet still her reviling screeches did not stop—until Guyon grimly took an iron lock and fastened it to her vile tongue, then halted even the gestures of her hands by tying them to a stake. No longer prompted by her, the madman Furor sought to flee, but Guyon pursued him and dragged him back. And now the knight's strength prevailed, and he bound Furor to an iron rack, with a hundred iron chains tied in a hundred stout knots.

The madman screamed and gnashed his teeth, struggling fiercely in his unbridled rage, but Guyon ignored him and went to the young squire whom Furor had so nearly killed. As Guyon made him comfortable and dressed his wounds, the young man, named Phedon, explained how he had come into such torment.

He had been tricked and betrayed—by one who, he had thought, was his dearest friend—into believing that his betrothed had been unfaithful. In a murderous rage he had slain the lady he loved. Later, when he had learned the truth, remorse and revenge drove him further into maddened rage, and he had also killed his treacherous friend.

Soon afterwards he had come upon the mad creature Furor and his vile mother. His rage had somehow kindled theirs to greater heights, so that Furor easily overcame him, which led to the scene of manic violence that Guyon had come upon.

"And now," Phedon added dolefully, "death itself would be better than the agony that grief and anger have brought upon me."

"So you have learned," put in the Palmer, "that emotions must be curbed, or they can grow too strong—all the more in a weak and intemperate man. Wrath, jealousy, grief, love itself can then make war upon the reason, and bring it down. Take heed now, young squire, of what you have learned through your suffering, so that your steps may be guided more wisely henceforth."

While he was speaking Guyon had seen in the distance a man running towards them at great speed. Soon he had come up to them, panting, sweaty and dust-covered, and proved to be a knight's servant, or page. He carried a shield slung on his back, presumably his master's, which displayed the emblem of flames of fire against a blood-red field, with the motto "Burnt, I do burn". And he held two light javelins, or darts, whose needle points were stained with blood and poison.

"Sir knight, if you are a knight," the servant said insolently to Guyon, "you would be wise to depart from this place, or you will find yourself in great danger."

Guyon was surprised at the servant's arrogance, but replied calmly, "What danger is it that threatens?"

"A knight of wondrous power," proclaimed the servant, "who has never failed to defeat his enemies. He is Pyrochles, brother of Cymochles, both of the race of the immortals, for they are sons of Acrates and Despite, gods older than Jove. And I am Atin, servant to Pyrochles, aid and encouragement to him in his warlike wrath. So now you must flee, in all haste."

"Let those flee who will," said Guyon quietly. "You yourself were in some haste, before—where were you going?"

"My master sent me," said Atin, "to find old Occasion, to stir him further to the furious battle that he craves."

"He is a fool," put in the Palmer, "who seeks Occasion to stir up strife. Too often she comes unsought, to the detriment of all men."

Guyon indicated where the hag sat, bound and silenced. "There sits Occasion," he told Atin. "Take that message to your master."

The servant exploded into furious anger. "Vile knight," he

The tale told by Phedon is an often-used plot—by the Italian poet Ariosto in his epic romance Orlando Furioso *(1532), from which Spenser borrowed freely, and later by Shakespeare in* Much Ado about Nothing *(c.1598–99). It also resembles the Knight's Tale in Chaucer's* Canterbury Tales: *illustration of the knight from a 15th-century manuscript of the poem.*

screamed, "you bring shame upon knighthood, to make war upon a weak old woman! My master will seek your blood for this!"

As he spoke, he hurled one of his javelins, the poison of ire and malice gleaming on the point. But Guyon swung up his shield, and the dart glanced harmlessly aside—while Atin turned and sped away.

*   *   *

Inevitably it was not long before Guyon saw the knight himself, Atin's master, galloping headlong towards them. His armour was flame-bright, his charger was blood-red, and dust rose like smoke-clouds beneath its hooves. He did not slow or hesitate as he came near, but levelled his lance and spurred at Guyon.

On foot, Guyon knew better than to stand against such a blow. He swayed lightly aside from it, and then lashed out powerfully with his sword. The blade glanced from the other knight's shield towards the charger's neck, and wholly severed its head.

Pyrochles crashed bruisingly to the ground into the pooling blood of his dead horse. He rose roaring threats and abuse, and struck at Guyon so fiercely that his sword hewed away the upper edge of Guyon's shield and carried on to make a deep gash in his helmet.

Guyon staggered a moment, for the blow would have killed him if his shield had not taken some of the force. Then anger spurred him, and he replied with a savage blow that slashed through the armour on Pyrochles's left shoulder and bit deep into the flesh.

The blood and pain fuelled the flame of Pyrochles's killing fury. Berserk, he seemed to forget all his knightly skills, and attacked Guyon like a maddened beast. With terrifying power he slashed and hacked and thundered blows that it seemed no man could survive. But Guyon, remaining composed, guarded and defended, awaiting his moment.

It came when exhaustion overtook the berserk rage of Pyrochles, and his sword arm sagged. Then Guyon counterattacked with a blow so huge that it forced Pyrochles to his knees. Another mighty stroke, and Pyrochles was stretched flat upon the ground, with Guyon's boot on his chest.

"Mercy!" cried Pyrochles. "Spare me—I yield!"

Guyon calmly lowered his sword. "Live, then, but first pledge allegiance to me, and learn also what this encounter can teach you, of the dangers of hasty and thoughtless wrath."

Pyrochles rose, glowering and grinding his teeth over the galling shame of his defeat. But Guyon said, "Do not be aggrieved: there is no shame in honourable defeat. But you, Pyrochles, defeat yourself. You must learn to curb the forces within you—blind fury, impatience, discord—that are your worst enemies. Tell me now, why did you attack me?"

"I was told," muttered Pyrochles, "that you had wronged a poor old woman. I came to fight on her behalf, to set her and her son free."

"Is that all?" said Guyon with a smile. "Then free them, if you will. They are there."

Pyrochles went quickly to break the bonds of the hag and her mad son. But as soon as Occasion was freed, she resumed her ways. Scolding, she chided Guyon for his victory and Pyrochles for his defeat; and when Furor was also free, the hag turned her tongue on him, kindling the manic rage within him. Soon both Furor and Pyrochles were so inflamed with the hag's railing that they sprang at each other with wild fury. And Occasion still tried to stir up wrath within Guyon, with biting scorn and shaming abuse; but Guyon remained calm, and her words had no effect.

Furor and Pyrochles fought on, ever more violently and bloodily. Then Occasion brought a flaming torch to her son, and with that weapon Furor's crazed power proved too much for the knight. Furor flung him to the ground, battering him viciously, dragging him through the dust—until Pyrochles desperately called to Guyon for help.

Guyon moved to respond, but the Palmer intervened. "Your pity is wasted," said the old man, "for Pyrochles chose wilfully to release Furor, and now must pay the penalty for his folly."

So Guyon held back, and with the Palmer turned away and resumed his journey.

Pyrochles and Cymochles recall the ancient world's idea of the four bodily "humours" that govern human temperament. Pyrochles is ruled by "choler" while his slightly less violent brother is more a man of "phlegm". Illustrations from Henry Peacham's Minerva Britannia.

Atin, servant of Pyrochles, had fled far away when his master first fell under Guyon's sword. Believing Pyrochles dead, Atin sought his master's brother, Cymochles—a knight of great prowess and also the lover of Acrasia, the evil enchantress who entrapped men through the idle and lascivious pleasures of her Bower of Bliss.

And in the Bower Atin found Cymochles, on a bed of lilies, surrounded by voluptuous half-naked damsels striving to outdo each other in wantonness for the knight's pleasure.

Atin burst in boldly and began to upbraid the knight for burying himself in lustful indulgence while even then his brother, Pyrochles, lay slain by an enemy. And Cymochles sprang up, brushing the damsels aside, fury blazing up within him under the poisonous sting of Atin's words. Donning his armour, he spurred fiercely away, just as he himself was spurred by the malice of Atin.

As Cymochles rode vengefully to find Guyon, he found his way barred by a broad stretch of water in full flood. But he saw a small boat at the water's edge—like a gondola, covered with woven boughs made into an arbour. Within sat a pretty damsel who seemed overcome by merriment though she was alone, singing and laughing to herself. Cymochles called to her, asking her to ferry him across the water; and she came to him at once, though she refused adamantly to take Atin as well into her boat.

They sailed swiftly out upon the water, though the gondola lacked both oars and sail. And as they went the damsel began to amuse and entertain Cymochles with songs and merry tales, jokes and playfulness, until all his grim warlike wrath faded.

When Cymochles asked her name, she laughed and said, "Foolish knight, you should know me, for I am Phaedria, a servant like yourself of great Acrasia. This place is the Lake of Idleness, where I dwell with my little boat."

As she spoke, the boat had brought them to an island in the middle of the lake, and there they disembarked, Cymochles marvelling at the lush and sensual beauty of the pastoral scene. Phaedria led him to a shady dale, and laid him down upon the soft turf, with her head in his lap, singing a melodic tune that soon lulled him to sleep. Then she returned to her boat, sliding again out on to the wide lake.

By that time Guyon had reached the other side of the same lake, and—seeing the gondola—similarly requested its owner's aid to carry him across. Again Phaedria willingly obliged, but would not allow Guyon to bring the Palmer as well. Guyon was unwilling to leave his guide behind, but it was too late: he had already entered the boat, and it magically flitted away from the shore before he could step out of it.

As with Cymochles, the damsel sought to bemuse and delight Guyon by her merry and playful charms. But while Guyon remained courteous, he drew back from her wanton excesses. And when the gondola as before drew up to her island, Guyon grew annoyed at having been so misled and taken aside from his intended path. But Phaedria laughed and teased him merrily, and insisted on showing him the rich beauties of the place.

As they moved through the island's lush glades, Cymochles awoke and went in search of the damsel. When he came upon Phaedria with Guyon, jealous anger rose up within him, and he flung himself at Guyon, sword in hand.

Guyon met him with his own sword, and exchanged stroke for thunderous stroke till their armour was gashed in many places and crimsoned with their blood. Cymochles had never fought such a valiant knight, and desperately increased the strength of his blows;

The merry and wanton Phaedria represents the goddess of love in her more amorous and immodest aspects. Painting of "Venus with a Mirror" by Titian (1477–1576).

but Guyon replied in kind, his own power seeming doubled.

At last both swung up their swords for murderous blows with all their hugest force, and both blows fell at once. Cymochles's sheared away a quarter of Guyon's shield—but Guyon's split the helmet of his adversary, and gashed his head to the bone.

Cymochles swayed, senseless as stone. Then Phaedria sprang between them, begging them to stop. "Dalliance and pleasure are the only battlefields where I wish my lovers to contend," she said. "Remember that Mars, god of war, is more famed for his love of Venus than for all his victories in battle."

So the knights relented and drew back from combat. But Guyon was as determined as before to return to his journey—and now Phaedria was all too ready to help him on his way, to rid her island of his stern presence. The little boat swiftly carried them to the far side of the lake, and the knight gratefully disembarked.

Guyon had landed near the place where the spiteful servant Atin waited, still wondering what had become of Cymochles. Atin began to pour forth a stream of vile insults and abuse at Guyon, but turned and fled as the knight strode away without reply.

Farther along the shore, Atin saw an armoured knight running at speed towards him, covered with dirt and dried blood. The knight did not pause, but rushed straight to the lake's edge and flung himself in, as if careless whether or not he drowned. Creeping closer, Atin saw with astonishment that it was his master, Pyrochles, whom he had believed dead.

He dashed down to the floundering knight, calling to him in fright and amazement. And Pyrochles cried out, as if in agony: "I burn, I burn—I am aflame, though I see no fire! Nothing can quench the flames that sear me, nothing but death, yet I cannot die! Help me, Atin, help me to die and end my suffering!"

And Atin wept at the pity of his master's plight, and plunged into the lake to aid him, not knowing that the water in that lake was so thick with mud and foulness that nothing, however heavy, could sink beneath it. So they splashed and struggled and cried out, until there hurried towards them an elderly, white-haired man, carrying a splendid sword.

Atin saw the old man, and knew him at once. "Archimago!" he cried. "Help us, or we shall die!"

Archimago came closer, and called, "Pyrochles, what is this madness? I know you for a wrathful man, but never driven to this excess."

And Pyrochles screamed again, "The flames, the flames—within my body, unseen, consuming me! Furor it was, the cursed fiend, who wounded me in battle, and kindled these hellish flames that char my very bowels!"

Then Archimago understood. With Atin's help, he dragged Pyrochles on to land and stripped his armour off. With charms and herbs and mighty spells he sought out the wounds made by Furor on the knight's body and quenched the hidden fire that lay magically within them, so that shortly Pyrochles was restored to health.

*   *   *

By that time Guyon, having now lost his guide as well as his horse, had travelled far from the lake into a dismal wasteland. Wandering into a shadowy glade, he came upon a man seated in the dimness whose face and beard were blackened with smoke and soot, whose hands seemed fire-scorched, with nails like claws. He wore a rusty, dirt-smeared iron coat—yet its inner surface, hardly visible for dust, was made of gold, wonderfully wrought. On his lap he held a mass of golden coins, which he played with and gloated over, while all around him lay further heaps of gold.

Seeing Guyon, the man hastily began pouring all the treasure down a wide hole into the earth. But Guyon stopped him. "What kind of man are you," he asked, "who keeps such a hoard of wealth hidden from the world in this wilderness?"

"You are rash and foolish, sir knight," said the man, "to impose yourself upon me. I am the god Mammon, from whom all riches, all worldly goods and high estate, flow out to mankind. Pledge yourself to me, and all this wealth or ten times more shall be yours."

"Offer it to those who covet it," Guyon replied, "but I have pledged my life to honour and knightly deeds, not to the weak craving for riches."

"Fool," said the god, "riches can bring anything you want: brave chargers, bright arms, crowns, and kingdoms."

"Not so," Guyon insisted, "for covetousness is the root of unhappiness. Wealth is acquired with guile, preserved with dread, spent with pride, leaving only grief behind. It is the source of infinite harm—bloodshed, treachery, wars—so that truly noble hearts must despise it."

"Why is it, then," Mammon said angrily, "if wealth is so evil, that mortal men crave it so desperately, and bemoan its lack?"

"Men are weak, and intemperance often traps them into avarice," Guyon said. "Here you are, with this vast treasure, which, for all I know, might have been stolen from its rightful owner, covered with blood-guilt."

"All this is mine," Mammon replied, "and far more, beneath the earth, than ever you could imagine. Come and see what no other human eye has ever seen."

Out of curiosity Guyon followed Mammon down through the cavern into the earth's depths, until the tunnel opened into a vast open space, with a broad highway leading to Pluto's dwelling place. By the roadside Guyon saw an assortment of terrible beings: dire Pain, with an iron whip, and Strife, with a bloody dagger; cruel Revenge, rancorous Spite, disloyal Treason, burning Hate; Jealousy, sitting apart from the others; Fear running in panic to and fro; Sorrow, weeping in darkness. Above them all soared grim Horror on black wings.

They came to a small door, beside the very gates of hell, that led to Mammon's house. As they entered, from the shadows moved a ghastly fiend, who stalked watchfully behind Guyon, ready with dreadful claws to rip him to pieces if ever he rested a covetous hand or eye on anything in that place.

Silently Guyon followed the god through another door, beyond which lay a mountainous hoard of gold that surpassed all the wealth of the entire world of men. "Here lies all the world's happiness," Mammon announced, "and if you will, it shall be yours."

"I seek a different happiness," Guyon said, "in the true life of knighthood."

Behind him the fiend growled and gnashed his teeth, deprived. Mammon then led the knight into a place where a hundred furnaces blazed hot and bright, tended by deformed and ugly demons, refining ore into purest gold. Again Mammon made his offer to Guyon—again the knight unhesitatingly refused it.

The god led Guyon onwards seeking to tempt him further. He offered the knight his daughter, who sat on a high throne while throngs of people sought to climb the golden chain of Ambition that she guarded. He took Guyon into the glorious Garden of Proserpine, where grew the golden apples with which foul Discord had stirred up strife among the Olympian gods and launched the Trojan War. But always Guyon steadfastly rejected these blandishments.

Then Guyon began to feel weak, for he had been a long time in that underground world, without food or rest or good air. He asked Mammon to return him to the outside world, and the god had to agree, for a mortal could remain only briefly in that dark world.

But when Guyon reached the surface, the effect of light and fresh air overcame him, weakened as he was by the foulness of the underworld. And he fell unconscious, as if life itself had left him.

*   *   *

Meanwhile Guyon's faithful Palmer had found his own way across the Lake of Idleness and had been hurrying to overtake Guyon. As

Mammon's offer to Guyon resembles the temptations that many mythical heroes undergo—as did even Jesus of Nazareth, tempted by Satan, in this 13th-century painting by Duccio di Buoninsegna.

he searched in the wasteland, he heard a clear voice calling nearby—and, following the call, found Guyon lying, apparently dead.

Beside Guyon the Palmer saw a gloriously handsome youth, with wings of snowy white rising from his back. The Palmer was stricken, but the youth reassured him.

"Your aid has been sorely lacked," said the youth, "by your pupil, who has undergone much hardship. Yet do not fear: he lives, and will awaken soon. I now return the guardianship of him to you, though I will watch over him still." And he spread his angelic wings and rose into the sky.

The Palmer, awed, watched the youth vanish from sight. But as he moved to Guyon's side, he saw two knights approaching swiftly, accompanied by a young page and a white-haired old man. They were the brothers Pyrochles and Cymochles, with Archimago and the spiteful Atin.

When they saw Guyon's fallen body, Pyrochles shouted, "Old man, stand away from the corpse of that treacherous knight!"

"Not so," said the Palmer fearlessly. "You dishonour yourself by maligning the dead—and you yourself have experienced both his nobility and his prowess."

"What do you know of prowess, old fool?" sneered Cymochles. "He is dead, therefore his knightly valour has proved false."

"And I will have my vengeance!" Pyrochles roared. "I will despoil him of his arms and shield, for a dead dog needs no bright armour!"

"To desecrate the dead is both shame and sin," the Palmer replied. But Pyrochles ignored him, and snatched up Guyon's shield, while his brother bent to unfasten the fallen knight's armour.

As they did so, Archimago saw another knight spurring towards them, followed by a squire who bore his lance and a covered shield. And the sorcerer called to the brothers, "Rise and prepare yourselves for battle! Yonder comes the noblest knight alive—Prince Arthur, the flower of chivalry!"

The brothers leaped up to challenge the newcomer. And Pyrochles, lacking a sword, demanded of Archimago the use of the bright blade that the sorcerer was taking, as he had promised earlier, to the false knight Braggadochio.

But Archimago would not let Pyrochles have it. "This sword itself belongs to Arthur, made for him by Merlin, and filled with great virtue. It can never be used against its rightful owner by another hand."

But the furious Pyrochles snatched the sword, turning with his brother to face Prince Arthur. The prince saluted them, then gazed down upon the face of Guyon, still lying as if dead. "Reverend sir," Arthur said to the Palmer, "how did this noble knight meet his end?"

"He is not dead, but clouded in deep unconsciousness," said the Palmer. "And your aid would be welcome, fair sir, to prevent this vengeful pair from despoiling him of his arms while he is helpless."

Arthur turned to the brothers. "Sirs, I know nothing of what cause you have for enmity to this fallen knight. But let not your wrath lead you to stain your honour."

"Who are you, to protect him?" Cymochles demanded. "I shall not be prevented from wreaking my vengeance on his corpse, as I would have done on his living body."

And Pyrochles cried, "If you protect him, then you partake of his crimes!" And without warning he swung Arthur's great sword in a blow that might have cleaved the prince in two, had it landed. But the enchanted sword swung aside from its true owner.

Arthur, angered by the cowardly attack, charged at Pyrochles, his lance thrusting fiercely. But Pyrochles half-blocked the thrust with Guyon's shield, so that the lance-point buried itself only in his shoulder, yet hurled him bleeding to the ground.

His brother Cymochles, raging, slashed at Arthur with his sword, the blow glancing from the prince's helmet and sending him in turn crashing to the ground. He rose at once, but without a sword was

The dying King Arthur returns his sword, Excalibur, to the Lady of the Lake—from a 14th-century French manuscript. Spenser gives Prince Arthur's sword another name—"Morddure"—but its magical qualities are no less obvious in the combat with Pyrochles.

badly handicapped for fighting on foot. Then Pyrochles too was up, his blazing fury overcoming the pain of his wound, and both brothers assailed the prince with a rain of thunderous blows.

Arthur gave ground slowly under the terrible onslaught, skilfully warding off the blows with his impenetrable shield. And when he saw his chance, he thrust again with his lance at Cymochles, who had lowered his own shield's guard for a moment. The steel struck deeply into Cymochles's thigh, and the lance broke, leaving the point embedded.

The wound seemed only to inflame both knights to even more berserk rage. The strength and number of their blows doubled and redoubled—and though the sword in Pyrochles's hand still would not make contact with Arthur, his brother's sword finally hewed through the shaft of the lance with which Arthur was defending himself and bit deep into the prince's side.

Yet Arthur still did not give way, but instead struck out so ferociously with the broken lance that he drove Cymochles back a pace or two. Then the Palmer snatched up Guyon's sword, and hurriedly took it to Arthur.

Properly armed, the prince was transformed. From defence he moved to attack, laying about him with inhuman might, battering at his enemies with twice as many blows as together they had rained on him. Back he drove them, until both would surely have been slain, except that Pyrochles still was carrying Guyon's shield, with its image of the Faery Queen—and the prince's hand always drew back from striking at that beloved face.

But Cymochles was not so fortunate. He lashed out at Arthur, his sword biting through the prince's helmet and into the skin beneath; but Arthur's counterstroke with Guyon's sword hewed deeper into his enemy's helmet and buried the blade in Cymochles's brain.

As his brother fell, Pyrochles's killing fury flared up beyond all bounds. He hurled himself at Arthur, slashing and chopping and lunging manically, all skill and strategy forgotten. Arthur waited, defending again till his enemy had spent himself in the crazed storm of his attack, knowing that the sword in Pyrochles's hand would do him no harm. But Pyrochles saw at last the futility of attacking the prince with that weapon, and flung it away, springing at Arthur bare-handed.

Arthur met his rush, and proved both the stronger and more skilful. It was Pyrochles who was hurled to the ground—and lay there unmoving, while rage and hatred seethed within his heart.

The prince, in the generous nobility of his spirit, said to him, "Renounce your villainy now, and yield yourself to me, and I will spare your life."

In the traditional coup de grâce *that ended a combat to the death between knights, the victor would wrench off the helmet of his defeated opponent and behead him—as in this illustration from a French medieval manuscript.*

"Fool," Pyrochles spat, "I defy you and reject your gift of life, which is meaningless to me!" And Arthur, anger and sadness mingling within him, had no choice but to sweep down his sword in the *coup-de-grâce*—and left Pyrochles's headless body gouting blood on to the ground.

At that point Guyon awoke, and rose unsteadily, looking around for his shield and sword. The Palmer greeted him with gladness, and quickly explained all that had happened. And Guyon went to Prince Arthur and bowed low. "My lord, for what you have done for me this day, there could be no repayment. I am forever in your debt."

"There is no debt, sir, and no repayment needed," said Arthur, "for is a knight not bound by his oath to do battle against evil and oppression?"

So they talked, in courteous fellowship, while, unseen, Archimago and Atin took hastily to their heels.

*　　　　　*　　　　　*

From there Arthur and Guyon travelled together, in deepening friendship. And as they journeyed, the prince inquired of Guyon why he bore the portrait of such a beautiful lady on his shield.

"If you think the image beautiful," said Guyon, "you would be overcome by the beauty of the reality, in face and mind and spirit. She is the mighty Queen of Faery, my liege and sovereign—renowned and praised throughout the world, more glorious than the morning star."

"Happiest of men," replied the prince, "to live in the service of such a queen. Since I first pledged myself to knighthood, my whole desire has been to serve her with all my power. Yet though I have travelled the world to seek her, still I have not succeeded."

"Keep constant and you shall reach your goal," said Guyon. "I would happily guide your steps, but I am called elsewhere on a quest from which I must not turn aside."

While they talked, they found themselves drawing near a handsome castle, set by a river in a peaceful dale, and turned that way, to seek its hospitality. But they found its gates locked and barred.

Arthur's squire approached the gate and blew the golden horn that he carried, so that the walls of the castle trembled. Then a figure appeared on the battlements, shouting down to them.

"Ride, ride away, good sirs! Happily would we make you welcome, but we are surrounded by a thousand foes who have besieged us seven long years! Ride, if you would save yourselves!"

And before the knights could move, around them swarmed a thousand yelling men, ragged and misshapen, bearing spears and knives, clubs and blazing torches. Wild-eyed and savage, they attacked with fury, throwing the knights back at first by the weight of numbers. But the knights rallied and charged the mob, like two lions bursting into a flock of sheep.

The rabble fell away from that powerful onslaught, and though their captain tried to spur them on, again the knights plunged in among them, laying about themselves with such might that the entire thousand fled in terror before them.

Then the knights were admitted into the castle, and made graciously welcome by the mistress of that house, whose name was Alma. She was a fair, graceful, and modest maiden, garbed in lily white, with a long train to her dress borne by two damsels, and a garland of roses in her golden hair. Taking the knights up to her hall, she showed them every hospitality—and when they were rested, she led them forth to show them her castle.

First she took them to the castle wall, showing them how it was formed not from brick or stone but from earth itself. She pointed out the proportions of the structure, using both the circle and the

The house of Alma is an allegorical representation of the human body, in which the ideal proportions are based on the circle and the triangle—figures with much symbolic significance in astrology, numerology, and alchemy. The geometrical design shown here, containing a male and female figure, comes from an alchemical book printed in Germany in 1618.

triangle based on the numbers seven and nine. The main gate of the castle wall, which opened to friends and closed to foes, had a smooth stone porch and a portcullis. And there a porter sat, on guard against liars, slanderers, and foolish babblers, with thirty-two stoutly armoured yeomen ranged around him.

Alma then conducted them to the dining hall, with broad tables laid and spread, overseen by a steward called Diet, of noble bearing, and a courteous, welcoming marshal named Appetite. From there they moved to the kitchen, with its vast furnace that blazed unceasingly beneath a mighty cauldron, and two huge bellows that cooled the air all around it. The master cook, named Concoction, oversaw all the work with great care, aided by a clerk named Digestion; and they directed the labours of all the other servants, including those who ensured that all waste was sent by a great conduit pipe to the castle's back gate to be expelled.

Next, Alma showed them into a spacious parlour, where many of the fair young men and women of the castle were seated. Arthur fell into conversation with a lovely damsel named Praise-desire, in whom he saw a reflection of his own tireless quest for knightly glory— while Guyon spoke with a shy and blushing maiden who outdid even his own modesty, and whose name was Shamefastness.

Finally Alma guided them up steps of alabaster to a high tower that contained many levels and chambers, illuminated by two beacons of living fire. In the most important rooms lived three honourable sages, the chief counsellors of Alma: one who could see into the future, one whose wisdom embraced the present, one who encompassed all the past.

The chamber of the first of these was decorated with colourful scenes from fantasy, dream, and imaginings, and filled with buzzing flies that were visions, prophecies, fancies, and idle thoughts—while the sage himself was a dark, saturnine young man with burning eyes and melancholic expression. The walls of the second room were covered with images from art and science, politics, law and philosophy, within which sat a grave, middle-aged man deep in thought and meditation.

The third room seemed ancient and decrepit, though its walls were as sturdy as the others, and were covered with scrolls and parchments of every kind, while more scrolls as well as countless quantities of books were heaped all round the room. There lived an aged man, older even than Methuselah had been, ceaselessly turning the pages of one book or another, attended by a small boy who brought to him the volumes that he wished.

Within that vast library Arthur caught sight of a book entitled *British Monuments*, the entire history of his land, while Guyon chanced on a book titled *Antiquity of Faeryland*. Both begged leave of Alma and the ancient sage to read those books, which was readily granted.

Arthur's book began with the earliest times, when Britain, then called Albion, was inhabited only by giants and savages. Then Brutus, descendant of the kings of Troy, came to the land and established his kingdom, naming it Britain, and overthrowing the giants. Brutus was succeeded by Locrine, under whom Albanact became ruler of the northern regions and Camber of the western. Locrine fought heroic battles against invaders, but later fell into dishonour when he deserted his wife for another lady. His wife raised an army against him, and he was slain.

Locrine's son Madan inherited the throne, succeeded by Memprise, both unworthy kings. But after them came the noble Ebranck, winning great fame in war against Britain's enemies, as did his son, the second Brutus, who victoriously carried the wars to Europe.

His son Leill restored peace to the land, made more permanent by the next monarch, Hudibras. His successor, Bladud, brought the arts and sciences to a peak that rivaled Athens. But then King Lear brought discord and violence back to the land by dividing the kingdom among two of his daughters, wrongfully excluding the third. And the royal house of Brutus declined into a series of pretenders to the throne, bloodying the land's history with intrigue, assassinations, and civil war.

Peace was finally restored by the mighty Dunwallo, who reunited the land and imposed the rule of sound law on his kingdom. His sons, Brennus and Bellinus, took armies into Europe and subjugated France, Germany, Italy, even Greece—while their successor, Gurgunt, subdued Scandinavia. After him reigned the just Guitheline, then Sisillus, Kimarus, Danius, and the violent Morindus.

He was succeeded by his five sons, in turn: Gorboman, Archigald, Elidure, Peridure, and Vigent. From them Hely gained the throne, followed by his son Lud, and then Cassibalane—who was king when the Romans under Julius Caesar invaded Britain and imposed their rule. From then Rome held sway over much of Britain, though many fought to throw off its grip, among them queen Boadicea and the later king Cole. Cole's son Lucius was said to be the first British ruler to embrace Christianity, though it was brought to Britain earlier with, legend says, Joseph of Arimathea, who carried with him the Holy Grail. As Rome declined, Britain was ravaged often by Huns and Picts, until they were driven back by Constantine. After him, Vortiger usurped the throne, and allowed in the Saxons Hengist and Horsa, who overran all Britain. But finally the sons of Constantine reclaimed the throne, and were succeeded by Aurelius and then by the great Uther Pendragon.

But there the book ended abruptly, much to Prince Arthur's surprise and displeasure, for he had marvelled long at the splendour of Britain's past. Meanwhile Guyon had been immersed in his own book.

It began with an account of how the god Prometheus had fashioned a living man whom he had named Elfe—and how Elfe had found in the gardens of Adonis a lovely woman whom he named Fay. From their union sprang all the race of Faery, and all the royal line that ruled Faeryland—Elfin, the first king; Elfinan, who began the Faery city Cleopolis, and Elfiline, who completed it; the warrior Elfinell; Elfant, the builder of the crystal tower Panthea; the giant-slayer Elfar; the master of magic, Elfinor; and seven hundred more monarchs of high fame and majesty.

From them, in more recent times, had sprung the wise king Elficleos, followed by Elferon and then his brother the mighty Oberon. He was succeeded by his fair daughter, unequalled in nobility, grace, wisdom, and beauty, Gloriana.

Spenser's chronicle of the rulers of Faeryland is entirely his own invention, save for its beginning with the Greek demigod Prometheus—pictured here as the creator of man from a 16th-century French edition of Ovid's Metamorphoses.

*   *   *

After an evening spent enjoying the pleasant company and hospitality of Alma, the two knights rose early the next day. Guyon, with his Palmer, took his leave of their fair hostess, and set out down the river by which the castle stood, towards the sea, in a boat with a ferryman provided by Alma.

But Arthur remained in the castle, which, soon after Guyon had left, was once again besieged by the wild and savage rabble that had been attacking it before.

Their foul captain had divided them into twelve troops, sending seven with battering rams against the gate, and the other five—all ghastly, deformed creatures with the heads of dire beasts—to assail the five main bulwarks of the castle, Sight, Hearing, Smell, Taste, and Feeling.

The guardians of the castle defended it heroically, repelling wave after wave of attackers. But Alma grew increasingly frightened, until Prince Arthur, with his squire, took a hand in the battle. Out from the main gate he rode in his bright armour, on his fierce charger Spumador. Arrows flew at him thick as falling snow, and the rabble closed round him in their thousands. But his shield balked all their shafts, and his sweeping, flashing sword cut a swathe through their ranks and turned and routed them, as the furious west wind drives autumn leaves before it.

Hearing the tumult of his forces' retreat, the captain of the attackers rode swiftly into battle, mounted on a snarling tiger and bearing deadly arrows able to cause injuries that could never heal. Maleger was his name, pale, withered and skeletal, garbed in thin canvas with a dead man's skull as his helmet. Behind him came two aged hags, barefoot and ragged yet swift as deer—although one was lame, and leaned on a staff. Her name was Impotence, while the other, armed with raging flame, was Impatience.

Maleger loosed arrow upon arrow at Arthur, who warded them off with his shield, then set his lance and charged the evil being. But Maleger turned and fled, and the tiger was so swift that not even Arthur's steed could catch it. Still Maleger fired his deadly arrows, which were gathered by the lame hag and returned to the foul archer. And the prince, seeking to deprive Maleger of this support, turned aside to capture the hag and bind her.

But her sister came to her aid as Arthur dismounted. Her attack caught Arthur unprepared, and threw him off balance—and as he fell, both hags sprang on him. Maleger sped towards them, and also leaped on the fallen prince, with furious, savage blows. Then it was the squire that saved the prince, dragging the hags from him and holding them at bay with his sword. And Arthur rose, enraged, to face Maleger.

The evil captain had no chance now to flee. Arthur raised his iron mace and with all the might of his arm struck Maleger to the ground. But the skeletal being rose again at once, unharmed, and plucked up a vast boulder to hurl it effortlessly at the prince. Arthur dodged the huge missile and attacked again, plunging his sword hilt-deep in Maleger's chest, yet no drop of blood gushed, nor did Maleger fall. Twice more Arthur struck, wounds so terrible that he could see entirely through the body of his foe—yet still Maleger did not fall.

Arthur's heart seemed to stop with the horror of it, yet his fighting spirit did not flinch. He tossed his sword aside, and grasped Maleger in his powerful hands, crushing the breath and life from the withered body, then casting it to the ground crushingly. But at once Maleger was up, restored to life, raining furious blows on the prince.

Then Arthur saw the truth: that Maleger was being restored to life each time by contact with the earth, from which his power sprang. So again the prince clutched the skeletal body, and crushed it to death. But now he held the corpse aloft, upon his shoulders, and carried it some three furlongs away to a deep lake. Into the waters Arthur cast the body of Maleger, where death claimed it finally and completely. And one of the two hags, screaming insanely, flung herself into the water after her captain, while the other, lame Impotence, took one of Maleger's arrows and ended her own life.

With the squire's help, Arthur made his way back to the castle, where Alma herself comforted him and dressed his wounds.

Guyon and the Palmer had meanwhile put out to sea, and sailed for two days without sight of land or other vessels. On the third day they heard a terrible roaring in the distance, and saw vast waves reaching up to the sky. And the ferryman told them that the waves were the Gulf of Greediness, which gulped down any boat straying within, then spewed it forth again. And on the other side was a huge magnetic rock, that drew all ships towards it to their destruction, called the Rock of Vile Reproach.

All the ferryman's skill was needed to guide their frail craft past the sucking maw of the gulf and the craggy cliffs of the rock. But they came through in safety, whereupon Guyon glimpsed land ahead, and urged the ferryman towards it.

But the man refused, telling them that they were seeing the Wandering Islands, resembling fair and fruitful lands but in fact not solid earth at all. Anyone landing there would be entrapped, forced to wander forever with the drifting, aimless islands.

Then again the boatman had to employ all his skill, for their course took them between the giant Whirlpool of Decay and the clinging Quicksand of Improvidence—in which they saw a great ship, laden with rich merchandise, caught beyond saving.

Soon a new danger appeared: an enormous host of sea monsters, whales, many-headed serpents, giant swordfish, sea-unicorns, and walruses, and a thousand thousand more of unimaginable horror, foaming the waves as they charged down upon the small boat. But the Palmer assured them they had nothing to fear, for they were only phantoms, sent by the enchantress Acrasia to force them to turn back. And the Palmer struck the water with his staff, and instantly the monsters vanished and the waves grew calm.

So they came to another island, on which Guyon saw a fair maiden desolately weeping, stirring him to pity. But the boatman told him that she, too, was an illusion, seeking to tempt men, then weaken them and lead them to ruin.

On yet another outthrust of land they saw a peaceful bay, within which five mermaids sang and played. They began a melodic song in Guyon's honour, praising his great deeds, inviting him to seek rest and pleasure among them. Guyon seemed for a moment to wish to hear more of their sweet music, but the Palmer warned him against giving way to vanity, and that danger too they bypassed.

By then they were coming near to the land they sought, until a choking fog descended on the water, blinding them, so they could not keep their course. Through the dark mist came a vast flight of birds, sweeping down upon them with talons and striking wings— all the birds of darkness and dolour, owls and ravens, bats and harpies and more. But they sailed firmly on, and finally the fog dissipated, to reveal before them the land that was their goal.

When the boat reached the shore, Guyon and the Palmer left the ferryman to guard their craft and moved inland. Soon they heard a dreadful bellowing, and saw charging upon them a frightful array of wild beasts. But the Palmer again raised his staff, which, made from the same virtuous wood as the *caduceus* of Mercury, had the power to subdue all monsters. And the beasts crept meekly to one side and allowed them to pass.

At last they came to the end of their journey—Acrasia's Bower of Bliss, a garden where everything that could be sweet and pleasurable to human senses and fancies was lavishly abundant. It was surrounded with a light fence, more for decoration than protection, and its gate was carved in ivory with figures that told the tale of Jason and the golden fleece. At the gate stood its guardian, an unnaturally handsome man in a loose robe bearing a staff and a giant bowl of wine

that he offered to newcomers. When this being offered his wine to Guyon, the knight overturned his bowl and broke his magic staff, before passing by.

Entering the garden, Guyon and the Palmer found themselves in a wide, spacious plain, clothed in smooth grass and bright with flowers, as if arranged by some artist who scorned Nature for being miserly but was himself too lavish. Like the landscape, the weather was always beautiful in that place: no storms or frosts, no excessive heat or cold, but a flawless summery warmth, the air fragrant and wholesome.

Guyon wondered at the beauty of the garden, but refused to let its delights undermine his will. Soon they came to another gate or doorway, formed of living boughs that intertwined and curved up into an arch, with grapevines woven among them. The fruit of the vines hung down in tempting bunches, and among them, half-hidden, were perfect replicas of grapes, fashioned from burnished gold, again as if art sought not to imitate Nature but to outdo her, to impose the glamour of artifice on natural beauty.

Within the arched doorway sat a comely woman, with rich garments immodestly disarranged. In her left hand she held a golden cup and with her right hand she plucked ripe grapes, squeezing their swollen fullness till the juice gushed into the cup. She offered this sweet wine to Guyon, as she did to all who passed by her. But the knight took the cup and flung it on the ground, where it shattered. And the woman—whose name was Excess—could only rage helplessly as Guyon continued on his way.

In the centre of the open land stood a glorious fountain, of a transparent substance that revealed the silvery water running through every part of it. The fountain was skilfully decorated with many strange sculptures, among which wound a trail of ivy, made of pure gold but painted perfectly in the natural colours of the plant.

Countless streams of water rose from this lovely structure, flowing down to form a pool at its base, so that the fountain seemed to be sailing on the water's surface. And Guyon saw that the pool held bathers—two naked, golden-haired damsels, splashing and playing.

As Guyon gazed at them, slowing his pace, unable to take his eyes from the enticing sight, the wanton girls stared with surprise at his appearance. One shyly lowered herself so that the water covered her body. But the other unabashedly stood upright, flaunting her lily-smooth breasts to Guyon's eager gaze—while her lower body, beneath the surface, stirred him even more because half-hidden. Her companion then rose upright as well, but loosened her long hair so that it flowed down to cover her body like a gown of gold, again no less desirable for being covered.

Aristocratic recreation within a beautiful walled garden, from a 15th-century Arras tapestry. Such gardens, where landscape and decorative art try to outdo nature, were often described in Renaissance poetry. But they were presented as paradise, not as the dangerous and illusory trap that is Spenser's Bower of Bliss.

By then Guyon had halted, his face clearly showing the desire kindling within him. Seeing this, the girls grew merry and playful again, beckoning to Guyon invitingly. But the Palmer intervened, reminding Guyon sternly of their serious purpose.

"Be advised, sir," the Palmer said, "that we will soon confront Acrasia; and we must come upon her without warning, or she may slip away and thwart all our intentions."

So Guyon turned away from the fountain and followed the Palmer towards the deepest heart of the gardens. As they drew near, they were surrounded by music: melodies so harmonious and beguilingly pleasant that they might have been devised only for a paradise, never for a real and human world. Neither slowed nor deterred by the music's charm, the knight and the Palmer moved carefully through the groves and thickets, until they could gaze through the foliage at the lascivious scene within.

Acrasia lay upon a bed of rose petals, with her singers about her—lovely damsels and youths who combined their music with much lewd play among themselves. The enchantress wore a gown of silvery silk, fine as cobweb, revealing her alabaster flesh more alluringly than if she had been naked. Her perfect breasts were openly displayed, and between them trailed some few pearly drops of perspiration, from her most recent excesses of love-making. And her eyes gleamed like starlight on the night sea as she looked down at the sleeping form of the young man beside her.

He appeared to be of noble birth, with a pleasant face that showed signs enough of manliness though his youthful beard was still downy upon his lip and cheek. But for him, ever since Acrasia had ensnared him with her sorceries, nobility and manliness had been left behind. His arms were hung uselessly from a nearby tree, the blazon on his shield had been crudely defaced. Only a lustful and luxuriating pleasure now inhabited his thoughts, and on it he was spending all his days, his wealth, his very substance.

So he sprawled in satiated sleep while the witch gloated over him, now and then brushing his lips or eyes with kisses as if she would drain his very soul. Then Guyon and the Palmer sprang from their hiding place and flung over the lovers a magical net, which had been wrought for this purpose by the Palmer.

As the singers fled into the woods in terror, the enchantress struggled with all her witch's arts, while the young man, awakened, also fought with all his strength. But neither his might nor her magic could overcome the Palmer's net. And when their struggles weakened, the Palmer bound the young man with cords that he found nearby, but fastened chains of unbreakable adamantine round the enchantress.

Spenser obviously took the idea of men transformed into beasts, in the Bower, from the episode in Homer's Odyssey *in which men are turned into swine by the witch Circe—here depicted by Dosso Dossi (c.1479–1542).*

Then the Palmer began to speak to the young man, whose name was Verdant, and soon untied his bonds while his wise words undid the spell that had made him Acrasia's captive. Meanwhile Sir Guyon had set about the task of destroying the Bower. Turning his mind away from its beguiling beauty, he pitilessly felled the groves and crushed the arbours, razed the secret thickets, despoiled the gardens, flung down all the artful structures.

When all that had been dangerously beautiful had been laid waste, Guyon and the Palmer returned the way they had come, leading with them the chained enchantress and her erstwhile lover, who was now both remorseful and ashamed. Soon they had returned to the place where the power of the Palmer's staff had quelled the attack of the horde of wild beasts. Again the creatures sprang towards them, even more ferocious, seeing their mistress captive. But as before the Palmer raised his staff and rendered the beasts powerless.

"What you see as animals," the Palmer said, "are in fact men—all former lovers of the enchantress, whom she transformed into beasts when she had tired of them. Each of them took on the shape of the creature which his inner, bestial self most resembled. It is a sad fate, but perhaps a just one for men who live intemperately, given up to the animal pleasures of the flesh."

"But since Acrasia is now our prisoner," said Guyon, "could not these creatures be restored to their proper form?"

In reply the Palmer touched each of the wild beasts with his staff, and instantly they became men again—in appearance if not always in manner. Some were fearful, some were struck with shame, some gave vent to fury. And one, named Grill, who had been in the shape of a hog, complained bitterly that he had enjoyed being a hog and wished he could be a hog again.

"How can a man have such beastliness within him," Guyon wondered, "that he can choose to be a beast, indifferent to the high excellence of the human mind and spirit?"

"Filthy and foul creatures of any sort take their pleasure in filth and foulness," said the Palmer. "Let Grill be Grill, and have his hoggish ways. But let us seek our ship, while wind and weather serve us."

ELIZABETHA ANGLIÆ ET HIBERNIÆ REGINÆ. &c.

The Legend of Britomartis, or Chastity; and the Legend of Cambell and Triamond, or Friendship

The central virtues allocated to Books Three and Four are named as Chastity and Friendship. But these are in fact only aspects (though certainly to Spenser the most important) of the poet's actual concern in these books. His real subject is True Love.

It is also the subject of *both* books. And that—along with the presence of Britomart in both, as the main linking character, the true hero—is why the two books are generally considered as a unit, and so have been run together here.

But Spenser knew that Love is not a neat, definable subject like Holiness or Temperance. Even True Love wears many forms—including romantic love between man and woman, married love between man and wife, bonds of affection and accord (i.e. Friendship) between man and man or woman and woman.

So Books Three and Four became a great intricate patchwork of different stories, all overlapping and interweaving as Spenser shifts back and forth from one to another. And moving through nearly all of them, linking and unifying, is the figure of the knight of Chastity, Britomart.

Being presented as a British warrior maiden, Britomart obviously is another representation in the poem of England's Virgin Queen. As such she is invincible; she never weakens or fails or needs rescuing by Arthur. Also, she is not from Gloriana's court and has no specific quest: she is instead searching for a knight, Artegall, with whose image she has fallen in love.

So we are made to see that her perfect chastity is not a permanent vow of celibacy (like that of a minor character, the huntress Belphoebe). Britomart's *virginity* will ultimately and properly give way to a different form of chastity—*fidelity* within married love. And that aspect of her role is reinforced in the other two most important stories in these books: that of Florimell, and that of Amoret and Scudamour.

Like Britomart, Florimell is wandering in search of her beloved, and is wholly virginal. Unlike Britomart, she is passive and defenceless. Florimell represents Beauty at its most perfect. But the effect of her beauty on the less virtuous men whom she encounters causes her to be the essential damsel in distress—most of the time either fleeing in blind terror or fighting off attackers. In her, we can see an allegory of "chaste romantic love and the dangers that threaten it".

In Amoret, young wife of Scudamour, we can similarly see "chaste married love threatened by dangers" (and, as it happens, rescued by Britomart). Beyond these central stories, there are other embodiments of forms of True Love: the "platonic" non-sexual love of Timias and Belphoebe, the friendship of Cambell and Triamond. (In Spenser's own published title the last-named was erroneously called *Telamond*.) These two knightly friends are proffered as the heroes of Book

Four, but they are not. Their story, though importantly emblematic, is in fact an interpolation, setting forth the ideal of Friendship (another kind of platonic love) between men. The relationship between Britomart and Amoret does the same for friendship between women, but more integrally to the narrative.

And among these stories in these two crowded books is a throng of characters who are different sorts of enemies to True Love—rogues and seducers, disguised temptresses, beasts and ravishers, personifications of Lust and comparable sins, even sexual perversions (the two giants who appear briefly). So Spenser underlines the dangers and pitfalls along the way of the proper virtuous progress that is his primary concern—from virginal youth via True Love to chaste marital bliss.

Sir Guyon returned with the faithful Palmer and their captive, Acrasia, to the house of Alma, where he rested awhile in company with Prince Arthur. But soon the two knights rode forth in search of new adventures, while the enchantress was sent under guard to the court of the Faery Queen.

As they journeyed, Guyon and Arthur encountered a strange knight, accompanied by an aged and frail squire who was bowed beneath the weight of the knight's shield—on which was the device of a lion on a field of gold. Guyon issued the knightly challenge to the stranger, and both couched their lances and spurred to battle.

Guyon's lance struck fairly, causing the stranger knight nearly to lurch from the saddle. But the spear of the other lifted Guyon bodily and flung him crashing to the ground. Shame and anger flooded Guyon, for he had never before been defeated so easily. But he could not know that the lance which unhorsed him was enchanted, and invincible, and that it was wielded by a woman—the lady Britomart.

Leaping up, Guyon drew his sword to continue the fight. But the Palmer intervened, calming him, for the old man had perceived the magical virtue of the other knight's lance. Soon the Palmer's words had brought the two opponents together in chivalric courtesy—and, with all anger dispelled and honour satisfied, the three knights rode away together.

Before long they entered a dense forest, where they rode for a long time without seeing signs of any other living thing. But then from a deep thicket burst a beautiful lady, on a white palfrey, at full gallop. She was golden-haired and clad in garments of gold, but her lovely face was aghast with terror. And behind her, fiercely pursuing, rode a wild, uncouth forester.

Arthur and Guyon, and Arthur's squire Timias, at once spurred away to rescue the damsel. But Britomart left them to that gallant chase, and took another way through the forest, unafraid of whatever perils it might present. For just as the warrior maiden bore no evil within her, so she feared no evil from without.

Preceding page: an allegorically patriotic Elizabethan engraving by T. Cecill of Queen Elizabeth, every bit as much a virginal warrior as Spenser's Britomart, receiving a lance from Truth (with the Spanish Armada in the background).

Spenser also modelled Britomart on a fictional warrior maiden, Bradamante, from Ariosto's poem Orlando Furioso *(1532)—seen here in a 16th-century illustration from the tale, centre foreground, in armour with a plumed helmet.*

Coming out of the forest at last, she saw in the distance a stately castle surrounded by beautiful grounds, and rode towards it. As she drew near, she found a furious battle raging on the greensward before the gate—one knight defending himself against six. The lone warrior seemed nearly exhausted, bleeding from many wounds, yet he fought heroically, dealing furious blows, yielding not one step to his enemies.

Britomart urged her charger into the midst of the battle, scattering the six, demanding to know the reason for their conflict. The lone knight, who bore on his shield and surcoat the symbol of a blood-red cross, replied first.

"These six seek to force me to change my allegiance, to love a lady of their choosing. But I will die before I yield, for I love a lady who is the truest on earth."

"Surely," Britomart said, "it is a great wrong for six knights to impose their will by force. Death will always be preferable to the shame of faithlessness, or to the loss of love by one who loves truly."

One of the six then said to her, "The lady of this castle, whom we serve, has decreed that any knight passing this way must give himself up to her service. Should such a knight already have a lady love, he must renounce her, unless he can overcome us in battle."

"And what would a knight receive in return for pledging himself to your lady?" asked Britomart.

"He would receive great advancement," said the other, "but his highest reward would be the love of our mistress. So you must tell us, sir," he went on, addressing Britomart, "whether you too have a lady love."

"I have a love, to be sure," said Britomart, "but I have no lady. And I will not forswear my love, nor will I pledge myself to your mistress. Instead, I will right the wrong you have done to this knight."

Levelling her enchanted lance, she charged forward—striking one of the six from his horse before he could move, then turning swiftly to strike down another, and a third, so fiercely that they lay unmoving on the ground. The Red Cross Knight, despite his wounds and weariness, had by then overcome a fourth. And the remaining two, in terror of Britomart's power, laid down their arms.

"Now you see," she said, "that truth is strong, and true love stronger still."

"Only too well do we see it," they replied. "And now our defeat requires that we must pledge our service to you, and—by her own law—that the lady of the castle will equally be yours." So they ushered Britomart into the castle, which was called Castle Joyous.

The interior was sumptuous beyond description. Its every arch and pillar was fashioned from purest gold, encrusted with luminous jewels, as might befit the palace of some enormously wealthy and ostentatious monarch. The walls were hung with luxurious tapestries, depicting the love story of Venus and Adonis, and the room was crowded with young damsels and squires dancing, drinking, making love on couches scattered round the room.

But when Britomart and the Red Cross Knight turned scornfully away from this lascivious display, their guides escorted them to the presence of the lady of the castle. They found her reclining on a bed of golden splendour that might have belonged to a Persian queen. She was a voluptuous lady of rare beauty, but with a wanton, suggestive expression in her eyes. Yet she greeted them graciously, and directed that they should be taken to chambers where they could remove their armour and refresh themselves with spicy wines. The Red Cross Knight willingly put aside his armour, to tend his wounds, but Britomart would not remove hers, not wishing to reveal herself as a woman in that company—and merely raised her visor so that no more than her face would be revealed.

Then the six knights with whom she had fought presented themselves again. They were brothers: lively Gardante, bold Parlante and Jocante, courtly Basciante, fierce Bacchante, and warlike Noctante. All were handsome knights, though Britomart remained unaffected by their appearance. And they were no more than courteous and friendly to her, still believing her to be a man.

The lady of the castle erred the same way, for when Britomart rejoined her, the lady saw the beauty of the face now revealed, and fell instantly in love. But the lady, whose name was Malecasta, was a wilful, passionate woman wholly without constraint or shame. Love to her was no more than fleshly desire, and that was the impulse that rose within her as the company sat down for supper.

The meal was as opulent as the surroundings, and the wines were copiously poured. And all the while the lady teased and flirted with Britomart, begging the handsome young knight (as she thought the warrior maiden to be) to set aside his confining armour. But Britomart ignored these blandishments—until at last Malecasta, with many piteous sobs and sighs, confessed the great love that had grown within her for her young guest, and asserted that unless her love was returned she would surely die.

Britomart was much affected by the lady's words. Being a victim of love's pain herself, she knew well what suffering it could bring. And being wholly without guile, she could not perceive how false Malecasta's protestations were. So she replied kindly to the lady, saying merely that she felt love should not be taken so lightly as to be offered to a passing stranger.

But Malecasta was encouraged by that kindness, and continued to feed the flame of passion within herself, while the supper ended and the company of knights and damsels returned to their carousing.

Not until the night was more than half spent did all the revellers take themselves to bed, and only then could Britomart go alone to her own chamber, and at last remove the heavy armour, safe from prying eyes. Weary from a long day of travel and combat, she climbed into bed and fell instantly asleep.

Soon the castle was silent, and everyone slept—except Malecasta. Restless and wakeful, she at last rose from her bed, and stole silently to Britomart's chamber. There, seeing the bed's occupant asleep, she carefully raised the edge of the coverlet, and slipped beneath it, sighing with pleasure at being beside the one she desired.

But Britomart stirred and turned in her sleep, and her hand brushed against Malecasta. Instantly she was awake, leaping up for her sword in the belief that a would-be ravisher had crept in beside her. Malecasta screamed in terror, and fainted—but not before her shrieks had roused the household.

To Britomart's chamber they rushed, among them the six brothers and the knight of the Red Cross, wielding whatever weapons they had snatched up in their haste. But in the chamber they halted, bewildered, at the sight of Malecasta lying in a swoon on the floor and Britomart, clad only in her white smock, her golden hair flowing loose and her eyes blazing, threatening them with the point of her sword.

The six knights gathered up their lady, who soon recovered. Then they began to mutter angrily among themselves, stirring up each other's spite and fury towards Britomart. None of them dared to reproach her directly—but one of the brothers, Gardante, took up a bow and arrow, intending to kill the maiden from a distance.

But his aim was not true, and the shaft merely grazed her side, so that vermilion blood seeped out to stain the white smock and the silken skin beneath. Stung to fury by the wound and the treachery of the attack, Britomart flew at the brothers, her sword flashing like fire as she laid about her. So swift and ferocious were her blows that none of the six could withstand them. Then the Red Cross Knight was at her side, and shoulder to shoulder they drove their enemies back and at last put them to terrified, shameful flight.

Quickly then Britomart dressed herself in her armour, wishing to spend not a moment more in that place of licentiousness and dishonour. And the dawn had barely begun to penetrate the darkness of the night sky when she and the Red Cross Knight rode out of the castle.

*   *   *

The dangers of unchaste love—Death lurks behind the tree, unseen by the careless lovers in this engraving by Dürer.

As they rode together, the Red Cross Knight asked Britomart why she had journeyed, in knightly garb, into the land of Faery. And Britomart told him of her background, in her own land of Britain, where she had been raised from infancy to learn the skills of war and chivalry rather than more feminine arts.

"Now I ride in search of adventure, like any knight," she added.

"And I have come here in search of one who has done me great injury —named Sir Artegall."

The Red Cross Knight was surprised, for he knew Artegall to be a man of high honour, prowess, and nobility. He assured the warrior maiden that she was mistaken, and secretly Britomart was gladdened by the words, for in fact she knew little of Artegall, and had spoken as she had done to learn the Red Cross Knight's true opinion of him.

Long before, in her royal father's house, Britomart had come upon a wondrous crystal globe that had been made by the magician Merlin. The crystal had the power to reveal the past and future of anyone who gazed into it—and to Britomart, among its revelations, it showed the image of a handsome, powerful knight. He wore strange armour, shaped in an antique fashion but solid and strong, with gold decorations, among which were the words, "Achilles' armour, won by Artegall".

Britomart was at once in love—and love came to her like an affliction. She spent her days in forlorn melancholy, her nights in sleepless misery. Her old nurse, Glauce, grew alarmed at her decline, until at last the desperate maiden confided in Glauce the cause of her wretchedness. The old woman knew then that there could be only one hope, to seek out the mighty one who had created the magic crystal, Merlin himself.

Merlin the magician (right) with Uther Pendragon, Arthur's father—in an illustration from a 14th-century English manuscript.

They travelled in secret, disguised as common folk, to the hidden cavern where Merlin dwelt in the far west of Britain. There they found him labouring among the high spells and mighty magics with which he could bind spirits or make the very sun and moon obey. Nervously they entered, but Merlin, through his power, knew them at once, and why they were there, and made them comfortable.

"Noble maiden," he said to Britomart, "though now you are sorely oppressed by love, know that from your love will come great excellence. The one you love is Artegall, who believes himself to be a knight of Faeryland, yet who is descended from the kings of Cornwall, and was stolen away as a baby by an elf. Your destiny, Britomart, will be to find your Artegall and wed him, and from your union will come a line of mighty warriors and renowned monarchs, who will rule this land in peace and glory."

And Merlin revealed to Britomart the names of the greatest among those who were to be her descendants—up to the time when a glorious queen should ascend the British throne, like Britomart herself a royal virgin, to rule with majesty and wise power.

Britomart vowed then to travel to the land of Faery, to seek the knight whom she loved. With Glauce she returned to her father's castle, where among many treasures was the armour and sword that had once been worn by the great queen of the Saxons, Angela, and an enchanted lance, made for his own use by an ancient sorcerer-king, Bladud. Britomart arrayed herself with armour, sword, and lance, and took up the shield with its lion blazon, while Glauce dressed herself as a squire. Then they set out on the journey to Faeryland, where Britomart was to seek her destiny.

All this Britomart recalled to herself as she rode with the Red Cross Knight, questioning him further about Artegall. But a time soon came when their paths diverged—and with many assurances of lasting friendship, they parted.

*   *   *

At length Britomart came to the seacoast, and there she dismounted, handing her helmet to old Glauce, and stared out at the foam-tipped waves that surged arrogantly against the craggy rocks. She saw in the heaving sea an image of her own inner torment, and herself a frail craft guided only by Love and Fortune, who are at once bold and blind.

But while she sighed and grieved within herself, too courageous to weep openly, she saw a brightly armoured knight galloping towards her. At once she was a warrior again: donning her helmet, she swung up into the saddle, readying her lance.

The stranger called to her sternly. "Sir knight, these lands are forbidden to strangers by my command. Other rash trespassers have met death at my hands: retreat now, while you still may."

"Those who need to flee can do so," replied Britomart curtly. "Only children need fear words. I will not beg you to let me pass."

And she levelled her lance and charged. The other knight spurred forward to meet the challenge, and his spear-point struck her fiercely, doubling her over with its power. But her own lance had driven ferociously through the stranger's shield and armour—and so irresistible was that thrust that the stranger was transfixed on Britomart's lance and carried along for several strides of her charger —until the lance tore free and the knight sprawled on the ground in his own pooling blood.

The virgin warrior hardly paused, but rode forward along the shore. Astonishingly, all round her lay priceless treasure—jewels, pearls, gold—strewn like pebbles over the sand. But treasure was not the goal of her tireless quest, and she rode on indifferently.

Behind her, the stranger knight lay mortally wounded. His name was Marinell, born of a union of a mortal man and a Nereid, a sea-nymph. The nymph had raised Marinell, and had caused her own father, the sea-god Nereus, to bestow the treasure upon him. Marinell had become a knight of great prowess and renown; but his mother

A 17th-century German carving of Neptune, god of the sea, ruler over all its fertile abundance, which is symbolized by the treasure of Marinell, scattered prodigally on the beach.

had always kept him from the company of women, for an old prophecy had foretold that he would have great injury and grief from a maiden.

Now the prophecy had come true, though not in the way that had been imagined. When Marinell's mother heard of her son's fall, she and the other Nereids stormed over the waves on their chariots to the shore where he lay. Loud and pitiful were their laments when they found him, but then they found that his heart was still feebly beating. Quickly the nymph gathered him up and swept him down to her bower on the sea-floor, calling the sea-god Tryphon and his healing arts to save Marinell's life.

Earlier, Prince Arthur and Sir Guyon had continued their wild pursuit of the terrified damsel in the golden dress, who had been in turn pursued by a savage forester. During the chase they had come to a cross-road—and, not knowing which way to choose, had separated. And the forester, seeing the knights, had fled in yet another direction, pursued by Arthur's squire, Timias.

Soon it proved that Arthur had chosen the right road, for he saw the damsel ahead of him. He called to her; but no matter what words of reassurance he spoke, she fled still, as terrified of a strange knight as of the forester. So they galloped without pause, until darkness fell and hid the lady from her would-be rescuer, leaving him to spend a restless and impatient night in the wilderness.

*　　　　*　　　　*

The following day Arthur resumed his search, and in the depths of a forest met a frightened and dishevelled dwarf, who told the prince that he was the servant of the very maiden whom Arthur had been pursuing. From the dwarf Arthur learned that the lady's name was Florimell, and that she had left the court of the Faery Queen to search for Marinell, the Nereid's son wounded by Britomart. Marinell was the only man the damsel loved, though he knew nothing of her love.

So the dwarf joined the prince in searching for the damsel, while elsewhere in the wilds Arthur's squire, brave Timias, also searched—for the forester whose woodcraft had enabled him to elude his pursuer.

The forester had gone to his two brothers for aid, and the three had hidden themselves at a riverside, near where the squire would cross. When Timias unsuspectingly rode to the river's edge, he was attacked.

The forester who had pursued Florimell sprang from hiding and flung a javelin that pierced the squire's armour, though without

The perils of the beautiful Florimell allow Spenser to dwell on the vulnerability of Beauty to false love, alluding to the also incomparably beautiful Helen of Troy—here being abducted by the Trojan prince Paris in a 15th-century painting by Benozzo Gozzoli. Later Spenser again uses the story of Paris and Helen, in a different context *(see p. 101).*

penetrating the skin. Timias turned, striving to climb the riverbank to do battle, but the first forester kept him at bay with a boar-spear, while the second loosed an arrow that struck deep into the squire's thigh.

But Timias fought heroically, and gained the top of the bank despite his wound. The third forester charged him with a heavy billhook, but Timias avoided the weapon and drove at its wielder with his lance, tumbling him dead on the bloodstained earth. The other two attacked with vengeful fury, one on each side, but Timias mastered them. His blade cleaved into the skull of the first forester, then swept across to the second one and sent his body toppling headless into the river.

Then the pain and loss of blood from his wound took effect, and Timias slid unconscious from his saddle, his life's blood still gushing forth.

Providentially, to the river at that moment came a fair huntress—Belphoebe, the same maiden who earlier had encountered the false knight Braggadochio. She saw the handsome youth dying in a pool of his own blood, and pity filled her heart. Quickly she gathered herbs from the woods around and, with all her skill and knowledge, staunched the bleeding and bound up the wound. And with some of the damsels who shared her forest life, she bore the squire back to the hidden valley that was her home.

Slowly, under the care of Belphoebe, the young squire's wound healed. But in that time he received another, no less painful, wound —for he fell in love with Belphoebe. And he dared not tell her so, for natural modesty told him that she was a noble, even heavenly maiden, while he was only a lowly squire. So he pined, seeing no respite for the pain of love but death. And Belphoebe grew ever more afraid, for none of her healing arts seemed able to restore Timias's strength. Nor did she guess at his true ailment, or its cure, for she was as pure and innocent a maiden as she was beautiful.

Painting of the goddess Diana, the virgin huntress (and foster mother of Belphoebe), by the 16th-century group of French artists called the School of Fontainebleau.

*　　　　　*　　　　　*

Belphoebe, daughter of a lady of Faery race, had indeed been born in magical circumstances. Her mother, Chrysogone, a lovely and virginal damsel, had been wandering in the forest on a fiercely hot summer's day and had stopped to bathe in a secret spring, hidden from all view. Afterwards, nude beneath the warm sun, she had fallen asleep—and the sunlight itself had embraced her and impregnated her.

When Chrysogone realized that she was pregnant, yet knew herself still to be chaste, she fled into the deep forest in her terror and shame. And there, alone, she eventually gave birth to twin daughters.

It happened that Venus, the goddess of love herself, was at that time searching for her winged son, Cupid, who often wandered the world beyond his mother's sight. She had sought him in royal courts, in cities, in the countryside; and everywhere she found people complaining that he had passed by, with his mischievous arrows, leaving behind him the pain and woe and distress of love.

Venus had even sought him at the dwelling of the virginal goddess Diana and her nymphs. Diana had at first been scornful, but then relented enough to aid Venus in her search. And together the two goddesses had come upon Chrysogone, asleep in the woods with her two new babes. Pitying the plight of the virgin mother, the goddesses took the infants away. Diana named one child Belphoebe, and gave her to one of her nymphs, to raise the child as a huntress. But Venus took the other baby, whom she named Amoret, to her own glorious paradise, the Garden of Adonis.

From that Garden, Nature in all her boundless fertility produced the newly born of every fruit and flower, every creature on land or water including man himself, multiplying under the governance of the goddess of fecundity, with the scythe of old Time their only enemy.

And there the child Amoret was reared—by Psyche, the beloved of Cupid—to be a paragon of feminine grace and beauty. Then Amoret came out into the world, to the court of Gloriana, where many a knight pledged his love to her. But she, the most perfect example of true love between man and woman, loved only one, for whose sake, as will be seen, she endured the most dire and desperate suffering.

*   *   *

All this while the lady Florimell, whom Prince Arthur had sought to save from the forester, had not halted her panic-stricken flight—although now the dangers that filled her with terror were mostly imagined, merely the normal sounds and shadows of the forest. But at length her white palfrey could run no longer, and collapsed beneath her. On foot, Florimell soon found herself in a deep and gloomy dale that held a tiny cottage, made of sticks and reeds. The maiden approached to seek shelter, not knowing that it was the home of a witch, a bent and ragged hag whose magical skills were as powerful as they were evil.

But the witch was astounded at the heavenly beauty of the damsel who had appeared from the wilderness, and dazedly invited Florimell to enter and make herself comfortable. In a while the witch's son

returned home, a lazy and loutish youth who was as struck by Florimell as his mother. But in the youth the vision of beauty kindled lust rather than mere amazement. Florimell treated him with kindness, but saw that his attentions would become threatening. So when her palfrey was rested, she slipped from the cottage at dawn and rode away into the forest.

The witch's son was overcome with his loss, wailing and crying, tearing his hair and flesh as if insane. And his distressed mother turned to her arts to save her son. She summoned a hideous beast, misshapen and spotted like a hyena, but swifter and deadlier than any natural creature. And she sent it after Florimell, either to bring her back or to destroy her.

When the monstrous creature came into sight, again Florimell had to flee in desperate terror. The dire race brought them to the sea, where Florimell leaped from her saddle, intending to hurl herself into the water rather than confront those loathsome jaws. But she saw a small boat at the edge of the water, in which an old fisherman lay asleep. She sprang in, using an oar to push herself to safety, while the foul beast slaked its rage and hunger on the body of the poor palfrey.

While it was at its cruel feast, and Florimell's boat had drifted out to sea, a knight chanced to pass that way—Sir Satyrane, who before

The witch's beast that pursues Florimell comes from the imprecise Elizabethan idea of a hyena—like this creature, feeding ghoulishly in a churchyard, from a 16th-century English bestiary.

had aided lady Una, the beloved of the Red Cross Knight. Satyrane recognized the dead palfrey as Florimell's, for he knew the lady from the court of the Faery Queen. And his eye also caught sight of a golden sash, lying crumpled on the shore, where it had fallen in Florimell's wild flight.

Satyrane fell upon the beast vengefully, and though the witch's spells ensured that the beast could not be killed, his prowess quelled its savagery, until he was able to bind it with the golden sash of Florimell.

As he dragged it away from the shore, Satyrane saw a strange pursuit in the distance. A giantess, on a grey steed, was in flight from a strange knight. And the giantess carried across her saddle a young squire, tightly bound hand and foot. Satyrane left the beast and galloped towards the giantess, his lance couched challengingly. And she threw the squire to the ground to make ready for battle, whirling a huge iron mace over her head.

Satyrane's spear struck her with all his renowned force, yet seemed hardly to affect her. And the terrible mace landed crushingly on the side of the knight's head, leaving him reeling and senseless in his saddle. Then the giantess plucked him effortlessly from his horse and slung him across her saddle, where the squire had been.

But now the other, strange knight had drawn closer. And the

giantess seemed unwilling to confront that foe. Angrily she threw Satyrane aside, to lighten her mount's burden, and fled, still tirelessly pursued.

Satyrane soon came to his senses, and went quickly to free the young squire. The youth told him that the giantess was named Argante, daughter of the Titans, and twin sister to the giant Ollyphant. Both giants lived lives of brutal and unnatural sin, stopping at nothing including incest in their monstrous search for fleshly pleasure. And Argante often took young men captive, as playthings for her insatiable lust—as she had the squire.

The squire himself forebore to tell Satyrane his name, but called himself the "Squire of Dames". A lady whom he loved had set him the task of wandering the world for twelve months doing noble deeds on behalf of other damsels. So successful was he at this task that he had won the hearts and the favours of a full three hundred ladies, in that year. Then his own lady, in jealous anger, set him a new task: to continue his wanderings until he had found an equal number of ladies who would chastely *refuse* him, no matter how fervently he wooed them.

Satyrane, laughing, asked how he had succeeded. And the Squire of Dames said ruefully that there had been only three in three years: a courtesan, who turned him away because he would not pay her; a nun, who rejected him for fear others would know; and a damsel of low degree, who refused him simply because she was chaste.

"She alone," added the Squire, "embraced chastity for its own sake, rather than as a means to other ends. So surely I will never complete my task and win my lady—for chaste damsels do not abound so plentifully as their opposites."

"Poor Squire," smiled Satyrane, "to labour so long and hard for such small reward." And together they rode away, back to where the knight had left the captive beast. But he found that the creature had burst its bonds, and had sped back to the witch with the news of Florimell's escape.

*   *   *

When the beast returned with its tidings, the witch's son was plunged even deeper into tumultuous grief, and in his madness threatened to slay both his mother and himself. The witch, in desperation, employed her darkest and most dire skills, and fashioned the form of a maiden identical with Florimell—but placed a wicked, guileful spirit within it.

The false semblance of Florimell deluded the son entirely, and kept him foolishly happy with coy and coquettish wiles. Then one

Facing page:
Engraving by Dürer of a sea-being abducting a nymph, much as Florimell was carried off by the god Proteus.

98

day, walking with the false Florimell, the son met what seemed to be an armed knight in the forest. In fact it was another deception, for it was the vain and puffed-up Braggadochio, who once had stolen Sir Guyon's horse and lance.

The false knight threatened the loutish youth with his spear, and sent him fleeing in terror. Then Braggadochio began making lustful advances, while the false Florimell affected great fear and grief. And before Braggadochio could extend his wooing, another armed knight appeared.

The newcomer challenged him to fight for his lady, and the vain-glorious Braggadochio pretended to agree. But when the other turned his steed, to move far enough away for a full charge, Braggadochio took to his cowardly heels, leaving the false Florimell to the stranger.

The true Florimell was meanwhile still drifting at sea, and soon the old fisherman whose boat she had entered woke from his sleep. When he accepted that he was not dreaming, and that a marvellously beautiful maiden was in his boat, lust fired his wrinkled body, and he sprang upon Florimell. The maiden screamed and struggled against the ravisher—and as she fought, her screams were heard. The sea-god Proteus, riding the waves nearby, hurried to see the cause of the tumult, and dragged the fisherman away from the damsel, beating him severely with his staff.

Florimell, seeing the grim face of the god, screamed still in fear, feeling that she had gone from one terror to another. But the god, trying to soothe her, carried her half-fainting into his chariot and bore her to his dwelling. There, no less struck with love than any other man who confronted her beauty, he sought to win her with all the promises and temptations a god could muster. Yet always she refused him. And in the end, frustrated and furious, the god flung her into a dungeon with a threat to imprison her until she relented.

During Florimell's sufferings at sea, Satyrane and the Squire of Dames had encountered another knight, whom Satyrane recognized —by the blazon of a burning heart on his shield—as Sir Paridell. They spoke together in friendly fashion, exchanging news. Paridell bore the sad tidings of the fall of Sir Marinell, and added that many knights of Gloriana's court, himself among them, had ridden out to find and protect the lady Florimell. Satyrane then sorrowfully told him what had happened beside the sea. And both knights gloomily agreed that the dead palfrey and the lost sash indicated that Florimell herself might be dead. But they vowed that they would continue the search, until they learned the truth.

As dusk gathered, the two knights and the Squire came to a castle, where they sought entry for the night. But the gates remained firmly locked against them. The knights were enraged at this abuse of the laws of hospitality, but the Squire of Dames explained.

He knew that the castle belonged to a suspicious old miser named Malbecco, who barred his gates against visitors for two reasons: he feared the loss of his treasure, and he feared the loss of his wife, Hellenore. Satyrane laughed at the idea that anyone might keep a woman virtuous, by locking her up, if she had a mind to be otherwise. But in any case they had to seek shelter elsewhere, for the night had brought a storm of rain.

Detail from the 15th-century Belgian Tournai tapestry, depicting the Trojan War—the destructive outcome of Paris's passion for Helen of Troy.

They found a small, crude shed near the castle, and there made ready to spend the night. Then another knight rode up, and—being also turned rudely away from the castle—sought the cover of the shed. But now it was fully occupied, and the knights within told the newcomer there was no room. The strange knight angrily replied that he would lodge with them, or he would dislodge them. And that challenge so enraged Paridell that he armed himself and rode out to confront the challenger.

They galloped at each other with furious force, both lances striking home. But the newcomer's thrust swept Paridell with bruising ease from his saddle, and he lay half-unconscious for some moments until the Squire of Dames helped him to his feet. Then he reached for his sword to continue the fray, but Satyrane intervened, pacifying both knights and assuring them that honour was satisfied. It would be more sensible, he said, to use their might together against the discourteous castle owner, rather than against one another.

When the fearful Malbecco saw three armed knights approaching, plainly intending to assault his castle, he swiftly opened the gates, offering nervous apologies. He showed the knights into a chamber where they could warm themselves and remove their armour. And then all were amazed to find that the stranger knight who had defeated Paridell was a lovely golden-haired maiden—Britomart.

At dinner, they were joined by Malbecco's wife, Hellenore, a comely and graceful woman. Malbecco watched the company jealously, but he was blind in one eye—so that while he kept watch over Satyrane, Paridell was hidden from him. And throughout the meal Paridell tirelessly cast flirtatious, suggestive glances at Hellenore, who understood their meaning well, and replied with similar glances of her own.

After the dinner Paridell entertained the company by recounting the history of the Trojan War, and how Aeneas fled from the ruin of Troy to Latium, the roots from which Rome sprang. Then Britomart added that a third Troy had since risen, the city of Troynovant, on the banks of the Thames in Albion, where the Trojan hero Brutus had brought civilization.

While these mighty tales were being told, Paridell and Hellenore had not ceased from their silent flirtations, while desire grew hot within them, unperceived by Malbecco.

When Satyrane and Britomart departed the next morning, Paridell remained behind, claiming that an injury suffered at Britomart's hand still troubled him. Inevitably, and despite Malbecco's vigilance, Paridell's charm had its effect on Hellenore, and before long the seduction was complete.

Facing page:
Sir Scudamour's shield bears the image of the cherubic but ever-mischievous Cupid, god of love—and so the source of lovers' anguish as well as joy—here complaining about bee-stings to his mother, Venus, in a painting by Lucas Cranach the Elder.

The central theme of Spenser's Book III: the combat between Love (Cupid again, in a more dangerous aspect) and Chastity (a warrior maiden) in a painting by the 15th-century "Florentine School" of artists.

Soon afterwards the lovers fled, pursued by Malbecco. But before he could overtake them, the fickle Paridell grew tired of Hellenore, and cast her aside, as he had many ladies before. She was found, wandering in the forest, by a troop of satyrs, and was kept by them as a communal maidservant and mistress.

When Malbecco came upon her in that wild company, she refused to leave, having grown enamoured of her wanton life among the inexhaustibly lustful satyrs. So Malbecco fled from the world of men, so filled with bitterness and rancorous gall that he came to be transformed from a man into the very figure of Jealousy itself.

*   *   *

Earlier, when Britomart and Satyrane had ridden away from the house of Malbecco, they had come upon a monstrous giant in savage pursuit of a young man. The giant was Ollyphant, twin brother of the giantess Argante whom Satyrane had encountered before. Like his sister, Ollyphant was a creature of foul and bestial lusts, fearing and abhorring chastity above all things. So when Britomart and Satyrane charged towards him, the giant left his pursuit and fled.

The chase led the two knights to a forest, where the giant had hidden, and they separated to search for their quarry. Britomart's path led her to a clear spring, beside which a knight lay, with his arms and armour scattered carelessly on the grass, his shield bearing the device of a winged Cupid. The knight was groaning and sobbing, clearly in the grip of some overpowering grief. And Britomart pityingly approached him, asking the cause of his sorrow, and offering her aid in overcoming whatever afflicted him.

The knight introduced himself as Sir Scudamour, and told how his beloved lady had been taken captive by a master of the black arts named Busirane, who held her in a dismal dungeon and subjected her to the most cruel tortures because she would not yield her love to him. And the lady was Amoret, adopted daughter of Venus, who had been nurtured in the Garden of Adonis.

Britomart, outraged, assured Scudamour that she would free his lady from the sorcerer or die in the attempt. And the knight gratefully guided the warrior maiden to the castle of Busirane.

The castle had no gates or bars to block their way, but instead a foul, sulphurous fire blazed furiously in the doorway. Undaunted, Britomart flung her shield up before her face and plunged into the inferno. To her surprise, the flames parted before her—yet closed again swiftly, preventing Scudamour from following her.

Britomart found herself in a vast room where the walls were clothed in a gorgeous tapestry woven of gold and silk, depicting all

the times when Cupid had wounded the Olympian gods themselves with his arrows of love's passion. At the upper end of the room was a golden statue of the winged boy himself, blindfold, with his foot entangled by the tail of a terrible dragon, which itself was blinded. Wondering at the splendour of the place, Britomart passed through a door into a room whose walls were gold, on which were carved images of all the monstrous forms of false love, and all the great kings and conquerors who had been brought down from their glory by love's power.

Still Britomart had seen no other person, and night was beginning to spread darkness through the room—when suddenly from the depths of the castle came the fierce blare of a trumpet. At once pandemonium filled the place. A violent wind swept the room, mixed with tumultuous thunder and lightning. The castle shuddered in the grip of an earthquake, and dark sulphurous smoke clogged the air with its stench. Then the wind struck again, and magically every door in the room crashed open.

Britomart watched, amazed but unafraid, as through one door walked a man splendidly costumed, with his name, Ease, written on his robe. He stood mouthing and gesturing, but in total silence, as if he were miming the introduction to a play—whereupon a group of musicians and singers burst in, filling the room with a melodic song of love. And they were followed one at a time by a series of costumed figures, like players in a courtly masque.

First came Fancy, a lovely and vain boy, followed by fiery Desire. Next came shrinking Doubt, accompanied by the armed figure of Danger. Pale Fear then entered, in the company of a smiling maiden named Hope. After them came Dissemblance, a woman whose apparent beauty was painted and false, in company with heavy-browed and watchful Suspicion. Black-robed Grief entered next, with pincers in his hand, along with Fury, a woman half-naked from violently tearing at her garments. After them came lumpish Displeasure walking with the cheerful lady Pleasure.

Behind them all came two ghastly figures named Malice and Cruelty. And they were supporting between them a beautiful damsel who was suffering an anguish and torment beyond imagining.

Her ivory breast was bared, displaying a wide and deep gash from which the red blood gouted to stain all her skin and clothing. And from that wound her heart had been drawn forth, to lie in a silver dish, transfixed with a deadly arrow. Yet still she lived, by some dark magic, though her step was feeble and her death was foreshadowed in her tortured face.

Behind her came the winged god himself, Cupid, on a ravening lion, his blindfold pulled aside so that he could gloat over the cruel effect of his power. As he shook his arrows in his right hand, and spread his great wings, into the room crowded other grisly figures—Reproach, Repentance, Shame; Strife and Anger, Care and Thriftlessness, Loss of Time and Sorrow, Change and Disloyalty; Riotousness and Dread; Infirmity, Poverty, even Death himself—all the maladies and afflictions of false love.

The entire company paraded round the room before Britomart's horrified eyes, then returned through the door, which slammed behind them, fastened with spells that would not yield even to the warrior maiden's strength. So Britomart determined to wait and see what the following night would bring.

When night fell again, and as before all the doors flew open, Britomart sprang through the one that before had admitted the fearsome masque. But none of the beings of the previous night were in the room beyond, save one—the tormented maiden with her gruesome wound, now fastened by iron bands to a brazen pillar. And before her sat the vile enchanter Busirane, writing down some evil lore of magic, and dipping his pen into the heart's blood of the maiden, who was Amoret.

Seeing the virgin knight, the sorcerer leaped swiftly towards his captive, drawing a dagger with murderous intent. But Britomart was swifter, and dragged him powerfully back. Then Busirane turned and slashed in fury at Britomart, and the blade sliced a shallow wound in her snowy breast.

Wrathfully Britomart drew her sword and struck the enchanter with such ferocity that he fell half-dead. The next blow would surely have meant his death, but a scream from Amoret stayed her hand.

"Do not slay him." cried Amoret, "or I will die! For only he who imposed this torture upon me can undo it!"

So Britomart grimly took hold of Busirane. "Death, or worse, is what you deserve," she said. "But if you restore this maiden, I will let you live."

The terrified magician quickly agreed, and reached for his book of spells. The words were dire and dreadful, and as he spoke the castle trembled and the doors rattled and creaked—yet Britomart's threatening sword did not waver from the enchanter's throat.

Then the metal bands holding Amoret split and fell away, and the brass pillar shattered. The cruel arrow drew out of her bleeding heart, the heart itself returned magically to its place, and the gaping wound in her breast closed up, leaving no sign that it had ever existed.

Amoret fell on her knees before Britomart in tearful gratitude, but the virgin warrior raised her up and soothed her, then led her out of the castle, from which all the splendour and richness had now vanished, as had the flames at the entrance.

But outside, Britomart found that neither Scudamour nor her trusty old nurse Glauce were to be seen. When Britomart had not returned, the knight had believed her to be dead, and had departed mournfully with Glauce to seek aid elsewhere.

* * *

The evil but beautiful witch Duessa reappears in company with the hag Ate, goddess of Discord—just as some attractive demons are joined by a hag in another version of the temptations of St. Anthony, painted in the 16th century by Joachim Patinir.

As Britomart and Amoret rode away, Amoret grew ever more fearful. She knew that by the code of chivalry she should pledge herself to her rescuer, yet she feared to do so, for her honour was dear to her above all else—and she was promised to Sir Scudamour, from whom she had been kidnapped on their very wedding day. And Britomart unknowingly added to her fear by failing to reveal herself as a woman, though she treated Amoret with every courtesy.

At length they reached a castle and sought shelter for the night. Within the castle were many knights, most of them in company with ladies, for the rules of the place insisted that a knight must be accompanied by a lady, or be barred from sleeping within the castle. And if a knight had no lady, he must seek to win one.

Many of the knights were struck by Amoret's beauty, and one young man, lacking a lady, brashly challenged Britomart, with Amoret as the prize. In their joust, Britomart effortlessly overthrew him; yet she felt sorry that the knight would be ejected from the castle, since he was valiant and chivalrous for all his youth. So before the company she removed her helmet, and the silken gold of her hair tumbled free. And she pointed out that the young knight, now pledged to her as a result of her victory, was no longer unaccompanied by a lady, and could be allowed to remain in the castle. So it was agreed with all friendly and honourable accord, and Amoret's fears as well were calmed.

The next day, Britomart and Amoret rode on, now fast friends, each sharing with the other the sad tale of the loved one for whom she was searching. As they rode, they saw two knights in the distance, in company with two ladies. They were unaware that one of the ladies was the dangerous Duessa, the sorceress whose false beauty had once ensnared the Red Cross Knight. And the other was the terrible Até, old Discord herself, mother of all dissension. She had been summoned by Duessa from her home by the gates of hell, to work her malevolence against knighthood. A foul and twisted hag was Até, with a forked tongue, deformed eyes and ears, and one foot twisted in the opposite direction from the other.

Duessa had become the companion of a knight named Blandamour, sturdy and valiant yet with a shallow and inconstant nature. So he was well matched with the knight riding with him, for he was the seducer Paridell.

Blandamour, seeing Britomart and Amoret, said to Paridell, "You have lacked a lady, but now fortune has brought you that lovely maid, if you can win her."

But Paridell declined, for he remembered meeting Britomart in combat before, to his cost. So Blandamour said, "Then you shall have my lady—" indicating Duessa—"and I shall win the maiden for myself."

He spurred forward to challenge Britomart. But the warrior maiden met the challenge with her invincible power, left Blandamour lying senseless on the ground, and rode on without a word.

Paridell and Duessa at last revived Blandamour, and they too rode on their way, Blandamour dejected and angry over his defeat and

An image of the medieval concept of "courtly love", on a 15th-century ceremonial shield. In its idealized form courtly love was both chaste ("Platonic") and inspirational, a central element in the code of chivalry by which a knight must defend all ladies but performs his valorous deeds for the sake of the particular lady to whom he is pledged.

the loss of Duessa. As they continued, they came upon two more travellers: Scudamour, and Britomart's old nurse Glauce.

Blandamour recognized Scudamour by the god of love blazoned on his shield, and his anger flared up more strongly, for he hated Scudamour deeply. Yet he could not challenge him, being not yet recovered from his defeat by Britomart, and asked Paridell to fight on his behalf. Willingly Paridell agreed, and rode in challenge against Scudamour.

Like two great waves lifted by opposing gusts of wind, the knights came together—and both were hurled crushingly to the ground by the impact. But Scudamour recovered and regained his mount, while Paridell lay unconscious and still. Paridell's friends ran to aid him, and Blandamour roughly abused Scudamour for the damage he had done. Then Duessa and old Até joined in, not with abuse but with treachery.

"Why do you strive so hard, Scudamour," said Duessa, "to seek your love, when all know that now she loves another?"

"I have seen it myself," Até put in, "how the lady Amoret now travels with another knight, shows him every affection, sleeps with him—and others have seen as well, and will say I speak truly."

Blandamour confirmed the hag's words, laughing to himself as rage and dismay swept over Scudamour, fed by the cruel spite of Duessa and Até, for he too did not realize Britomart was a woman.

*   *   *

Blandamour and Paridell then rode on, with their evil companions, and soon encountered yet another knight with a lady. She seemed to be the fairest damsel either had ever seen; but in fact she was the false Florimell, in company with Sir Ferraugh, the stranger who had taken her from the cowardly Braggadochio.

Blandamour at once desired her, and galloped without pause against Ferraugh, hurling the knight to the ground. Then Blandamour was swollen with pride at winning the lady whom he deemed the fairest in the land, while the false Florimell used all her coy flirtatiousness, all her subtle wiles, to intoxicate him. But in Paridell, envy began to build—and Até saw it and inflamed it with her discordant ways, till his bitter enmity led him at last to challenge Blandamour.

The challenge wrathfully accepted, the knights charged with such ferocity that both lances struck through shields and armour, deep into the flesh of both antagonists. Yet so hot was the rancour that had now replaced their shallow friendship that they fought on, afoot, swords hewing and slashing till the ground was awash with their blood.

Nor did the three women seek to end the combat, but spurred them on to even greater savagery. And there they might have slain each other had not the battle been halted by the arrival of a squire, who begged them to stop and tell him the cause of their strife.

It was the same Squire of Dames whom Sir Satyrane had befriended, earlier. The two knights, pausing, told him that they fought for the lady Florimell, and the Squire, believing her to be the true Florimell, greeted her with joy, for he and Satyrane had thought Florimell to be dead.

Then the Squire informed the knights that they should not be fighting over the lady, but should join forces against others who might seek to take her from them. He explained that Sir Satyrane had found the golden sash worn by Florimell, and that other knights —admirers of that lady, who also believed her dead—begrudged him the memento, and challenged him for it.

So Satyrane had declared that a grand tournament would be held, with the sash as the prize for the fairest lady there, and that lady the prize for the victorious knight. Since Florimell was the fairest in the land, the Squire added, and the sash was rightfully hers, she would certainly belong to the victor.

So Blandamour and Paridell put their animosity aside, professing friendship again—though it was as false and thin as gold foil spread over base metal. And with the Squire they rode on, towards the tournament of Satyrane.

On their way they met yet more travellers—two doughty knights, each accompanied by a comely lady. The Squire recognized them as the famed Cambell and Triamond, with their ladies Canacee and Cambina.

The story of Cambell and Triamond comes—as Spenser states—from the Squire's Tale in Chaucer's Canterbury Tales. *Illustration of the squire from a 15th-century manuscript of the poem.*

These were the knights whose story has been told by the great English poet Chaucer. Cambell was the brother of Canacee, a fair and virtuous maiden to whom many knights had professed love. But she had not returned their love, which stirred them even further, so that battle and bloodshed raged constantly around her. At last Cambell had put an end to the furor by declaring that he himself would fight against the three strongest of the suitors, and the victor would claim his sister.

Many knights dared not accept the challenge, for Cambell was brave and powerful, and also had—from his sister—an enchanted ring that could staunch the blood from all wounds. But there were three brothers, triplets named Priamond, Diamond, and Triamond, who were not so fearful.

Their mother, Agape, had given them a great gift. She had gone to the Fates themselves, the three sisters who hold the life-threads of all men and determine their lengths. When Agape had begged the Fates to prolong her sons' lives, the fearsome trio had undertaken that, should one son die, his life-force would enhance the lives of the other two; and should a second son die, both lives would go to extend that of the surviving third. These, then, were the three knights that took up Cambell's challenge, for the hand of Canacee.

*　　　　*　　　　*

On the day of the combat, Priamond entered the lists first, to oppose the valour of Cambell. Both knights were skilled with the lance, and charged each other with furious might, inflicting savage wounds— though Cambell's did not bleed. But at last a ferocious thrust sent Cambell's spear deep into Priamond's throat, and flung him dead and bloody to the ground.

Then Diamond strode vengefully into the lists, his strength doubled by his dead brother's spirit. The combat now was with battle-axes, which seemed to create a terrible storm, thunderous blows striking fire like lightning from metal on metal, blood pouring like rain. Again they seemed evenly matched, until the moment when Cambell moved skilfully aside from one murderous blow by

Diamond, and his axe sliced Diamond's head from his shoulders.

The remaining challenger, Triamond, now bearing the life-force of both his brothers within him, leaped into the lists, where Cambell, having lost no blood, seemed as fresh as when he began. Triamond's sword slashed and hewed in a hail of blows, driving Cambell back with his fury. But when that fury abated, it was Cambell's turn to advance with a flurry of mighty strokes. To and fro the battle went, neither gaining the advantage, except that Cambell did not seem to tire or weaken, so strong was the virtue of his ring.

At last the power of his sword-strokes found the mark, and the blade slashed across Triamond's throat, felling him. Yet he did not die from the mortal blow, for two souls remained within him—and he rose again to battle. Astounded, Cambell fell back, and Triamond pressed him hard, at last swinging up his sword for a killing blow. As he did so Cambell thrust fiercely, and his sword stabbed up under his opponent's armpit just as Triamond's blow crashed down on Cambell's helmet.

Knights in action in the controlled turmoil of a tournament—a scene painted on the side of a 15th-century decorated chest.

Both fell thunderously, and the watching throng was sure that both were dead. But then Cambell regained consciousness, and rose, just as Triamond also rose, animated now by the third soul that remained in him.

So they fought on grimly. But then a disturbance arose in the midst of the crowd, and through it, on a richly adorned chariot drawn by lions, came a lady so lovely as to seem heaven-born. She was Cambina, sister of Triamond, who from their mother had learned deep skill in magical lore. In one hand she bore a rod of peace, with two serpents entwined, and in the other a cup of nepenthe, the drink that sweeps away all care and grief.

Bursting into the lists, she entreated both knights to end their senseless battle, and make peace. When she touched them with her wand, the swords fell from their astonished hands; and when they drank from her cup, anger fell from their spirits. So the knights embraced, swearing fealty and true friendship to one another. Then Canacee came to them as well, and she and Cambina too made vows of undying friendship.

In accord at last, the four turned away from battle. And when the knights were recovered, Triamond took Canacee as his wife—and love for Cambina arose within Cambell, which was returned, so they too were married. And true love and friendship bound them all together for all time.

*   *   *

Such was the tale of Cambell and Triamond, who were riding towards an encounter with Blandamour and Paridell.

When the two parties came together, no knightly challenge was issued, since both Blandamour and Paridell were still suffering the effects of their previous combats. But Blandamour was insulting at first, until the fair Cambina created the pleasant concord that was her nature, so that they all rode together towards the tournament of Satyrane.

On their way they encountered a knight alone, who also avoided the risk of challenge, for he was the vainglorious Braggadochio. Soon this cowardly knight was casting eyes at the false Florimell, who had been wrested from him earlier, until at last Blandamour angrily offered Braggadochio the chance to win Florimell in battle—but added that the hag Até would be the loser's prize. And Braggadochio nervously blustered that while he would willingly risk his life for a beautiful lady, he would not do so for an ugly crone, at which all the company laughed, recognizing his cowardice.

Finally they all came to the place of Satyrane's tournament, where many brave knights had gathered with their ladies, to contest for the prizes. When the tournament began, Satyrane himself entered the lists with his heavy lance. A knight named Bruncheval engaged him first, while Blandamour jousted with another named Ferramont, and was unhorsed by that knight. Paridell suffered the same fate, but then Triamond took the field and overwhelmed Ferramont, and then in succession defeated knights named Devon, Douglas, and Paliumord.

By then Satyrane had overcome his opponent, and in turn charged against Triamond, his lance-thrust stabbing through the plate armour to gash Triamond's side. So Satyrane was declared victor of the tournament's first encounters, and all withdrew from battle for that day.

On the following day, the wounded Triamond did not enter the lists, but his friend Cambell took up the fight. He and Satyrane clashed at full gallop, and both fell thunderously—but rose again, regained their saddles, and engaged one another with swords. Their swirling, furious combat continued until mischance caused Satyrane's horse to stumble and throw him.

But before Cambell could wrench away Satyrane's shield, as prize of victory, a hundred knights gathered to assail him. Like a lion at bay Cambell fought, heroically defending himself—and the news of the battle came to Triamond on his sickbed. At once he rose and armed himself, unmindful of his wound, and rode to his friend's rescue. And together the two beat back the attackers, as fierce and unstoppable as two ravening wolves loose in a sheep-fold. Then again the day's fighting was done, though neither Cambell nor Triamond would claim the victory, each insisting that it was rightfully the other's.

On the third day Satyrane again overshadowed all knights on the field, with unwearied power, so that the ground was strewn with the broken lances and lost weapons of his opponents. But at that point a strange knight entered, his armour curiously decked with moss and leaves, his shield bearing the legend "Salvagesse sans finesse", which could be translated as "wildness without wiles".

No one could stand against the newcomer. Almost without effort he flung down sturdy and valiant knights. When his lance was broken, his sword hewed and smote with such power that others shunned him as if he were death itself. And all wondered who it might be beneath the strange disguise, for none could guess that it was the great Sir Artegall, among the doughtiest knights in all the land.

But equally none knew the name of another unknown knight who then entered the lists, at just the moment when all felt that the "savage" knight had won the day. The newest arrival charged unerringly against Artegall, and hurled him crushingly from his horse. Other valiant warriors then tried the newcomer—Cambell, Triamond, Blandamour in turn—and all fell as readily and painfully before that invincible lance. For it was Britomart herself who had joined the battle, and who finally, at the tournament's end, had won the day.

*   *   *

When the unknown knight who was in fact Britomart had been judged the victor, it was time for the ladies to compete for the title of the fairest of all, with the golden sash as prize. They all knew that the sash was the same as the girdle of Venus, which the goddess wore in her chaste and wifely moods: so it represented chaste love·and wifely virtue, and could not be worn by any woman who did not exhibit that virtue.

When the ladies came forth, Cambina and Canacee seemed to outshine even the loveliest of the rest, though some knights seemed to favour Duessa. Then Britomart brought Amoret forward, and her angelic beauty seemed sure to carry the day—until Blandamour produced his lady, the false Florimell. Then everyone believed her to be the true owner of the sash, and unquestionably the fairest of them all.

But when the false Florimell tried to fasten the sash of virtue round her waist, it loosened itself and fell away. Again and again she tried, and each time it would not remain. And equally many of the other ladies who took it up could not wear it, which mightily amused the Squire of Dames, in his cynicism about the chastity of womankind.

Then Amoret shyly tried on the sash, and it fitted perfectly and remained securely fastened. But the false Florimell snatched it from her, insisting that it was hers as rightful prize, and all had to agree that the judgment had gone to her as fairest of all.

Equally, she herself was the prize for the victorious knight. But Britomart naturally refused to accept her, and turmoil ensued. The wild knight, Artegall, had departed, or he might have been awarded Florimell; and Triamond also refused the prize, remaining true to his Canacee. Satyrane might then have claimed Florimell, but both Blandamour and Paridell objected fiercely—while old Até stirred all the knights to furious argument and rage.

In the end, to avoid an all-embracing brawl, Satyrane decreed that the lady herself would decide which knight should claim her as a prize. And the false Florimell created even greater furore and consternation by unhesitatingly choosing Braggadochio, who took her quickly away before every knight on the field might challenge him to fight.

Earlier, seeing the trouble that was stirring, Britomart and Amoret had ridden away, both still bound on their searches for the ones they loved. Britomart had no idea that she had just encountered, in battle, the object of her search, Artegall. Nor had Amoret any idea that, not far away, her beloved, Scudamour, was bitterly and vengefully seeking Britomart, whom he believed to have stolen Amoret's love.

*   *   *

In his search, the woebegone Scudamour, still accompanied by old Glauce, came to a forest and saw an armed knight resting in the shade. The two warriors challenged each other, and charged with couched lances, but at the last moment the stranger—whose armour was decorated with leaves and moss—raised his lance and pulled up his steed.

"Your pardon, Scudamour," he said, "I will not ride against you this day."

"No pardon is needed," said Scudamour, mystified, "when a knight seeks to prove himself against another. But since you know my name, will you tell me yours, and why you are here?"

"Call me the Knight of the Wilds," said the other—who was of course Artegall, in the same disguise that he had worn in the tournament. "I have chosen to keep my name hidden awhile. And I am here to regain my honour against a knight who shamed and defeated me sorely."

He told Scudamour of the tournament, and when he described the knight who had defeated him Scudamour instantly recognized Britomart. "I will wait with you," said Scudamour, "for this same treacherous knight has stolen my lady love from me, and besmirched the fair name of knighthood."

Nor did they have long to wait. In a while Britomart appeared, riding through the forest—and Scudamour requested and was granted the chance to make the first challenge.

Fiercely he charged, and Britomart in turn spurred to meet him. And in seconds both Scudamour and his steed were sprawling dazed on the ground. Then Artegall galloped furiously against her, and was as swiftly flung from his saddle.

Raging, Artegall sprang at her with his sword, and though she was still mounted and he was afoot the power of his attack forced her to give ground. As she swerved and wheeled, defending herself, one mighty stroke glanced from her helmet and sliced deeply into her charger's back.

Then Britomart too had to dismount, and put aside her enchanted lance. But with sword and shield she met Artegall's fury with her own, beating him back, finally slashing past his guard so that her sword hewed through his armour into the flesh beneath. But Artegall replied with renewed power, and forced her on to the defensive. And so the battle went, one and then the other taking and losing the advantage. But slowly Artegall's strength began to prevail, as Britomart grew more weary, until at last he struck a blow of tremendous force that would surely have killed her if it had not been turned slightly by her helmet.

But the blow sheared her helmet entirely away. And Artegall, sword poised for the next killing blow, was frozen in astonishment to see the virgin warrior's lovely face, dewed with sweat from her exertions, and her tumbled golden hair. Horrified at what he had nearly done, he dropped to one knee, begging forgiveness for the outrage. Britomart, still in her battle fury, demanded that he rise and fight; but he would not.

Then the others gathered, and Scudamour, amazed at the sight of Britomart, overjoyed that he had been misled about the knight who rode with Amoret, also knelt in homage, while old Glauce greeted her mistress with cries of gladness. With peace restored, all the knights raised their visors—and Britomart saw Artegall's face.

She knew it at once as the face she had seen in the magic mirror, of the knight she loved. And she was overcome, speechless and trembling, all the more so when Scudamour recognized Artegall and greeted him by name. And equally Artegall had been struck by Britomart's beauty and grace, so that he found himself in love, yet neither of them were able to speak of it, or reveal their feelings to one another.

Scudamour broke into their thoughts by asking about Amoret. And Britomart sorrowfully had to tell him that his lady was lost again. Earlier she and Amoret had paused to rest, in a peaceful wood, and when Britomart had awakened Amoret had been nowhere to be seen. But, she reassured the stricken knight, she would not rest till she had found the damsel, and brought vengeance upon whoever had stolen her away.

For some time the three knights remained together, resting while their wounds healed. During that time Artegall gently paid court to Britomart, manifesting his love. And she, at first modestly rejecting his advances, at last relented and confessed her own love. So finally their troth was plighted.

But Artegall had already begun a dangerous quest of his own, which he had to complete before they could marry. So at length he rode forth on his adventure, leaving Britomart forlorn and miserable, but vowing to return to her swiftly when his purpose was achieved. And Britomart joined Scudamour to ride in search of her true friend and his true love, the maiden Amoret.

*   *   *

Amoret's bestial abductor, an allegorical figure of unbridled Lust, resembles the more evil kinds of "wild men" common in medieval fiction and folklore—like this creature in a woodcut by Cranach.

Amoret had met grave danger on the day when she had wandered into the woods, while Britomart slept. Out of a dense thicket had rushed a hideous creature, more beast than man, shaggy with hair, huge fangs bloodstained from the human flesh that was his food, a knotted oaken club in one hand. He had snatched up the fainting Amoret and carried her off, rushing through the forest to his distant cave, into which he had flung her and left her, blocking the entrance with an enormous boulder.

When Amoret awoke in terror, she heard another maiden's voice sobbing quietly near her in the darkness. The other told her that they were both captives of a being who lived only to pursue and carry off maidens, deflower them, and then consume their flesh. He had devoured seven women in the previous twenty days, she said, so that now there were only herself and Amoret, and an old woman who was also in the cave with them.

In reply to Amoret's timid question, the other maiden said that her name was Aemylia, and told her story. She was the daughter of a great lord, but had fallen in love with a lowly born squire, and had been forbidden to marry him. So she and her love had planned to elope together—except that when she had come to the grove where they were to meet and make their escape, she had encountered the vile beast-man, who had carried her off to his cave. And there she had remained ever since, but still with her chastity unblemished, for the old woman had always given herself to the creature's bestial lusts.

As they spoke, mourning their fates, the boulder was rolled back from the cave-mouth and the monster entered. His foul intentions were obvious, and Amoret did not hesitate. She slipped past him and sprang for the entrance, terror lending almost superhuman speed to her flight.

The beast-man pursued her, hardly less swift, and as they ran the forest echoed with Amoret's piteous cries for help. At last those cries were heard. The huntress Belphoebe had been roaming the woods with her nymphs, in company with the squire Timias. But during the hunt they had become separated, so it was Timias who arrived on the scene just as the beast-man had caught up with Amoret and gathered her up under one huge arm.

Timias intercepted him, threatening him with his boar-spear—but the monster attacked the squire with his club, and used Amoret as his shield against the javelin. Time and again the squire stabbed and thrust, yet had to pull back the stroke to keep from harming the maiden. But he waited his moment, and at last the spear found the opening he had sought, and the beast-man's black blood flowed.

Then the monster went amok, throwing Amoret aside and raining a terrible onslaught of blows against the retreating squire. But at that moment Belphoebe arrived, and at the sight of her the beast-man turned and fled, fearing her chastity above all things. The huntress pursued him with relentless speed, and just as the creature had reached his cave one of her arrows buried itself in his neck, toppling him dead on his own threshold.

From the filthy cave Belphoebe brought forth Aemylia, and also the old woman, a befouled and loathsome hag. And with them she returned to Timias—to find her squire cradling the swooning figure of Amoret in his arms, with what seemed to be love and adoration.

Anger and indignation filled Belphoebe's heart. "Is this the faith you would show me?" she cried to Timias, and, turning, sped away.

Timias sprang after her, dismayed at her misunderstanding. But she would not let him approach her, brandishing her weapons to keep him at bay. And finally she vanished into the woods and was lost to his sight.

Then Timias too was lost, in woe and anguish. He wandered forlornly away into the heart of the forest, and there he remained, determined to forego the unhappy world. He broke his weapons, tore his squire's garments. And as time passed, he built himself a tiny cabin in the wilderness, and lived on the fruits of the forest and the water of its streams.

Eventually a day came when Prince Arthur passed through that forest and came upon the cabin. He did not recognize his own squire, for by then Timias was ragged and wraith-thin, with hair and beard grown long and straggling over his face. Nor did Timias speak a word, though he bowed low to the prince—and Arthur was greatly puzzled by the mystery, as he was by the name, unknown to the prince, that was carved on every tree around the cabin: *Belphoebe*.

*   *   *

Unable to aid the wretch who had been Timias, Arthur left him there in his misery. But one day the squire's loneliness was interrupted by the visit of a dove, who seemed to echo his sadness with her soft cooing. Timias fed the bird and befriended her, and as a sign of his affection took a ruby once given him by Belphoebe, on a golden chain, and fixed it round the dove's neck.

Surprisingly, the dove flew swiftly away, far through the forest, till she came at last to the feet of the wandering huntress Belphoebe. And the maiden, seeing the jewel, knew it and sought to catch the bird. But the dove flew before her, leading her deep into the woods to the cabin of Timias.

Belphoebe too did not recognize the squire who loved her, but felt pity for the lonely and ragged hermit that she believed he was, and more pity when the squire, still speechless, threw himself weeping at her feet.

"Are you here," Belphoebe asked gently, "because of some punishment from heaven, or some villain's crime against you? Or have you wilfully chosen to turn your back on the world and also on God's grace?"

And Timias at last broke his silence. "All three reasons are true— for heaven chose to bring me down from the happiness that I knew, so that I came to loathe my life, while you yourself were the cruel one who drove me to wretchedness, by a misunderstanding that led you to reject me."

Belphoebe knew him then, and saw with horror what she had done to him. So they were reunited, in perfect love and accord for all their life together.

Prince Arthur knew none of this, still believing his squire lost.

But by then he had come upon Amoret and Aemylia, wandering lost in the forest. He listened with pity to their tale, and took them up on to his charger to carry them to safety.

On their way, they came upon a mounted squire, in the headlong gallop of panic, with a dwarf set on the saddle before him, and being pursued by a frightful giant. The huge pursuer, mounted on a camel, bore a vast iron mace, and from his eyes blazed twin beams of merciless, deadly fire.

Arthur set the damsels down and rode to intercede. As he came up to the squire, the giant struck viciously down at the youth—but Arthur was quick enough to fling his shield up and partially block the blow. The giant turned then on Arthur, but the prince eluded the great blows and, choosing his moment, slashed entirely through the giant's neck and sent his headless body crashing down in streaming blood.

The grateful squire then approached, and told his story. His name was Placidas, and he had come into danger because of his dearest friend, who also looked exactly like him, a squire called Amyas. Amyas had loved a high-born lady, but her family had forbidden them to marry, and before they could elope together, Amyas had been captured by the giant whom Arthur had just slain.

The giant, Placidas went on, was named Corflambo, an evil enemy of all beauty and honour, whose flaming eyes sought to kindle lust within men and women. But the giant had a daughter, Poena, fair and lovely if more vain and wanton than a maid should be. And within men and women. But the giant had a daughter, Poeana, fallen in love with him.

Amyas had resisted her, remaining true to his own lady. And then Placidas, searching for his friend, had found him in his captivity, and had devised a plan. Leaving Amyas unseen, Placidas posed as his friend, completely unsuspected by Poeana or the dwarf, who was the squire's gaoler. And since Placidas had no lady, he was able to feign deep love for the giant's daughter, pleasing her so that she allowed him more and more freedom, though always watched by the dwarf. Finally a chance for escape came, and he fled—taking the dwarf with him—but the giant saw his escape and pursued him, and would have killed him had not Arthur intervened.

Then the lady Aemylia was overcome, for Amyas was the very Squire of Low Degree whom she loved. But Placidas assured her that her squire still lived, and Arthur undertook to free him from his captivity.

Spenser borrowed the character of the Squire of Low Degree from a popular medieval romance. Title page of a printed version (1550) of the tale.

*   *   *

With the two maidens and Placidas, Arthur advanced upon the giant's castle, and found the lady Poeana singing a sad song of love. The prince took her captive without difficulty, and compelled the dwarf to open the dungeons—from which nearly a score of knights and squires emerged, including Amyas. Both Aemylia and Placidas embraced him with warmth and gladness, and Poeana gazed at them, unable to be sure which was the man she loved, so alike were they.

Arthur stayed in the castle awhile, so that the maidens might rest from their travels, and while there brought peace and concord to the place. With Amyas and Aemylia reunited, he set Poeana free, and eased her sorrow by granting that she and Placidas could be married. Placidas was willing, as was she, and so the squire became lord of that castle and its estate, while Poeana reformed her wanton ways, and both lived in joy and wedded harmony from then on.

But soon Arthur returned to his own quest, still taking Amoret with him to protect her and aid her own search. On their travels they came upon a scene of violent battle, four knights against two.

The four knights were the fickle Blandamour and the seducer Paridell, along with Sir Druon, a woman-hater, and Sir Claribell, known for his lechery. Each had been searching for the false Florimell, ever since the tournament when she had gone with Braggadochio. They had met during their search, and had been stirred by Duessa and foul Até into angry conflict among themselves.

But as that battle had raged, Britomart and Scudamour had passed that way. And the four, recognizing Britomart as the knight who had shamed them all in the tournament, had left their own combat and turned on her and her companion. The warrior maiden and Scudamour had fought with heroic prowess, so that even four knights against two had not gained an advantage.

When Arthur came on the scene, he tried to halt the unequal battle —and the four false friends, in their rage, turned on him, raining fierce blows upon him from all sides. But the prince was valiant, and they were battle-weary, so that his wrathful sword counter-attacked with such power that he drove them back, and might have slain them had not Britomart intervened to calm him and to impose a truce among the combatants.

When the four false friends explained the reason for the battle, Arthur reproached them for seeking to gain dishonourable redress, by unequal combat, for their defeat. So peace was restored—and in the course of the conversation that followed, the four knights asked Scudamour to tell them the tale of how he had gained the love of Amoret.

*   *   *

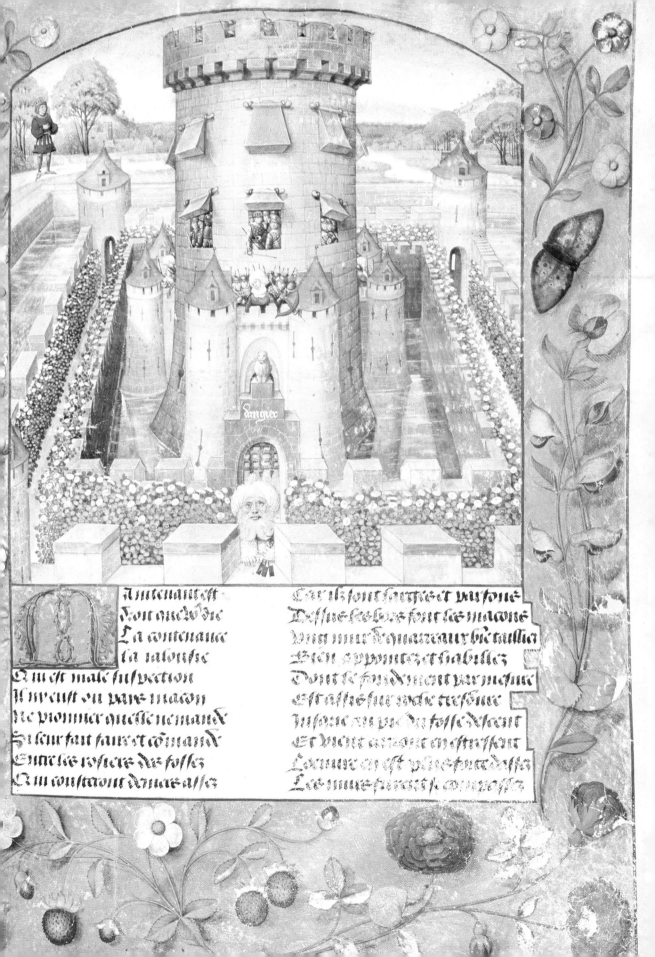

Maintenant est
son oncle dit
La contenance
la ialousie
Qui est male suspection
Il y eust en paine maçon
Ne pionnier quelle ne mande
Si leur fait faire et comand
Entre les riviere du fosse
Qui conseront a maint asse

Car ils sont faittes et du fone
Dessus les bos sont les maçons
Vng mur de quareaux bien taillie
Bien appointez et habillez
Dont le fondement par meisme
Est assis sur arde tresferme
Jusque au pie du fosse defont
Et vont amont en estrecsont
Comme en est plus hault redisse
Les murs plus fort compresse

Scudamour related how, as a young knight, his search for adventure led him to the island on which stood the glorious Temple of Venus. The island was walled and fortified, with a beautiful bridge leading across to a sturdy castle, with twenty knights standing guard before it. And in an open space by the castle door was a pillar on which was hung the shield of love, with its blazon of the winged Cupid, and beneath it the words: "Whoever can win this shield will also win the fair Amoret."

Scudamour boldly rose to the challenge, and met the twenty knights one after another in single combat, leaving all of them groaning on the ground. Then he took down the shield and advanced upon the castle. The porter, Doubt, with two faces gazing in opposite directions like Janus, saw the shield and admitted him. He brushed past old Delay, who sought to hold him back with prattle and wheedling, and came to a second gate, called the Gate of Good Desert, guarded by the ferocious giant Danger.

The young knight assailed the giant bravely, and forced him to give way. So he entered into the island's interior, a paradise where every lovely tree, every fragrant flower, grew in abundance—where sweet brooks and streams wound over soft greensward—where bowers and glades and labyrinths offered shade and privacy to the thousands of pairs of lovers who walked there, in chaste and sweet contentment. Equally, nearby, pairs of true and devoted friends strolled together: and among them were Hercules and Hylas, David and Jonathan, Theseus and Pirithous, Damon and Pythias.

Much affected by the heavenly sights around him, Scudamour made his way to the magnificent Temple itself, more beautiful than any other on earth. In its porch sat a comely and sober matron, richly gowned, flanked by two young men. They were half-brothers, and total opposites in every way, for their names were Love and Hate; yet the matronly woman had brought them into harmony, so that they stood with joined hands. Her name was Concord, mother of the divine twins Peace and Friendship, and she is the true guardian of the gate to Venus's grace.

Reaching the inner temple, Scudamour was amazed by the glories of the building: tall, decorated pillars bedecked with flowers and garlands, a hundred altars and steaming cauldrons tended by fair priestesses. In their midst was a statue of the goddess herself, on an altar of pure crystal. She was lightly veiled—because, some said, she combined within herself attributes of both male and female, perfectly blended—and round her legs twined a serpent with its tail in its mouth.

At Venus's feet was a bevy of lovely women who attended her: steadfast Womanhood, shy Modesty, sweet Cheerfulness, gentle

Scudamour's entry into the Temple of Venus is based on a similar assault by a lover on a castle where his beloved is being held, from the medieval French allegorical poem Roman de la Rose. *Illustration from a 15th-century manuscript of the poem.*

Courtesy, soft Silence, and Obedience. And in the lap of the first, Womanhood, was a beautiful young maiden in purest lily white, alight with virtue and grace—the fairest Amoret.

Scudamour advanced boldly and took the maiden's hand; and when Womanhood rebuked him, he displayed the shield that he had won. "It is fitting," he said, "that Cupid's knight should be joined with Venus's maid. Your goddess is not one to be served only by virgins."

The statue of Venus had seemed then to smile at him, as if in approval, and so he had led Amoret forth into the world, to be his bride.

*   *   *

During all this time, quite unknown to all the knights adventuring in the land, the true Florimell had remained a prisoner in the dungeon where she had been cast by the sea-god Proteus, when she would not give herself to him. For seven months she had lain in that prison, yet still she remained true to her only love, the knight Marinell.

For much of that time Marinell had remained close to death from the terrible injury he had suffered earlier in battle with Britomart. But Tryphon, medically the wisest of the sea-gods, had come at the behest of Marinell's Nereid mother, and had at last healed that injury and restored the young knight to health.

It then happened that all the immortal sea-beings of the world were to attend a glorious feast, for the spirits of two great rivers were to be married. The god of the Thames himself was to take the nymph of the Medway as his wife, and the wedding festivities were to be in the house of Proteus.

On the wedding day, the sea-gods gathered—with great Neptune at their head, beside his wife Amphitrite, her father Nereus, and even old Ocean and his dame Tethys, the oldest of all in that divine procession. With the gods came also the famous rivers: the Nile and the Amazon, the Ganges and the Euphrates, the Rhine and the Tiber, and many more. And in the train of the Thames came all the rivers of Great Britain, large and small, to do honour to the wedded couple, while the bride, Medway, was attended by Nereids, including the mother of Marinell.

Marinell himself was unable to attend, for he had had a mortal father. So while the immortals were at their feasting, he wandered idly round the palace of Proteus, until he came to a mighty overhanging cliff. From beneath it he heard a piteous, plaintive voice, speaking as if to itself about sufferings undergone for love, and determination to suffer and to die rather than to be untrue. And the voice concluded with the words: "Wherever you may be, Marinell, this is all for you."

Marinell was shaken by the knowledge that he had caused a damsel such dire torment, and he sought to work out how he might free her. He knew that he could not merely beg Proteus to release her, and that it would be folly to fight the god for her. Nor could he steal her away from that impregnable ocean prison.

So he was helpless, and had to return to his home with his mother, when the feast had ended, without aiding the damsel. By then the pity within him had begun to mingle with love, at the thought of her steadfastness through all pain. In his home, he began to pine, neither sleeping nor eating, languishing and weakening as if in the grip of some illness. His frightened mother called Tryphon again, but the god could not help. Only when Apollo himself came, at the nymph's request, was the malady correctly diagnosed—the affliction of love.

At first the nymph was angry with Marinell, and then more frightened, remembering the prophecy that he would be brought near to death by a woman. But then she came to believe that the maiden whom Marinell loved must be a sea-nymph, not a mortal woman. So she promised her son that she would use all her power to bring his lady love to him—and she had to keep that promise even after Marinell told her who it was he loved.

His mother duly went to Neptune himself, to plead her case, saying that for love of a maiden imprisoned by Proteus her son would surely die. And the king of the sea took pity on her, and gave her a warrant to take to Proteus, ordering him to free Florimell.

Despite Proteus's grumbling, the order was carried out, and the nymph took Florimell back to her own home. She was deeply struck by the maiden's beauty and grace, which seemed to excel all living creatures, and was delighted to have gained so fair a wife for her son. And Marinell threw off his enfeebling misery when Florimell was brought to him, and declared his love for her. But what befell them next must wait till later to be revealed.

BOOK FIVE

The Legend of Sir Artegall, or Justice

The allegory of the Book of Justice, perhaps necessarily, refers more explicitly and consistently than anywhere else in all six books to the *political* reality of Elizabethan England. The central hero, Artegall, has been assigned the quest of freeing the lady Irena from oppression by the tyrant Grantorto. And while he may personify the abstraction of true Justice through much of the book, in the Irena episodes he is explicitly Lord Grey of Wilton, who was sent by Elizabeth to Ireland to put an end to the "great wrong" (in Italian, *gran' torto*) of rebellion and sedition.

Similarly, Prince Arthur's parallel adventure on behalf of the lady Belge, against her oppressor Geryoneo, is explicitly the story of the campaign fought by the Earl of Leicester in the Protestant Netherlands, against the forces of Philip II of Spain and the Catholic Inquisition. Arthur cannot be said to be identifiable with Leicester throughout the *Faerie Queene*, except in Book Five.

And further, the character of Mercilla is yet another representation of Elizabeth—and the trial of Duessa, over which she presides, is a clear allegory of the trial of Mary, queen of Scots.

Comparable, if less integral, references to political realities (and their religious overtones) occur throughout the book, interspersed with other allegorical instances that reflect the virtue of Justice and the dangers that beset it. But even these may be specific *social* references more than generalized *moral* meanings—as with the episode of the Amazons, commenting revealingly on the "proper" place of women in sixteenth-century society.

Essentially Artegall follows a similar pattern to that established by the Red Cross Knight. He rides on his quest, has adventures along the way that illustrate aspects of his central virtue, is tested and (humiliatingly) found wanting, is rescued (by Britomart!), is restored in the House of Mercilla in order to complete his quest. Along the way, though, he tends to be upstaged. The invincible iron man, Talus, does much of his fighting for him; Britomart must ride to his rescue; and Arthur's battle with Geryoneo is far more exciting than Artegall's final encounter.

Lord Grey de Wilton, lord deputy of Ireland (1580–82), a fanatical anti-Catholic, whom Spenser served as private secretary. Grey became his close friend and influential patron, and Spenser remained unswervingly loyal to him even after Grey had been recalled to England. Portrait by Gerlach Flicke.

But much of importance is being presented in this way. We are made to see that the justice of Talus is grim and inflexible, the "letter of the law", while Artegall's justice is tempered with wisdom, humanity, and ultimately mercy. When Artegall is defeated we perceive that his sense of right has been blurred by a *misplaced* pity. And when his final victory is diminished by his being recalled from Irena's land before peace is wholly secured, we are asked to remember that Lord Grey was similarly recalled by Elizabeth—because of the bloody and murderous fervour with which he pursued and executed Irish rebels—before he had restored "peace" to Ireland.

When the warrior maiden Britomart had at last met and become betrothed to her love, Artegall, he was already committed to a great adventure of his own—for which he had soon had to leave Britomart. That adventure had begun when a distraught lady named Irena had come to the court of the Faery Queen. She was seeking the Queen's aid against an evil tyrant, Grantorto, who had wrested her lands and heritage from her. And Artegall had been the champion selected by the Queen to aid Irena and restore what was rightfully hers.

As a child, Artegall had been adopted by the goddess Astraea, who had nurtured in him a sure knowledge of right, justice, and equity. And as he reached manhood, she had given him a mighty sword, called Chrysaor, tempered with adamantine and decorated with gold, and sent him forth into the world, where his just weighing of right and wrong became as renowned as his knightly prowess. Astraea then left the world of men, and returned to heaven, where

Artegall learned the virtue of justice from Astraea, identified with the zodiacal sign of Virgo—here personified, with her neighbouring sign of Libra, the Scales, in 15th-century reliefs by Agostino di Duccio.

she is now remembered in the form of the constellation Virgo. But before she left, she also gave Artegall a servant named Talus, a man entirely of iron, invincible and relentless, who carried an iron flail that no wickedness or falsehood could withstand.

At the outset of their journey to the land of Irena, Artegall and Talus came upon a squire, bitterly weeping over the headless corpse of a lady. When Artegall asked how she had died, the squire told him that she had been slain by a cruel knight, whose shield bore the device of a broken sword on a blood-red field.

The squire had been travelling with his lady when he had encountered the knight, whose name was Sanglier. The knight had also been accompanied by a lady, but announced that he preferred the squire's companion. Casting his own lady callously aside, he forced the squire to give up his beloved. And when Sanglier's lady desperately tried to prevent him from forsaking her, he drew his sword and viciously beheaded her, before carrying the squire's beloved away.

Artegall at once sent his iron servant in pursuit, and the swift Talus soon overtook Sanglier, and ordered him to return and face judgment. The knight replied with a savage attack, but his lance had no more effect than if it had struck a great rock. And Talus felled Sanglier with a terrible blow, bound him, and brought him back to Artegall.

When he had recovered, Sanglier denied his guilt, insisting that the squire was lying. Knowing that a trial by combat was not possible, for a squire would be no match for a knight, Artegall sought other means to reach the truth.

"Since both of you claim this living lady," he said, "this is my decision: that she shall be divided in two, and each shall have a share. And he who dissents from this judgment must, as a penance, carry for twelve months the head of this other lady who lies already slain."

Seeing a way to escape paying for his crime, Sanglier immediately agreed to give the living lady up to be slain and her body divided. But the squire, who loved that lady, would not agree. To save her life he yielded her to the knight, forlornly choosing to bear the penance.

"So it is proved," said Artegall, "that the living lady is truly the squire's, for only he loves her enough to save her at any cost to himself. Yours, then, Sanglier, is the penance, to bear the head of the lady you slew."

Under the forbidding gaze of both Artegall and Talus, the knight dared not refuse, but took up the severed head and hurried away like a cowed dog.

*   *   *

Artegall's encounter with Sir Sanglier and the squire is based on the biblical story of the judgment of Solomon (First Book of Kings), shown here in a French manuscript of the Bible Historiale *(c.1400).*

After leaving the squire happily reunited with his lady, Artegall and Talus encountered a dwarf travelling with nervous haste. He was Dony, servant to the maiden Florimell, who announced that he was on his way to the wedding of Florimell and Marinell.

But Dony was troubled, for the road ahead was barred by a cruel Saracen, named Pollente. The Saracen held a bridge across the river, and forced all travellers either to pay a huge toll or to do battle. In that way he had built up a vast treasure hoard for himself and his wicked daughter Munera, and had also slain many a valiant knight. For the bridge held a hidden trapdoor, through which Pollente would plunge his opponents into the dangerous river below, and then—being a skilled swimmer—would leap into the water after them and slay them easily.

Angrily Artegall made his way to the bridge, and there the Saracen awaited him, demanding his toll. But Artegall couched his lance instead, and charged. Pollente released the trapdoor, but Artegall, forewarned, leaped rather than fell into the river, maintaining his guard. Then Pollente was upon him, like a seal in the water. But Artegall too was a skilled swimmer, and attacked Pollente furiously, grasping the Saracen's iron collar in one mighty hand and raining a torrent of blows on him. The water was whipped into frenzied foam by the fury of their battle, but at last the Saracen began to weaken. Gasping for breath, he fled to the shore—but there Artegall caught him, and the bright sword Chrysaor sliced through the pagan's neck, tumbling his headless body into the blood-reddened river.

By then Talus had assailed the Saracen's castle, indifferent to the hail of stones and arrows from its defenders, or to the dark magic with which the pagan's daughter, Munera, tried to divert his wrath. The iron man's terrible flail beat down the door, and Artegall entered, while all the occupants hid themselves in terror. No pity rose in Artegall as the implacable justice of Talus took its course: the iron man dragged Munera out and flung her to her death in the river, then razed the castle to the ground and burned the ruins, together with all the Saracen's ill-gotten treasure.

Then they rode on their way, taking a path that led them near the sea. There they found a huge giant standing on a rock, addressing a crowd of awed people. The giant held a vast scales in his hand, and boasted that he could weigh the world itself in them, if he could find something to counterbalance it. He declared that his scales could weigh the land against the sea, fire against air, heaven against hell— and that by doing so he would correct the balance of things. For, he said, the world had become full of inequalities: the sea wore away the land, fire burned away the air, everything seemed to oppress or be oppressed by something else.

Facing page: like Artegall and Pollente, two knights confront each other at a bridge—from a French illustrated manuscript (c.1465).

apres quilz neurent pas grammēent alle quilz se regarderēt
et virent deuant eulx vng moult hault pont de fust atra
uers de la riuiere foible fraesle dancienne faccon et estoit
a merueilles Sicque a paine y pouoit passer vng cheual
de front la riuiere estoit creuse et roide durcmēt Sicque a
la roideur de leaue elle faisoit tout crouller et trēbler le pont

Comment le cuer et desir trouuerent le pont ou Il se combatit
Et de laultre part du pont rauoit vng cheualier
tout arme dunes armee noures fors auc sur son
escu qui estoit noir auoit trois fleurs de souffre et estoit

Artegall grew annoyed at the giant's proud boasting, and the credulity of the common folk who clustered round to listen like flies round honey. "Even were you able to change the balances of the world," he said, "you ought not dare to do so. All things have been placed as they are by the Creator, in just proportions ordered by Him."

"Foolish knight," the giant thundered, "can you not see the imbalances? How the sea encroaches on the land—how the earth is increased when the dead return to it? I will restore equality: I will throw down mountains to make them level with the plains, I will tumble kings and nobles from their high places, I will wrest wealth from the rich and give it to the poor."

"It is you who cannot see," Artegall replied angrily. "The sea may take soil from one place, but the tide deposits it in another, and the land remains the same. The dead do not enlarge the earth, for they came from earth originally. So all things keep the positions appointed by God: hills and valleys, kings and commoners. If your scales have the worth that you claim, let me see you weigh the wind, or the light of dawn. Weigh a thought, or weigh one of your own empty words."

Arrogantly the giant set out to prove Artegall wrong. He placed his words into his scale, but they vanished from it, as if winged. He placed truth in one balance and falsehood in another, but falsehood slid away, unable to be weighed against truth. He put the right into one balance, and heaped into the other all the wrongs he could muster —but the right outweighed them, however many they were.

"So you see," said Artegall sternly, "that truth, and right, and the words of men, are to be weighed in the mind and heart, not in your worthless scales."

The giant, raging, began to threaten the knight. But Talus leaped up to his pinnacle and pitilessly flung him down into the sea, where his crushed body sank along with his broken scales. The crowd that had been listening to the giant then wrathfully took up arms and moved in a riotous, vengeful tumult against Artegall—but again Talus intervened, scattering them with his relentless iron flail.

*   *   *

The primitive communism of the giant with the scales probably alludes to the beliefs—in full equality, common ownership, and so on—of the Anabaptist sect of Protestant extremists, prominent in Europe in the 16th century. Illustration from a book describing the sect by Daniel Featley (1646).

From there Artegall made his way to the celebration of the wedding of Florimell and Marinell. Never was such a high and glorious gathering, never such feasting and entertainments, culminating in a mighty tournament, in which Marinell met all challenges, in honour and praise of his beautiful lady. All the knights of the land were there, yet on the first two days of the jousting Marinell emerged the supreme victor.

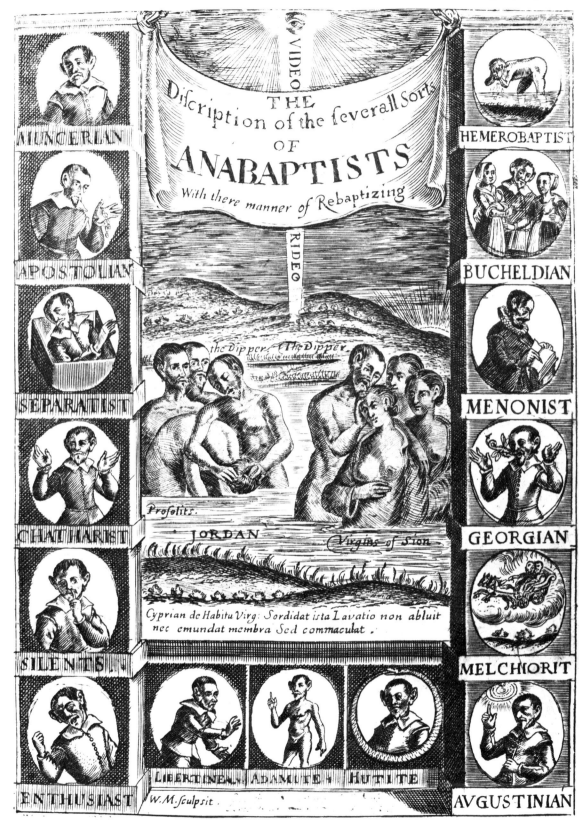

But on the third day, Marinell was assailed by a hundred knights, and even his valour did not suffice. He was defeated, and his opponents took him captive and began to lead him away—until Artegall took a hand.

He had arrived at the wedding at the same time as the vainglorious Braggadochio, still in company with the false Florimell. And, to disguise himself, Artegall borrowed Braggadochio's shield, before riding to aid Marinell. He stormed into battle like a raging lion, sweeping fifty of the knights aside, and releasing their prisoner. Then Marinell fought at Artegall's shoulder, and in that heroic onslaught the entire hundred knights were overcome and driven from the field.

So the victory was Artegall's, and the fair Florimell herself came forth to give the victor the garland. But by then Artegall had moved back into anonymity, giving Braggadochio his shield; so it was Braggadochio, with that shield, who rode out to receive the prize. Boastfully he told the gathering that his heroism had been all in his own lady's honour—and with that he presented, and unveiled, the false Florimell.

Consternation filled all the crowd, no one more than Marinell, to see a lady wholly identical with the bride. But Artegall could not allow the deception to continue. He presented himself to the throng, crushing Braggadochio's swollen vanity by revealing himself as the victor of the jousting. And he brought the true Florimell to confront her false replica.

When the two were placed side by side, the false Florimell simply vanished—melted away, for the evil magic that created her could not maintain itself in the face of the truth. Only the golden sash of Venus, which the true Florimell had lost and which had been claimed by the false Florimell at the tournament of Satyrane, remained behind. While the crowd watched, astounded, and Braggadochio stood in a daze of fright, Artegall took up the sash and fastened it in its rightful place round the waist of Florimell.

At that point another knight shouldered through the crowd, angrily threatening Braggadochio. It was Sir Guyon, who had recognized the horse that Braggadochio rode as his own charger, stolen long before by the false knight. Artegall interposed, restraining Guyon from attacking the terrified Braggadochio, and asked if there were any way that Guyon might prove the horse to be his own. And Guyon stated that it had a black mark within its mouth that would reveal its identity.

Several knights moved to open the horse's mouth, but the powerful charger shattered the ribs of one with a furious kick, and crushed the shoulder of another between its teeth. Then Guyon spoke to the horse, and it came to him at once, frisking, neighing

A disgraced knight, bound and placed in a cart as a punishment akin to the fate of Braggadochio. From a 15th-century Flemish manuscript.

with gladness at seeing its rightful master. And at Guyon's bidding it stood quietly while the mark in its mouth was examined. So Artegall declared that the horse was truly Guyon's and that henceforth Braggadochio must travel on foot.

The false knight began to complain and revile the others foully, and Artegall grew angry. But it was left to Talus to silence Braggadochio. The iron man wrested from him all the marks of his assumed knighthood—shaving his beard, tearing his armour apart, breaking his sword, erasing the heraldic emblem on his shield. Then with his flail he whipped both Braggadochio and his guileful servant Trompart out of that gathering, so they were banished from the company of true knights and ladies forever.

*   *   *

Afterwards, Artegall and Talus returned to their journey, riding again along the sea coast, where they came upon two young squires in furious battle, while two maidens sought in vain to calm their fury. Artegall parted them, and in reply to his enquiry the squires told their story.

They were brothers, named Amidas and Bracidas, whose father had left them each an island, lying near one another just off the shore. Bracidas had loved a maiden named Philtera, and his brother had loved another named Lucy. But as time passed, the eroding sea had swept away much of the land from the island of Bracidas, and had deposited it on the other island, so enlarging the lands held by Amidas. And Philtera, seeing Bracidas's lands and wealth diminished, had left him and eloped with his brother.

The maiden Lucy, finding herself deserted, had sought to take her own life by drowning—but when she plunged into the sea, she repented, and tried to save herself by clinging to an old sea chest floating near her. Then Bracidas had rescued her, and they had found the chest to be filled with treasure. But his brother Amidas had declared that the treasure belonged to Philtera, who had been bringing it to him as a dowry when it was lost at sea.

So the strife between the brothers had erupted. But when Artegall offered himself as a judge of the case, they willingly undertook to abide by his judgment.

Turning first to Amidas, Artegall said, "By what right do you lay claim to the land that has enlarged your island, at the expense of your brother's?"

"It is mine by right," said Amidas, "because the sea brought it to me."

"Very well," said Artegall, turning to the other squire, "by what right do you lay claim to the treasure, which originally belonged to your brother's wife?"

"By the same right," replied Bracidas, "because the sea brought it to me."

"There then is my judgment," said Artegall. "The sea has taken from each of you, and given to each. And what the sea gives to a man remains his to keep."

Amidas and Philtera were deeply annoyed, but Bracidas and Lucy happily took up the treasure and went on their way together. And Artegall resumed his journey.

Before long he saw a tumultuous crowd of people approaching— and, drawing near, found them to be a troop of warlike women, fierce and fully armed. In their midst was a knight, his hands tied and a noose round his neck as if the Amazons intended to hang him.

Seeing Artegall, the Amazons swarmed round him, intending to drag him down and subject him to the same treatment. But Talus met them with his flail and routed them, so that they fled, leaving their first victim behind.

Artegall recognized that knight as Sir Terpin, who explained how he had fallen into the Amazons' hands. The mighty Amazon queen, Radigund, had once loved a knight who had rejected her. So her love had turned to hatred for all knights—and any whom she could overcome, by force or trickery, she would keep as her prisoners, dressing them in women's clothes and requiring them to labour at women's work, sewing, spinning, washing and the like. And if any tried to resist, or to escape, she would hang them, as Terpin was to be hanged.

Artegall vowed to confront the Amazon queen, and avenge the shame she wreaked upon the honour of knighthood. Guided by Terpin, he rode to the city of the Amazons, and thundered upon its gates. Radigund herself came to the gates and ordered them opened —and when Artegall and Terpin entered, she and her army fell upon them.

The knights, with Talus, fought valiantly against the enormous odds. But a ferocious blow from Radigund felled Terpin to the ground, and the queen would have beheaded him had not Artegall fought his way through the swarming Amazons to hurl her back with a blow of frightening power.

But the rush and press of the battle then carried them apart, so that the queen could not again confront Artegall. The combat raged on till nightfall, with Talus always in the thick of it, shattering the Amazons' bows with his flail, driving them before him like a flock of sheep. And when darkness drew in, Radigund called her warriors

In Spenser's allegory the Amazons were an "unsuitable" form of woman warrior (the opposite of Britomart or Belphoebe), who overturned the "proper" relationship between men and women, and so threatened the "just order" of society. Painting by Rubens.

back into the city, leaving Artegall and his companions outside the gates.

During the night the wrathful queen devised ways that she might defeat the might of Artegall. At length she called one of her maids, Clarin, and ordered her to take Artegall a challenge—to meet the queen in single combat, the loser to be bound in servitude to the victor.

*　　　　*　　　　*

At sunrise the Amazon queen emerged from her city, with a short coat of mail over her silken tunic, armoured buskins on her legs, sword and shield gleaming. And Artegall confronted her, in full armour, while her people crowded round to watch.

Radigund began the battle, heaping blows on Artegall in a berserk battle fury. The knight defended himself, waiting for the storm to diminish—and when the Amazon began to tire, counterattacked as if his sword was a blacksmith's hammer and she the anvil. Many of his blows she warded off with her shield, until one ferocious stroke sheared half her shield away. She replied then with redoubled fury,

and her blade glanced off his own defence and sliced through his leg
armour, drawing a stream of blood from his thigh.

Such was Artegall's rage that his next blow shattered into
fragments what was left of the queen's shield, and another mighty
stroke thundered against her helmet, and flung her senseless on the
grass. Artegall quickly dragged off her helmet, intending to deliver
the *coup-de-grâce* that would have slashed her head from her shoulders.
But her womanly beauty halted him. Chivalrically realizing that he
could not slay a lady, he cast his sword aside as if it repelled him.

Then Radigund came to herself, and rose. Artegall sought to make
peace, but she refused, and assailed him as furiously as before. Though
he defended himself as best he could, in the end, knowing that he had
lost the battle when he had abandoned his sword, he had no choice
but to yield.

So the proud and vengeful queen made him her slave—and at the
same time sent her Amazons to take Sir Terpin again, and hang him as
they had previously intended. But they could not overcome Talus,
who laid about himself with his flail and escaped untouched, seeming
unwilling to rescue Artegall, who had brought his defeat upon
himself.

Radigund then ordered that Artegall be dressed in woman's garb
and put to the task of spinning, along with many other knights in
similar positions. And Artegall had to bear the humiliation, for he
had agreed to the terms before the battle.

For a long time he worked at his galling labours. And during that
time Radigund, watching him, began to find herself strongly
attracted to her newest captive. Her pride would not let her show it,
but love for Artegall began to torment her. At last she called her
maid Clarin and revealed that she wished to win the knight's love
while keeping him bound to her. She directed Clarin to become
friendly with Artegall, to sound out his feelings and learn how his
love might be won.

Clarin did as her queen ordered, treating Artegall with friendly kindness and talking with him whenever she could. In the course of their talk she asked him why he had not sought the queen's favour, and perhaps win respite from his shame. He replied that he had merely lacked opportunity, and would be grateful to the maid if she could provide it.

But by then it was too late—for in that time Clarin had felt love for Artegall burgeoning within herself. So when Radigund asked her, later, how Artegall had responded, Clarin falsely reported that the knight had obstinately rejected her overtures, saying he would rather die than seek the queen's favour. Radigund at first was furious, but calmed herself and told Clarin to try again. And also, she ordered that he should be given more and harder work, poor food and less of it, and only straw for a bed, so that his pride might be more swiftly broken.

But Clarin, going to Artegall, pretended that Radigund had ordered these further punishments out of her merciless cruelty. To win Artegall's regard, Clarin disobeyed the queen, by improving Artegall's food and lessening his labours. And when the knight responded with grateful courtesy, the maid convinced herself that he returned her love.

*   *   *

While Artegall languished in the feminine snare to which his own sense of right had brought him, Talus had travelled at great speed to find the knight's beloved, Britomart, who had been restlessly awaiting Artegall's return from his adventure. When the iron man appeared, alone, she ran to him fearfully, demanding to know what news he brought.

"My lord and your beloved," Talus said gloomily, "lies now in wretched bondage."

"Has he been vanquished, then," Britomart cried, "by the tyrant whom he rode out to quell?"

"Not by a tyrant," said the iron man, "but by a tyranness."

Anger flared in Britomart. "He has fallen victim to some harlot? Then tell me no more of him." And she stormed away.

For a long time rage and grief alternated within the breast of Britomart—sadly bewailing her love's breach of faith, then angrily thinking of riding out and seeking revenge by challenging him. At last, in her torment, she sought out Talus, to learn the details of Artegall's betrayal. When the iron man told her the whole story, she was abashed, then armed herself and galloped away, guided by Talus, to free her knight.

As she travelled, she came upon a knight who was well advanced in years. The knight greeted her courteously and, as darkness was beginning to fall, offered her the shelter of his home. She accepted, but at the old knight's home she refused to remove her armour, and her host, whose name was Dolon, was secretly annoyed. He had mistaken Britomart for Artegall, who had once slain the eldest of Dolon's three sons, in battle. And the old man had devised a treacherous plan for revenge.

During the night Britomart remained sleepless, brooding and grieving over her beloved's plight. Talus, of course, also did not sleep, but stood guard outside her door. And in the middle of the night, the warrior maiden was startled to see the bed, where she should have been lying, suddenly disappear downwards through a hidden trap-door in the floor. Realizing her danger, she snatched up sword and shield, just as a commotion arose in the hall outside. Two armed knights, the remaining sons of Dolon, were approaching her door, followed by a rabble of armed villains.

But Talus barred their way, and with his terrible flail beat them back and drove them into flight, out of the house. Then, as dawn lightened the sky, Britomart rode out, blazing with anger. Beyond the house she came to the bridge on which Artegall had fought with the Saracen Pollente—and there she saw the same two armed knights, Dolon's sons. They challenged her abusively, promising to wreak their vengeance for the death of their brother. And though Britomart knew nothing of that death, she had no intention of letting them bar her way.

She charged with all her fierce power, and the two knights on the bridge could not withstand her. One of them she flung to his death in the river, and the other was transfixed on the point of her lance, carried along the full length of the bridge until the corpse fell away on the other side.

*   *   *

Riding onwards, Britomart came soon to a glorious structure, like a heavenly temple, dedicated to the goddess of ancient Egypt, Isis, who held in her person all justice and equity. Britomart entered and was made welcome by the priests, though Talus was required to remain outside. Awestruck, she gazed at the golden pillars and other splendours within the temple, and especially at the statue of Isis herself, so wondrously carved that it seemed almost alive. It was entirely of silver, garbed in linen, with a crown representing the moon, a white wand in one hand, and a writhing crocodile beneath its feet.

Isis and Osiris, from the Egyptian Book of the Dead *(1550–1090* BC*). Elizabethan scholars, taking their cue from Roman writings, knew that Osiris was a god of justice, and Isis at times represented the principle of Equity, a role similar to that played by Britomart in Book V.*

Britomart found herself growing sleepy, and reclined near the statue, closing her eyes. And there she dreamed a strange and terrible dream, in which the statue came to life, garbed now in red with a crown of gold. Then the temple of the goddess was assailed by a furious tempest and deadly leaping flames—but the crocodile gaped wide and swallowed both wind and fire. It seemed as if the beast might then threaten Isis, but she quietened it with her wand, so that it began showing her a humble affection and love, which she accepted. Soon the goddess and the beast were united, and from their union she gave birth to a mighty and kingly lion.

When Britomart awoke, much bemused by her dream or vision, she recounted it to the priests. They were amazed, and explained to her that by the dream Isis had confirmed Britomart's lineage and her destiny. The crocodile represented Artegall, they said, overcoming the opposition of storm and flame which were his enemies. And the goddess in red was Britomart herself, who, united with Artegall, would bring forth the royal line of British monarchs.

Gladdened by this confirmation of her future, the virgin warrior took her leave and rode forward to the city of the Amazons. There the people were much disturbed by the challenging arrival of another formidable knight, also in company with the terrible iron man whom they remembered well. So queen Radigund armed herself again for battle, and strode out to meet the challenger.

As before, the Amazon queen laid down the terms for battle— that Britomart should become her slave if defeated. But the warrior maiden rejected the terms outright, for she would be bound by nothing save the laws of chivalry. Then the battle was joined, like a tigress and a lioness in all their savage ferocity.

Time and again Britomart was driven back by the wild, berserk power of the Amazon's attacks. Time and again she counterattacked, and Radigund had to fall back from the merciless might of the British maiden. For hours they fought with undiminished fury, their keen blades so often hewing through armour into flesh that the ground beneath them was slippery with their blood.

But at last Radigund saw an instant when Britomart was briefly off balance, and her sword swept down in a fearsome blow that struck Britomart on the left shoulder, biting deep into the bone. The warrior maiden could scarcely then support her shield, but the agony lent extra strength to her sword arm. Her own blade flashed with deadly accuracy, cleaving through Radigund's helmet and burying itself in the Amazon's brain.

As Radigund fell, Britomart in her battle rage did not hesitate, but swung her deadly sword again and slashed the queen's head cleanly off. As the Amazon army saw the death of Radigund, they turned

Previous page: The attempt to kill Britomart recalls various Spanish-inspired attempts to assassinate Elizabeth, illustrated in this contemporary tract on "Popish Plots"—figures 6, 10, 11, and 13.

and fled in terror—but not swiftly enough to escape Talus, who fell upon them with the irresistible force of a hurricane.

Entering the undefended city, Britomart sought out the place where Radigund kept her slaves, deeply pained to see so many fine knights so humiliated—but even more distressed when she found her own beloved Artegall in similar shame and misery. At once she released him, and found his arms and armour so that once again he could be properly garbed as a noble and manly knight.

They remained in the city while her wounds healed, and in that time Britomart took charge of its government, reordering its affairs with wise justice. Those other knights whom she had freed she made magistrates of the city, after they had sworn fealty to Artegall, and left them there to maintain justice and the right. But soon it was time for Artegall to resume his journey towards his true quest—and with heavy heart Britomart took her leave of him and returned home.

* * *

As Artegall proceeded, he saw in the distance a strange and deadly race. A damsel on a palfrey was fleeing in terror from two Saracen knights, while they in turn were pursued by a knight with a covered shield. Artegall rode to intercept the Saracens, but as he did so one of them turned to confront the lone knight, while the second Saracen swung aside to face Artegall. They hurtled towards each other with lances ready, and the pagan's spear struck firmly—but Artegall's power sent the Saracen sprawling from his saddle. Nor did he rise again, for the fall had broken his neck.

By then the lance of the lone knight, who was Prince Arthur, had slain the second Saracen. Then Arthur hurried in pursuit of the damsel, and found Artegall before him. Each thought the other to be a second enemy, and so they leveled their lances and charged, both lances shattering in that fierce impact. But as they drew swords to continue the combat, the damsel quickly calmed their hot blood, explaining that both were her rescuers.

Seeing their mistake, the two knights raised their visors and made courteous apologies, pledging friendship and fealty to one another. And the damsel told them that she was in the service of a great queen named Mercilla, famed for the wisdom and grace of her rule. But Mercilla was much oppressed by an evil and idolatrous Souldan, who sought to overthrow her and place himself on her throne. Mercilla had sent the damsel, whose name was Samient, to seek some way to achieve peace without warfare—but the Souldan's proud and cruel wife, Adicia, had turned Samient away and sent the two knights after her to capture or slay her.

Artegall and Arthur then undertook to aid the damsel and her queen against the tyrant. They devised a plan by which Artegall would disguise himself as one of the dead pagan knights, and return to the Souldan's palace with Samient, as if she were a prisoner—while Arthur would assail the palace from without, and challenge the Souldan.

So the plan went forward, and Artegall entered the tyrant's palace unsuspected. Soon Arthur rode up to the gates and challenged the Souldan, demanding the release of Samient. In great fury the Souldan armed himself and charged out against the prince, riding on a chariot with hooked blades jutting from its wheels and drawn by vicious horses that were fed on the flesh of men.

The prince moved swiftly aside from the first rush of that deadly vehicle, and as easily dodged the javelin that the Souldan hurled at him. But the speed of the chariot carried the Souldan away from Arthur's counterattack, and the tyrant's second javelin flashed past the prince's guard and drove deep into his side.

Unmindful of the blood pouring from the wound, Arthur pursued the Souldan—and as he did so drew the covering from his enchanted shield. The virtuous light blazed forth, against which no evil thing could stand. And the cruel horses of the Souldan went insane with terror, and bolted, dragging the chariot at a headlong gallop over rocks, through forests, across hills and valleys, while the terrified Souldan fought in vain to halt them. Though Arthur pursued relentlessly, his valour was not needed, for in that wild flight the chariot overturned, and the Souldan was caught up and dragged along, his body shredded into gory rags by the blades fixed to the vehicle.

Arthur carried the tyrant's shield and armour back to the palace, hanging them on a tree to display the Souldan's defeat and death. When the Souldan's wicked wife, Adicia, saw them there, a murderous madness rose in her heart. Seizing a dagger, she ran in fury to find and kill Samient. But the disguised Artegall forestalled her, wresting the knife from her hand. And in her madness she fled raging from the palace into a wild forest, where she was transformed to a savage and cruel tigress.

Artegall then rode against the Souldan's men, fully a hundred knights, attacking with such heroic courage and power that he routed them and put them to shameful flight.

*   *   *

Artegall and Arthur gave the Souldan's palace and all its treasure into the hands of Samient, and prepared to take their leave. But the maiden begged them to ride with her and visit her mistress, Mercilla, and they agreed. On their way Samient mentioned to them an evil being who dwelt nearby and preyed on the folk of the country all around. His name was Malengin, she said, a smooth-tongued and subtle deceiver of great cunning and guile, who lived in a deep cavern set within the natural fortification of a mighty rock.

The knights resolved to put an end to the villain, but knew they must meet guile with guile. They sent Samient ahead to Malengin's rock, weeping pitifully as if in great distress. And as they had hoped, her cries brought Malengin from his cave. He was hollow-eyed and ragged, with long shaggy hair, and bore a staff tipped with many hooks and a great net, with which he caught any who might fall victim to his wiles.

Samient cried out in earnest when she saw him approach, but he began to speak to her with false reassurance, his clever words soon bemusing her so that she was no longer on guard. Then swiftly he flung his net over her and snatched her up, hurrying back to his cave.

But the knights were waiting for him, barring the entrance. Instantly Malengin dropped the maiden and sprang away, pursued by Artegall. But the villain sped over the rocky hillsides and crags as swift and surefooted as a mountain goat, so that not even Artegall could hope, in full armour, to catch him. Instead, he sent Talus in pursuit—and the tireless iron man wore down his quarry and drove him down from the mountain.

Malengin sought to throw off pursuit by changing his form, in quick succession, to a fox, a bush, a bird, a stone, a hedgehog. But Talus followed inexorably; and when Malengin took at last the form of a serpent, the iron man struck so mightily with his flail that the snake was crushed upon the rock.

Afterwards the knights and the maiden continued on their way to the palace of Mercilla. They found it to be a magnificent structure of many high and solid towers, whose gates were guarded against malice and deceit by a mighty giant named Awe. A marshal named Order guided them through a crowd of noisy petitioners, come to seek judgment in their disputes, and brought them into the presence of Mercilla.

She sat on a golden throne, beneath the canopy of a red cloth of state held by cherubs. Lovely as an angel herself, Mercilla grasped the sceptre of clemency, while at her feet were a sheathed sword and a mighty lion held by an iron collar. Around her was a group of white-clad maidens, with Temperance and Reverence among them.

The knights made deep obeisance to the majestic figure, and Mercilla greeted them cordially and brought them up to sit beside her while she concluded the complex judgment that was before her. The prisoner at the bar was a woman who seemed strikingly beautiful,

The witch Duessa returns again to Spenser's poem, to face a trial that is a clear allegory of the trial of Mary, Queen of Scots, kept prisoner by Elizabeth (Mercilla) for 19 years. Drawing by an eye-witness of the trial of Mary (seated on the right) at Fotheringhay Castle, Northamptonshire, in 1586, where she was executed a few months later.

yet with signs of vileness and foul sin in her face. And the knights realized that she was Duessa, the enchantress who had tempted so many fine knights with her false allure, now brought to trial.

The prosecutor, deeply learned and a skilled orator, named Zeal, detailed Duessa's crimes—including at the last a plot to overthrow Mercilla herself, with the aid of the shallow-minded knights Blandamour and Paridell. Then others came to attest to Duessa's evil: sages named Authority, and Kingdom's Care, and Law of Nations; great Religion, and stern Justice.

But others spoke on her behalf, in mitigation, among them Pity and Regard of Womanhood. Grave Danger warned of her threatening alliances, high Nobility spoke of her misfortunes, sad Grief pleaded for her. But Zeal at last brought out the loathsome hag Até, once Duessa's companion but now—true to her nature that loved discord and ruin—treacherously willing to reveal Duessa's plots and treasons and all her wickedness. And other witnesses came to accuse the prisoner: the sins of Murder and Sedition, Adultery and Impiety.

Artegall and Arthur were firm in their decision that she was guilty, and Zeal called for justice against the villainess. So Mercilla could not do otherwise than pass the just sentence of death. Yet she did so not vengefully but sorrowfully, while tears like pearls fell from her eyes.

*   *   *

A 16th-century engraving of the siege of Graave during the English wars in the Netherlands—of which Arthur's battles on behalf of the lady Belge are an explicit allegory.

For some time afterwards Mercilla entertained the knights royally in her house, until a day when two young men arrived with a humble entreaty. Their widowed mother, whose name was Belge, was being oppressed by a tyrant named Geryoneo, who had invaded her lands and slain twelve of her seventeen children, after having won the widow's confidence by sly and false offers of protection.

Portrait of the Earl of Leicester (c.1575), who led Elizabeth's forces against the Spanish in the Netherlands, and who Arthur—here—represents.

The oppressor was a fearsome giant, son of the monster Geryon who had been slain by Hercules. Like his father, Geryoneo had three huge bodies, and three pairs of arms and legs, and was said to be invincibly mighty in battle. But Prince Arthur did not hesitate to offer himself for that adventure, and Mercilla willingly granted that he should pursue it.

While Artegall rode again on his own quest, the prince travelled with the two youths to where Belge was hiding from the tyrant's cruelty, in marshy lowlands, alone and fearful. She greeted Arthur with sad gratitude, but when Arthur suggested that they find some more suitable place for her, she gloomily told him that all her cities and palaces had been sacked and razed by the oppressor, or else occupied by his own forces.

Nonetheless, Arthur took her to a nearby city, overlooked by a tall castle that was now controlled by Geryoneo. The tyrant had set up his idolatrous altar there, and beneath it had placed a ghastly, devouring creature to which many innocents had been sacrificed. And the castle was held by Geryoneo's captain, or seneschal, his most feared warrior, who had vanquished many a brave knight.

Arthur resolutely approached the castle, issuing a ringing challenge to the seneschal, and that warrior armed himself and charged wrathfully out to confront the prince. In their first clash the seneschal's lance struck against Arthur's enchanted shield, and though the point stuck fast the lance itself shattered into fragments. But Arthur's lance drove irresistibly through the enemy's shield and his armour, hurling him lifeless to the ground.

When Arthur rode forward towards the castle, three more knights galloped out and attacked him together. All three lances struck at once, yet like some great bulwark Arthur held firm against them. At the same time his own lance impaled the middle knight, tumbling him dead from his horse, and the other two turned and fled. The prince pursued them to the threshold of the castle, where Arthur's lance found the hindmost, and the corpse fell across the doorway so that the gate could not be closed. Then the prince hunted the third knight through the castle, and slew him in the great hall.

All the rest of the occupants fled in terror, and Arthur brought Belge and her two sons to take their rightful charge of the now deserted castle.

Facing page:
The giant Geryoneo (who is allegorically both Philip II of Spain and the generalized armed might of Roman Catholicism) is modelled on many mythological giants slain by heroes—not only Geryon from the Hercules myths but also the club-wielding, one-eyed Cyclops from the Odyssey (here from a medieval manuscript).

*　　　　*　　　　*

News quickly reached Geryoneo of Arthur's victory over the seneschal, and the lady Belge's return to the castle. A towering rage then took hold of the giant, and he rode at furious speed to the castle,

e flyes pas long ne prolyxe
dtop gruitier dela malice
Blapes qui lueil au Jeant.

where he demanded that it be immediately restored to him, before his wrath should descend on those who were within.

He had no sooner spoken than the gate was flung open, and Prince Arthur rode out in full armour. "Are you the being," asked the prince, "who so cruelly wronged the lady Belge, and drove her into exile?"

"Whatever my actions," roared the giant, "I am here to justify them—with my own hand!" And without warning he hurled himself at Arthur, his huge iron axe slashing murderously down.

The sudden ferocity of the attack forced the prince to give way, and the giant pressed forward, the axe battering at Arthur with power enough to cleave through solid marble. Six giant hands grasped the haft of that weapon, and superhuman strength was in each of the hands. And there was skill as well, for often the giant would pass the axe from hand to hand with bewildering speed, to make his opponent lose sight of it, and so expose himself to a deadly blow from an unexpected direction.

But Arthur kept careful watch on the flailing axe—so that wherever its blade sought to strike, his shield would be there to meet and parry it. Then, while the axe was flickering from one giant hand to another, the prince's sword flashed in a counter-stroke, and sliced off one of the tyrant's arms.

Geryoneo bellowed with pain and fury and swung the great axe high. Arthur pulled back from the terrible blow, and the blade crashed down on his charger's head. But as the horse fell, Arthur leaped lightly from the saddle, ready to continue the battle on foot.

Again the axe struck mightily, a blow that might have cut the prince in two had Arthur not blocked it with his enchanted shield. But his own blow in reply was just as ferocious, hewing through two more of the giant's arms like twigs pruned from a fruit tree.

Cursing, foaming, his teeth gnashing, his eyes bulging, Geryoneo began to lash out in maniacal abandon with his axe. Arthur coolly dodged or parried the enormous blows, always waiting his moment to strike.

The moment came when one tremendous swing of the axe missed its mark and carried the giant off balance for an instant. Before the axe could swing again, Arthur sprang forward and plunged his sword deep into Geryoneo's exposed side. The might of that thrust drove the blade like a skewer through all three of the giant's bodies, and all three fell as one, dead on the blood-drenched ground.

The lady Belge rushed with her two sons from the castle to kneel at Arthur's feet, and all the people from the towns and villages around, who had been watching, hurried as well to cheer the victor. Weeping with joy, the lady said: "Sir knight, you have restored my life just as you have restored my sons to their rightful place. What reward could I give for such a deed, except to offer into your hands all that which you have saved from the tyrant?"

But Arthur raised her to her feet. "Dear lady," he said, "the worth of any deed must not be measured by the might of the one who performed it, but by the justice of the cause itself. I seek no other reward then that which is always virtue's reward—virtue itself."

Timidly then the lady said that another deed remained to be done, for the sacrificial altar of Geryoneo still remained, with its infamous idol, and the accursed flesh-eating monster lurking beneath it. The prince unhesitatingly rode to the altar, and slashed at the golden idol with his sword. And from beneath the altar came a creature bred of hell.

It was vast, and blood-freezingly hideous. Its body was like that of a giant dog, but with the claws of a lion, the barbed tail of a dragon

The monster beneath Geryoneo's altar represents the Roman Catholic Inquisition—and no less ghastly a combination of forms is this portrayal of "Rome" in a 16th-century German etching.

and the wings of a huge eagle. And surmounting that horror was the head and face of a woman—so that it resembled the terrible sphinx, whose riddle was solved at last by Oedipus.

When the creature emerged, Arthur bared the blazing light of his shield, and the monster turned at once to flee in panic. But the prince sprang at her, his sword lashing out, and she had to turn again and fight to save herself. Flying at him in fury, she clutched his shield, and all his strength was not enough to drag it free from that mighty grip. But then his sword flashed across, and sliced off the creature's lion claws.

She screeched demonically, and her enormous tail lashed at Arthur. For an instant the impact staggered him, but before she could strike again he had recovered, and with one mighty blow he hewed through the tail. The monster's screams rose even higher, and in a frenzy she spread her vast wings and hurtled down upon the prince. But he took her weight on his shield, and stabbed upwards with his sword. The blade gashed open her belly, releasing a flood of stinking, poisonous filth as the huge grisly corpse of the monster fell.

Then the cheers and rejoicing of the lady and all her people echoed up to the heavens. All the damsels of the city danced and sang round the victor and crowned him with garlands, and great feasting and merriment continued while Arthur remained, resting, as the honoured guest of the joyous lady Belge.

Meanwhile Artegall, with Talus, had steadily proceeded towards his purpose, to defend the lady Irena from the villainous Grantorto. On his way he encountered an aged knight, Sir Sergis, who sadly told him that Irena had been taken prisoner by the tyrant, who had proclaimed that if no champion appeared within ten days, to do battle on her behalf, she would be put to death.

Vowing to reach her before the ten days had passed, Artegall hastened onward, until he came upon a violent tumult in his path. A lone knight was being hard pressed by a great rabble of wild and uncouth common folk, who seemed to have captured a fair lady, for she was crying and wringing her hands in their midst. Artegall did not recognize the knight, who bore no shield, but he did not hesitate to gallop to his aid. The vast crowd turned at once against him, and might have overpowered him by sheer weight of numbers, had not Talus met them with his flail and scattered them like chaff before the wind.

The other knight approached, humble with gratitude, and told Artegall that his name was Burbon, and that the lady was named Fleurdelis. She had been his beloved until she had been seduced by the evil Grantorto, who had sent the rabble to carry her away.

Under Artegall's questioning, Burbon admitted that he had cast his own shield aside. It had been given him by the Red Cross Knight, and bore the same device. However, too many evil enemies had assaulted him because of that shield, he said, and he had abandoned it. Artegall reprimanded him sternly for that dishonour, but by then the vast mob had regathered, swarming around them threateningly.

Artegall and Burbon set upon them then, with Talus wielding his wrathful flail, and soon they were driving the great throng before them, while the two knights singled out and subdued the leaders. As Talus continued the pursuit, Burbon sprang to the lady whom they had rescued, but she drew haughtily back from his embrace, disdaining his love.

"You have disgraced yourself, lady," said Artegall sharply, "by being untrue to your love. Nothing is more precious than honour, nothing more foul than a breach of faith."

The lady, abashed by his rebuke, then allowed Burbon to lift her to his saddle and carry her away. And with Talus, who had driven the mob into the sea, Artegall returned with all speed to his own appointed task.

Contemporary engraving showing Sir Henry Sidney (father of Sir Philip, and three times lord deputy of Ireland) entering Dublin. Sir Henry is probably the elderly knight Sir Sergis, whom Artegall encounters (p. 154).

*   *   *

Reaching the coast, Artegall and his grim companion took ship to the land where Irena was held prisoner. On its shores they found a vast host of armed men barring the way to their landing. But Talus

O Sydney worthy of tryple re-
nowne,
For plagyng the traytours that
troubled the crowne. 1581.

sprang down and laid about him with the relentless flail, until the armed host fled in disarray, like a flurry of doves under the shadow of an eagle.

As Artegall rode forward through that land, the tyrant Grantorto learned of his presence and sent an army against him. But it was in vain, for the knight and the iron man set upon their enemies with invincible power, strewing the dead over the landscape like seed under the sower's hand. At last Artegall called a halt to the slaughter, and ordered a herald to take a challenge to Grantorto: that he should meet Artegall in single combat for the life of Irena.

The following day, Artegall took the field before the house of the tyrant—and Irena, greatly cheered at seeing him there in battle array, found hope renewing itself within her. Then Grantorto came forth, fully armoured and bearing a heavy, iron-studded poleaxe. He was an immense and powerful giant who had never before been defeated in single combat, his appearance so terrible that many of his opponents had been defeated by fear before striking a blow.

But Artegall met him with fierce courage and determination, and battle was joined. The vast axe whirled in a terrifying flurry of blows, each of them so powerful that no armour could have withstood them. Wisely Artegall dodged and parried that first gigantic onslaught, biding his time; yet even so the cruel axe-blade found its way past his guard, glancing blows that were still enough to draw blood.

But when Grantorto at last swung the axe up to its highest arc to deliver a death blow, the knight stepped close and hewed at the giant's flank with his bright sword Chrysaor. It slashed a deep wound, and both dark blood and loud outcries of pain and rage poured forth abundantly from Grantorto. Yet that mighty blow of the axe fell at the same time, and Artegall warded it off, finding that the blade had driven so deep into his shield that it had stuck fast, and not even Grantorto's strength could wrench it loose.

With the giant encumbered, the knight took his advantage and pressed him hard with a storm of blows. At last one found its mark cleanly, when Artegall's sword thundered with matchless might against the giant's helmet. Grantorto staggered, dazed, and Artegall struck again with the same power—felling the huge villain prostrate on the ground. Swiftly Artegall's blade flashed down to complete the victory, severing the giant's head from his shoulders.

For some time afterwards Artegall stayed in the land of Irena, aiding her to restore peace and to impose the rule of law and justice, and winning the praise of the people for his judicious government— while Talus ranged through the land seeking out and punishing criminals and rebels. But before the task of restoration was complete,

Artegall was recalled to the court of Gloriana, where other tasks awaited him.

When he returned by ship to his own land, a strange encounter took place near the coast. By the wayside stood two loathsome, malevolent hags. One was leathery and thin, holding in her filthy, clawed hands the living body of a poisonous snake, on which she gnawed, the venom dripping from her jaws. She was Envy, who took no pleasure save in others' misfortune, and who as often fed on her own bitter entrails. With her stood the equally ugly hag called Detraction, with a tongue forked like an asp's, holding a distaff on which she spun malicious lies and false calumnies—and who took her pleasure in slander, rumour, and the destruction of reputation.

These horrors had with them a ghastly monster called the Blatant Beast, a creature with a thousand tongues, which the hags had trained to their purposes. And as Artegall passed, this unholy trio turned all their venomous, spiteful evil against him, and against his achievement in the land of Irena.

Detraction cursed and reviled him, accusing him of dishonour and cruelty, and of bringing down Grantorto by treachery. And Envy ran at him, flinging the still living serpent, which strove to sink its fangs into his flesh. At the same time the Blatant Beast raised such an uproar of howling and bellowing that the very earth seemed to tremble with dismay.

But Artegall rode calmly on, ignoring the vicious hags and their creatures, even forbidding Talus to turn back and chastise them, feeling that such action would be both unnecessary and unworthy. So he held unswervingly to his proper course, and to the path that would lead him back to Gloriana's court.

BOOK SIX

The Legend of Sir Calidore, or Courtesy

The Courtesy that is the theme of the sixth book does not mean mere politeness. In Spenser's time it meant "courtliness", the social *savoir faire* and ideal behaviour displayed by perfect gentlemen—which was supposedly found at its best among "courtiers", and therefore naturally best of all at the court of Elizabeth. Sir Calidore represents Courtliness at its highest, a sweet and gentlemanly bearing combined with the manly prowess and heroic virtues of a knight.

His assigned quest is to catch and subdue the Blatant Beast, which represents the slander, calumny, and scandal that is the gravest danger to a gentleman straying from the path of true courtesy. ("Blatant" merely meant "outrageously noisy" in Elizabethan times.) Calidore is of course immune to the Beast's threat, and is as unassailable in his central virtue as Britomart in hers—necessarily, for Calidore also represents Spenser's friend and patron, Sir Philip Sidney, widely acclaimed as the most perfect living embodiment of all the virtues, courtly and knightly, admired by Elizabethans. So Calidore is never found wanting, never needs rescuing, does not even have a companion like all the other books' heroes.

And so, again as with the equally invincible Britomart, Spenser found it necessary to remove Calidore from the action for a considerable time. In his place he introduces Sir Calepine, whose name shows him to be something of an *alter ego* for Calidore. He is a more ordinary man—whose courtesy can be tested and found inadequate, who needs the aid of Arthur, who needs a "redemption" of sorts before he can complete his own adventure.

Before Calidore returns to the action, there is another "diversion" in the story of Timias, which connects the moral virtue of Courtesy explicitly with social (and topical) meanings—for Timias here is Raleigh, imprisoned by Elizabeth because of the "scandal" of his love affair with his wife-to-be.

When Calidore returns to the story, he seems to have forgotten his quest, bemused as he is by the beauties of the pastoral life among shepherds and shepherdesses. Spenser here is both reflecting on the "natural virtue" of these common folk, and reminding us of his mastery of the popular pastoral mode—even introducing his character Colin Clout from the much-admired poems he had written earlier. Then it is necessary for Calidore to rescue his shepherdess (an episode consciously parallel to Calepine's rescue of *his* beloved), after which Calidore returns to his duty and rather hurriedly completes the capture of the Beast.

Certainly Book Six seems less carefully orchestrated than the earlier books. Its strengths and beauties are found more in its digressions, its interludes, than in the central story. But we need not regret that fact overmuch. Far more regrettable is the fact that there was no more to come of the *Faerie Queene*—a fact that seems to be foreshadowed in the slightly bitter admonition of the final stanza.

Portrait of Sir Philip Sidney (1554–86), soldier, scholar, statesman, and poet, who died—heroically —in the Netherlands, fighting the Spanish. Admired by Elizabethans as the embodiment of chivalric virtue and nobility, he was the ideal model for Spenser's knight of Courtesy.

As Artegall rode on his way, he met a knight whom he recognized from the court of the Faery Queen—Sir Calidore, a powerful and doughty warrior, equally admired for his noble virtues and gracious manner. In response to Calidore's friendly interest Artegall related his recent adventures, and their outcome. Then, in turn, he asked Calidore about the purpose of his own journey.

"I am pursuing the Blatant Beast," said Calidore, "a monster bred in hell, which plagues all good knights and ladies with venomous spite and malice."

"I have seen such a beast," Artegall replied, and told Calidore of his encounter near the coast with the many-tongued creature that had howled and railed at him. Delighted to know that his quarry was so near, Calidore took his leave of Artegall, to continue on his own perilous adventure.

Soon afterwards Calidore came upon a young squire bound hand and foot to a tree, calling piteously for help. Calidore released the young man, who explained his plight. A castle nearby, he said, was owned by a proud lady named Briana, who loved a knight named Crudor. But Crudor had wickedly refused to return the lady's love until she presented him with a robe lined with the hair of ladies and the beards of knights. So Briana had placed in the castle a powerful seneschal named Maleffort, with orders to stop every passing knight and lady and demand from them that shameful toll—the loss of their outward badges of manhood or womanhood.

The squire and his lady had been set upon by the seneschal, who had tied the youth to the tree before pursuing the fleeing damsel. And even as the squire spoke, the desperate screams of the squire's lady could be heard in the distance.

Calidore hurried to her aid, and found the seneschal dragging the maiden by the hair towards the castle. When Maleffort saw the knight, he drew his sword and attacked fiercely, but Calidore warded

If Sir Philip Sidney was the perfect courtier, Elizabeth's (Gloriana's) was the perfect court, from which all achievement and glory flowed. Illustration from a volume of writings dedicated to Elizabeth (1580): the queen rides a triumphal car attended by Fame, while the (unknown) author presents his book to her.

off the huge flurry of blows and replied, like a dammed-up river released from restraint, with twice the power and fury of the other.

Fright gripped Maleffort under that mighty onslaught, and he turned and fled to the castle. The guards hastily opened the gate—but then Calidore overtook him, and his powerful sword split Maleffort's skull down to the chin. When the castle guards assailed him, Calidore's flashing blade brushed them aside as if they were no more than flies.

Then he entered the great hall, and confronted the lady Briana. "My beloved will punish you," she shrilled, "and bring shame upon you for what you have done here."

"The shame is yours, lady," Calidore replied, "for seeking to shame others. No man's love is worth having if it means bringing disgrace upon your fellows."

But the furious lady ordered a servant to ride to Sir Crudor, and bring him to seek vengeance on her behalf. And Calidore waited calmly, untroubled by Briana's continuing flood of scorn and reproach.

When Sir Crudor arrived, Calidore rode out to confront him. Lances couched, they charged without a word, and both struck with such accurate force that each was hurled bruisingly to the ground. Rising and drawing swords, they began a relentless fray in which neither warrior seemed even to pause for breath, slashing and hewing savagely till blood covered the ground around them like a lake.

Finally both knights swung up their swords at once, each seeking to end the battle by one supreme blow. But Calidore was the quicker, and his blow landed first—thundering down on to Crudor's helmet and felling him to the ground. Swiftly Calidore wrenched off his enemy's helmet, for the *coup-de-grâce*. But Crudor desperately begged for mercy, and Calidore calmed himself.

"I will grant your life," he said, "on certain terms. You see now how your pride and cruelty have brought you to defeat. Now learn the lesson that no man can hope to overcome others till he can overcome himself, and the frailties that are within all men. Virtue and nobility are as much part of knighthood as is prowess in arms; and so I charge you from now on to show proper courtesy to all knights, and to honour and aid all ladies, whom you encounter."

Crudor willingly swore to the terms in a binding oath. Then Calidore directed him to take the lady Briana to be his love, without any shaming conditions. So both Crudor and his lady were overcome by Calidore's kindness in victory, and humbly pledged loyalty to him. Briana offered Calidore the castle itself, in reparation—but Calidore turned it over to the young squire and his damsel, to recompense them for the wrongs that had been done to them.

Riding on after his wounds were healed, Calidore came upon a dire battle, in which a tall young man, garbed in the Lincoln green of a hunter and armed only with a boar-spear, was confronting a fully armed knight on horseback, while a fair lady stood nearby, watching fearfully. Yet even as Calidore rode up the youth brought the knight down and slew him.

When Calidore remonstrated with the youth for disdaining the laws of chivalry, by attacking a knight when he himself did not bear knightly arms, the youth replied that he meant no disrespect for the law. "But I would break it again if need be," he said, "to defend myself. For it was the knight who first attacked me, as this his lady will attest."

And he told Calidore how he had been hunting in the forest when he saw the knight riding towards him—with the lady afoot. Even more shamefully, when the lady stumbled or slowed the knight would drive her on with blows. The youth had tried to intervene against this ignoble behaviour, but the knight had attacked him.

The lady confirmed the youth's words, and told Calidore of her ill treatment, and how, earlier, her knight had attacked and wounded another knight, while the other was unarmed, in order to win the other knight's lady. But that lady had fled and had hidden, so that the knight had taken out his guilty wrath upon herself.

So Calidore agreed that no blame attached itself to the youth, for the knight had brought his death upon himself by his own breach of the law of arms and his vile behaviour. And turning again to the youth, whose composure and bearing had impressed him, Calidore asked his name and lineage.

The youth replied that he was the son and heir of a king of Cornwall, in Britain, and that his name was Tristram. On his father's death, when Tristram had been but a child, an uncle had usurped the throne—and to protect him from danger Tristram's mother had sent him away, to the land of Faery. There he had remained, undergoing the proper education and training of a young nobleman, though enjoying most of all ranging the wilds as a hunter. But now, he added, it had become time for him to take up knightly arms and follow the way of life that properly befitted his rank.

Calidore, liking the youth even more, and remembering the warlike strength with which he had dispatched the armed knight, at once offered to make Tristram his own squire, and to give him the arms and armour of the knight he had slain, as his victor's due. So the delighted Tristram knelt and swore the chivalric oath, to uphold truth, faith, and honour, and pledged his fealty to Calidore.

But then Tristram was saddened, for Calidore told him that they could not ride together. Calidore had been sent on his quest by the

The lovers Tristan and Isolde, from a medieval French illustrated manuscript. Spenser's Tristram is one of several examples in Book VI of natural, inborn courtesy: the young man has all the chivalric qualities, though he was raised in the wilds, not at court.

Faery Queen, who had enjoined him to pursue it unaccompanied. Instead, Calidore directed the new squire, now wearing the bright armour of his erstwhile enemy, to guide and protect the lady through the wilderness. So they parted, with every expression of courtesy and good will, and Calidore rode on.

After some miles he came upon a knight without armour and badly wounded, while a fair lady, weeping grievously, sought to staunch the bleeding. Realizing that this was the same couple who had suffered at the hands of the brutal knight slain by Tristram, Calidore went to their aid, helping the lady bind the knight's wounds, and easing her grief by assuring her that the one who had brought such misery upon them was now dead.

The lady wanted to convey her beloved to a place where he could be properly tended, yet was reluctant to ask Calidore for further aid —fearing that he might think it demeaning for a noble knight to bear such a burden. But Calidore did not hesitate: placing his own shield on the ground and gently lifting the wounded knight on to it, he and the lady together bore the burden towards a nearby castle.

*   *   *

At the castle they were made welcome by its elderly lord, a wise and gentle knight named Aldus. Then Calidore found that the injured knight whom he had aided was named Aladine, and was the son of that old knight. Despite his shock and grief over his son's wounds, Aldus showed his guests every courtesy, and both he and Calidore sought to ease the distress of the lady, whose name was Priscilla.

She was the daughter of a great lord of that region, who had wished her to marry another highborn nobleman. But Priscilla loved only Aladine, although neither his rank nor his means compared with those of the other suitor. And now she blamed herself for his injuries, since it was because of a tryst with her that he had been in the forest, unarmed, when the brutal knight had come upon them.

But in the morning Aladine regained his senses, and the lovers were reunited in glad affection. And Calidore undertook to return Priscilla safely to her home and reassure her father that no harm or dishonour had befallen her.

On their way Calidore passed by the place where Tristram had slain the brutal knight, who had been the cause of all the young couple's misery, and he beheaded the corpse and took the head with him. Soon they reached Priscilla's home, and there Calidore related to her noble father all that had happened, making it clear that she was no less pure and guiltless than before, and proffering the severed head of the villainous knight as proof of his words. Both the damsel and her father were deeply grateful for his kindness, and in due course he rode on his way.

His path brought him to a hidden glade, where by chance a comely knight was resting, his weapons and his armour put aside, in quiet pleasantry with his lady love. The couple were much embarrassed to be discovered, but the grace and politeness of Calidore's apology for disturbing them soon put them at ease, so that they invited him to pause and converse awhile.

The terrible three-headed dog Cerberus, guardian of the gates of Hades, which Spenser makes the sire of the no less monstrous Blatant Beast, representing scandal. From a sixth-century BC Greek vase.

As he and the other knight, named Calepine, were talking of adventure and knightly deeds, the lady, whose name was Serena, drifted away across the glade, with its wealth of wild flowers. Then from the depths of the forest rushed a foul and hideous beast, its mouth gaping hugely. It snatched her up between its jaws and sped away.

Both knights sprang instantly after her, alerted by her horrified screams. Calidore soon outdistanced the other knight, and overtook the beast—attacking it fiercely, until it dropped its prey and fled at its utmost speed. For it was the Blatant Beast itself, which dared not face Calidore in battle.

Knowing that the other knight would tend to his lady, Calidore followed the Beast. And that relentless pursuit went on as if it would never end, taking the knight and the monster through woods and over hills, far into the distance.

Meanwhile Calepine had come up to the fallen form of his beloved Serena, bleeding profusely from the great gashes that the Beast's fangs had left in her sides. Urgently Calepine lifted her on to his steed, and hurried away, leading the horse, to seek help for her.

Towards the end of the day Calepine saw a stately castle ahead. But a rushing river lay in his path, and he was not sure whether he could ford it on foot. While he considered, an armed knight and a fair lady on a palfrey rode up to the riverside—and Calepine politely explained his and Serena's plight, and asked if he might mount behind the other knight to cross the river.

But the other's reply was cruel and churlish. "Peasant knight," he sneered, "do you think I am so baseborn as to carry such a vulgar burden? Make your own way across, or not at all."

The other knight's lady, distressed by her companion's rudeness, offered Calepine her own palfrey. But anger had blazed up in Calepine. He thanked the lady, but refused, and stalked into the river on foot, leading his own steed with the wounded Serena. During that risky crossing the other knight laughed and mocked so that when Calepine reached the farther shore he wheeled in fury. "You are a blemish on the name of knighthood!" he cried. "I challenge you to alight from your horse and face me on foot in equal combat!"

But the other merely laughed scornfully, as if it were beneath him even to consider a challenge from Calepine, and rode away towards the distant castle, with his lady. So Calepine had no choice but to follow, still seeking some aid for Serena.

At the castle, however, the porter rudely slammed the door in Calepine's face, declaring that no knight could enter until first doing battle with the lord of the castle. For Serena's sake Calepine swallowed his wrath and mildly pointed out that he was exhausted, that his lady was near death, and that he sought hospitality according to the code of knightly courtesy.

Wild men and women, in a 15th-century Swiss tapestry. The wild man who aids Calepine is a clear example of "natural virtue", the "noble savage" whose goodness owes nothing to noble birth or civilized upbringing. It is a major theme in Book VI, counterpointing the courtesy of Calidore and other knightly courtiers.

The porter disdainfully replied that his master, whose name was Sir Turpine, would show courtesy to no errant knight, for one such had once done Turpine a great wrong. But Calepine entreated the porter at least to inform Turpine of their presence. "If he will shelter my lady this night," he added, "I will readily meet him on the field of combat in the morning."

When the porter delivered that message to his master—who was of course the same mocking knight whom Calepine had met at the riverside—he brusquely ordered that Calepine and Serena should be

forbidden to enter. Turpine's lady, Blandina, tried to change his mind, but he would not be persuaded. And so Calepine was turned away, and spent a bitter night in the open, striving however he could to keep Serena sheltered and preserve what life remained within her.

When the life-giving sun rose at last, Calepine carefully placed Serena on his horse again, and moved away in search of other aid. But before long he saw an armed knight galloping furiously after him, and realized that it was the mocking knight from the river, whom he now knew to be Sir Turpine.

As dishonourable as before, Turpine charged without pause at Calepine, who, on foot, could do little but try to dodge the savage thrusts of the lance. But Turpine pursued him as a hunter pursues a beast, until at last the cruel lance found its mark and stabbed deep into Calepine's shoulder. Still the vicious attack continued—and Calepine's life-blood was pouring out, so that he saw death looming inevitably.

*　　　*　　　*

But rescue came in time to Calepine, and in a strange form. A wild man of those woods came on to the scene, drawn by the tumult. He seemed no more than a naked savage, lacking possessions or weapons, apparently knowing nothing of pity or gentleness or other civilized ways. But Calepine's plight and that of Serena touched some chord within the wild man, and moved him to compassion. He sprang to Calepine's aid, careless of Turpine's weapons—for the wild man was invulnerable, thanks to a strange magic that had attended his birth.

Turpine struck fiercely with his lance, but the point rebounded, leaving neither wound nor blood on the wild man's breast. Enraged, the wild man grasped Turpine's shield in a relentless grip, tugging at it with such power that the knight was nearly dragged from his saddle. Terrified, Turpine released his shield and also flung down the encumbrance of his lance before galloping away in headlong flight.

The savage pursued him furiously awhile, but then turned back to where Calepine and his lady lay. He crept to Serena's side, almost fawning like a friendly dog, the pity that he felt showing in his face —for he had no language, and could not speak. Seeing the still bleeding wound of Calepine, the wild man hurried into the forest, returning with a special herb that miraculously stopped the bleeding at once. Then he took up the discarded lance and shield of Turpine, and helped Serena and Calepine to accompany him deeper into the forest to his dwelling.

It was a small clearing where the trees and shrubs grew thickly round and over it, providing perfect shelter. And there the knight and the lady rested while the savage ministered to their hurts. Soon the magical herbs had wholly healed Calepine—though Serena's wounds from the Blatant Beast's fangs were not to be cured so readily.

During their stay with the wild man, Calepine one day wandered into the woods, enjoying the air and the birdsong. Suddenly across his path ran an enormous bear, gripping between its jaws the tiny, screaming form of a child. Calepine gave chase and, unencumbered by his armour which he had left behind, was fleet enough to overtake the bear before long.

Fearlessly Calepine approached, and the bear dropped its prey and turned on him in fury, huge fangs gleaming. Calepine was unarmed as well as unarmoured, but near him lay a large jagged rock. Snatching it up, he thrust it with all his strength between the beast's gaping jaws. And while the bear fought to dislodge the rock, Calepine sprang upon it, evading the deadly claws, and throttled it.

Then he lifted the baby, relieved to find it unscathed by the bear's fangs. But when he set out to return, he found that the pursuit had led him into an unfamiliar part of the forest—and he was lost.

For a long time he wandered, vainly seeking a path that would return him to Serena, while the baby wailed without pause. At last he reached the edge of the forest, and there he met a fair lady, who seemed overcome by grief and woe.

Gently Calepine asked the lady what had troubled her, and she told her story. Her name was Matilde, and she was the wife of Sir Bruin, lord of those lands, which he had wrested from a cruel giant. But recently Bruin had become gloomy, because he and Matilde had not been able to have children—and Bruin feared that if he had no heir the giant would reclaim the lands after Bruin's death. Bruin had been given a prophecy: that he would have a son, who would "be gotten, but not begotten". But his and Matilde's unhappiness had deepened when the prophecy showed no signs of coming true.

Touched by the sad tale, Calepine at once saw how to remedy it— and proffered Matilde the baby whom he had rescued, explaining how he had come to have it. The lady realized that the prophecy had been fulfilled; overjoyed, she took charge of the infant, and returned with it to her husband, where in the years that followed the child grew to become a noble and valorous knight.

Before she left, Matilde offered Calepine the hospitality of her home, and horse and armour if he wished them. But he refused, while thanking her graciously, preferring to remain in the forest and continue his search for Serena.

*　　　　*　　　　*

Meanwhile the wild man had continued to show Serena every courtesy and kindness. At last, worried by Calepine's absence, the wild man searched the woods for him, but failed to find him. And Serena grew ever more woebegone at the loss of her knight, so that the healing of her wounds was retarded even further. Weak as she was, she determined to leave the woods and seek aid elsewhere. And the wild man loyally accompanied her—helping her on to Calepine's horse, then clumsily arraying himself in the knight's armour, though without the sword that Calepine had put carefully away.

But as they travelled, some part of Serena's saddle became dislodged, and the wild man put aside his encumbering armour to help her rearrange it. As they were thus occupied, an armed knight and squire appeared, riding towards them. They were Prince Arthur and his squire Timias, who had been reunited in a strange manner.

Timias, who had earlier regained the love and trust of the virgin huntress Belphoebe, had found their chaste happiness marred by many enemies—three in particular, who sought to harm them not by violence but by guile. They were named Despetto, Decetto, and Defetto, malicious and powerful beings. But even their power was not enough to damage or entrap Timias, until they brought in the reinforcement of the Blatant Beast.

They had sent the Beast to roam the forest where Timias hunted, knowing that the squire would not hesitate to attack the creature once he had seen it. And so it proved: Timias had confronted the Beast, with such valour that the creature had to flee from him, though not before its poisonous fangs had wounded him.

Timias had pursued the monster, which led him to a glade where the three evildoers lay in wait. They had sprung out at the squire, attacking him with a frightening rain of murderous blows. Timias had set his back against a tree like a wild bull at bay, and fought back with grim power. But the villains, assailing him from three sides, had worn down his strength and soon threatened to overpower him.

At that moment, a brightly armoured knight had ridden by and, seeing the unequal combat, had spurred to the squire's rescue. The evil threesome had fled away into the deep woods—and the knight, who was Prince Arthur, found that he had rescued his own long-lost squire. So they were reunited, with great gladness and deep affection, and Timias then accompanied Arthur awhile on his journey, which brought them at last to the encounter with the wild man and Serena.

Seeing an injured lady, and knightly armour scattered on the ground, Arthur and Timias concluded that the wild man had stolen both from some knight whom he had overcome. Timias stepped forward to wrest the possessions from the supposed villain, but the

1602

S.ʳ Walter Raleigh Knight Lord Warden of
the Stanneries   of the
& of the Isle of Iarsey & her M.ᵗⁱᵉ Lieute-
nant general of the Counties of Devonshyre & Cornwall

Æ SÆ 8

Sir Walter Raleigh (1552–1616) with his son Wat, aged eight. The attack on Timias by the Blatant Beast and the trio of villains is an allusion to the scandal created by Raleigh's affair, at the age of 40, with Elizabeth Throckmorton, one of Queen Elizabeth's Maids of Honour, whom he later married. The queen angrily imprisoned both partners in the Tower of London for several weeks.

wild man struck the squire to the ground with a fierce blow of his fist. When Timias sprang up, sword in hand, Serena cried out, halting the conflict, and explained the true circumstances.

So the knight and squire assisted her on to her steed, and rode with her to help her find aid. For Arthur could see how the poison in her wounds made her ever weaker—and the same poison of the Blatant Beast in Timias's wound was also affecting the squire.

As they rode, Serena recounted to Arthur how she and Calepine had fallen foul of the rancourous Sir Turpine. And the prince was outraged, vowing that when he had conveyed her to safety he would return and punish the shame that Turpine brought upon knighthood. Soon, as night closed in, they came upon a small hermitage, standing in a clearing with a little ivy-covered chapel beside it. There an aged and holy hermit lived—once a knight of great prowess and renown, who had eventually turned his back on the world and devoted himself to concerns of the spirit.

The aged man made them welcome, ushering them into his small but cosy hermitage, inviting them to partake of his simple meal. They stayed there overnight, but neither Serena nor Timias could rest with the torment of their wounds. And in the morning, when Arthur sought to depart, both the lady and the squire seemed too weak to be moved. So the prince left them in the old hermit's care, and rode on his way, accompanied by the savage, who had come to admire Arthur's noble bearing, and did not wish to be parted from him.

*   *   *

The wise and kindly hermit is a common figure in medieval and later writings. This hermit is allegorically named "Understanding", in a 16th-century Flemish book entitled Le Chevalier Delibéré.

The wounds inflicted by the Blatant Beast were like all the injuries caused by slander and poisonous infamy—almost without a cure. But the old hermit was deeply learned in all the arts of healing, whether of afflictions of the body or illnesses of the passions and the spirit. He spoke at length to Serena and Timias, telling them more of the dire Beast that had injured them. It was hell-born, he said, of the ghastly Echidna, who was half-woman and half-dragon, and the monstrous Typhaon. And no knight or lady, however upright and honest, had ever been safe from the poisonous gall in the Beast's tongue and wounding fangs.

"Only in yourselves does your healing lie," the hermit told them. "By self-restraint, and discipline, and proper honourable behaviour. Far better would it be to use these means to avoid the Beast in the first instance; certainly only they can cure its effects."

Serena and Timias listened carefully, and took the hermit's words so much to heart that the infection in their wounds began to abate. Within a short time the healing was complete, and they could take their leave of the hermit, going forth together, for Timias would not leave the lady unprotected.

Earlier Arthur and his savage companion had ridden in search of Turpine, to punish him as the prince had vowed. At Turpine's castle they found the gate standing open, and Arthur entered, leaving his horse in the wild man's care. He feigned a slow and feeble walk— and when an uncouth groom stopped him and demanded to know what he was doing there, the prince mildly claimed to be suffering from wounds and seeking shelter and hospitality.

True to his master's way, the groom abusively ordered Arthur out of the castle, and seized him as if to hurry him on his way. But the wild man had come in, and he sprang at the groom in a savage fury, and tore him to pieces. The uproar brought others from within the castle, who saw the groom's corpse and vengefully attacked the intruders. But Arthur stood against them with invincible might, slaying many and driving the others back.

By then Turpine had armed himself and advanced to the hall, accompanied by forty yeomen. At once they assailed the prince, heaping blows upon him like hailstones in a tempest—although the shameful Turpine crept behind the prince to strike a cowardly blow at his back. But the prince saw his intent and turned on him with his furious sword, and pursued him through the struggling throng. From room to room the prince chased him, cornering him at last in the room of his lady, Blandina, and felling him with a thunderous blow against his helmet.

But Blandina flung herself across Turpine's body, begging Arthur to spare her lord's life. So Arthur stayed his hand, while Turpine tottered to his feet, dazed and terrified. Arthur reproached him fiercely for his unknightly behaviour, and ordered him to forego bearing arms and professing knighthood, if he wished to remain alive.

Then Arthur left them, for the wild man was alone and still facing the forces of their enemies. Hurrying back to the hall, he found the savage unharmed, tirelessly battling with a few remaining yeomen while the corpses of the rest lay strewn bloodily around the hall. Arthur stopped the slaughter and calmed the savage's fury, then took him back to the chamber where Blandina and Turpine remained. There the savage might have leaped at Turpine's throat, remembering him as the one who had dishonourably harmed Calepine and Serena, but again Arthur restrained him.

Believing that peace and order had come at last to the castle, Arthur remained there overnight, where he was lavishly entertained by the courteous and charming Blandina. The guileless prince did not see that the lady's charm was a mask, for she could feign whatever beguiling emotions that she wished. Nor did he realize how bitter resentment was gnawing within Turpine.

In the morning Arthur and the wild man departed, and Turpine followed them, waiting for an opportunity to do them harm. Soon Turpine came upon two comely young knights, riding together in fellowship. Greeting them, he told them how dishonour had been brought upon himself and his lady by Arthur, and promised them both renown and reward if they would avenge him. The young knights at once boldly rode after the prince, and when they overtook him issued their challenge.

Both charged together, and Arthur spurred to meet them. The lance of one missed its mark, so that its wielder hurtled harmlessly past; but the lance of the second struck fairly on Arthur's shield, and shattered into pieces. At the same time Arthur's lance drove accurately against the helmet of the second knight, thrusting through the metal and tumbling him dead on to the ground.

The first of the young knights, recovering, charged again, but his lance-point glanced harmlessly from Arthur's shield, and the prince's lance swept the young man from his saddle to the ground with crushing force. Arthur sprang down, sword in hand, but the young knight begged for mercy—and Arthur granted him his life. Then the prince demanded to know why the two had attacked, and the young knight, whose name was Enias, revealed Turpine's plot.

Irate at such villainy, Arthur ordered Enias to bring Turpine to him, and the young knight swore to do so. At length Enias found Turpine, and told him that the vengeance had been accomplished, and that Turpine's enemy lay slain. Eagerly Turpine followed Enias back to the scene of the battle, where he found the corpse of Enias's companion, and also what seemed to be the body of Arthur.

But the prince had merely lain down on the grass to rest, after setting aside his armour, and had fallen asleep, while the wild man had wandered off into the woods to gather the fruit that was his principal diet. Realizing that Arthur was not dead, Turpine tried to steal away; but Enias held him back, angrily declaring that since Turpine's lies had caused the death of the other young knight, Turpine would not escape punishment. Turpine tried to wheedle Enias into letting him go, even suggesting that the two of them might slay Arthur while he slept. But Enias rejected such treachery—and while they spoke, the wild man returned.

Instantly the savage dropped his burden of fruit and snatched up a weapon he had acquired: a heavy club made from an oak tree, which he wielded as if it were a hazel wand. But the noise awoke Arthur, and he sprang up, grasping Turpine by his collar. The base knight fell to his knees, begging for mercy, but Arthur would not this time be swayed. He stripped the villain of his arms and all emblems of knighthood, and strung him up by his heels to a tree, to be an example of dishonour to all who passed.

Meanwhile the squire Timias and the lady Serena, on their journey, had encountered the strange sight of a lovely lady clad in mourning, riding on a mangy donkey led by a giant and followed by a cruelly laughing fool.

The lady's name was Mirabella, who though she had been lowly born had won great fame throughout Faeryland because of her great beauty. She had been wooed by many a fine knight—but she had grown over-proud, and scorned the love of all her admirers, enjoying more the power that she could cruelly wield over them. Those whom she rejected languished in the depths of their misery, and many died. And their deaths made Mirabella even more proud and arrogant, feeling herself almost godlike in the power of her beauty.

But a time came when Cupid held his court on St Valentine's Day, and found that the numbers of lovers who were expected to attend were woefully diminished. When the god sought the reason, he was told—by Infamy and Spite—of the deaths caused by the cruel Mirabella. So the wrathful god sent a bailiff named Portamour to bring the lady to justice.

At her trial Mirabella's stubborn pride gave way, and she pleaded

Mirabella echoes the theme of Beauty turned cruel and disdainful, a conventional subject in the great Elizabethan sonnet sequences (including Spenser's). Painting by Titian, often called "Profane Love" or "Vanity".

for mercy. And Cupid, who is not cruel unless provoked, granted that she should live, but imposed a penance. She would travel the world accompanied by the giant Disdain, and the fool Scorn—and she would continue until she had saved the lives of as many lovers as she had slain.

When Timias and Serena encountered her, she had been wandering for two years, and in that time had saved only two—though those whom she had destroyed, before, numbered twenty-two. So she continued on her doleful way, while Disdain railed at her with cruel abuse, and Scorn lashed her with his whip.

Indignation and pity rose in Timias when he saw a fair lady so mistreated, and he attacked the giant, hurling him away. But Disdain was vast and terrible, a kinsman of the giant Orgoglio who had taken the Red Cross Knight captive. He wore a quilted leather jacket, with a Moorish turban on his head, and he wielded a mighty iron club.

They knew nothing of the Beast, but they saw Calidore's weariness and kindly invited him to stop and rest with them. He gladly accepted, taking pleasure in their natural courtesy and the homely refreshment they offered him. Then his eye was caught by a fair damsel, garlanded with flowers and clothed in green homespun. She was surrounded by shepherds and shepherdesses, playing musical instruments and sweetly singing a song of love and praise to her, to which she listened with a gentle grace and modesty that equalled her loveliness. All the shepherds seemed smitten with love for the maiden, whose name was Pastorella, none more than a swain named Coridon; but she in her maidenliness returned the love of none of them. And, watching, Calidore too felt the power of love take hold of him.

As dusk gathered, the shepherds gathered up their flocks to drive them home. Pastorella accompanied her father, old Meliboe—though he was not in fact her true parent, for he had found her in the fields, an abandoned infant, and had raised her as his own. Coridon and the other shepherds vied with one another to help the lovely damsel, while Meliboe courteously invited Calidore to shelter in his home that night, which the knight gratefully accepted.

After the evening meal he and Meliboe fell into conversation about the happiness that could be found in the simple life of a shepherd. Meliboe was eloquent about the peace and contentment in such a life, asserting that he envied no man, however rich or great, preferring the humble joys of nature's bounty, which, with his flocks, satisfied all his needs.

Nymphs and shepherds painted by Titian. The romantic idealization of the beauty, peace, and natural virtue of pastoral life was a universally popular theme in Renaissance art and literature.

Calidore was much impressed by the old man's description of rural bliss, just as he was still overcome with love for the fair Pastorella. "I can see," he said to Meliboe, "how happiness might be more readily found in this humble place than among the great and the mighty, where glory and ambition rule."

"A man's happiness must be found within himself," said Meliboe wisely, "whatever his rank or degree. Many that have much yet want more; many who have little are content with it."

"If it is given to each man to shape his own life," Calidore replied, "then by your leave I would wish to make my life here with you awhile, and rest from the stormy world of trouble and pain."

Meliboe willingly invited him to stay, nor would he take any of the gold that Calidore offered in payment for that hospitality. So the knight made his home among the shepherds, and from then on paid attentive court to Pastorella, with all the gentle and pleasing courtesies that he could muster. To make himself more welcome in her eyes he put aside his arms and donned rough shepherd's garb, and accompanied her into the fields to guard the flocks.

The shepherd Coridon grew jealous at Calidore's constant devotion to the damsel, yet could find no fault in the knight's manner, no sign of malice or a comparable jealousy. Whenever Coridon joined them Calidore was kind and friendly, even praising the small gifts that the shepherd would bring to Pastorella. But the maiden showed little interest in Coridon, growing more and more affected by Calidore's attentions.

One day all the shepherd folk took themselves to merrymaking—dancing to the tune of the best piper among them, Colin Clout. And they all called for Pastorella to lead the dance, with Calidore. But the knight graciously stood back, and sent Coridon instead to dance with the maiden; and when Pastorella made a garland for his brow, Calidore generously placed it on Coridon's head, to ease the shepherd's unhappy jealousy. Later, the dancing gave way to sports and games, and Coridon challenged Calidore to wrestle, seeking to demean him. But Calidore's knightly skill prevailed, and he threw Coridon with such force as nearly to break his neck; yet when Pastorella placed on him the victor's oak-leaf crown, again he modestly gave it to Coridon in praise of the shepherd's efforts.

So Calidore's fair and graceful courtesy won the hearts of all those simple folk, and stirred in the heart of Pastorella the seeds of a perfect love. And little blame should be attached to Calidore for turning aside from his high quest, since with the shepherds he learned the importance of love, simplicity, and true virtue.

*　　　*　　　*

Spenser made his first major impact on Elizabethan literature with his sequence of twelve pastoral poems, the Shepheardes Calendar *(1579). Illustrations from a later edition of the* Calendar: *top, from the "April" section, obviously in praise of Elizabeth: the shepherd piper is Colin Clout—the central character of the* Calendar, *and a pseudonym for Spenser himself. Below, from "December", Colin in less merry a mood.*

One day, ranging over the fields while Pastorella was busy elsewhere, Calidore came upon a place where nature had poured forth all her skill to create ideal beauty. It was a grassy hill, surrounded by a wood, with a silvery brook at the foot of the hill that had never been polluted with uncleanliness. The hilltop was level, offering an inviting place to stroll or dance—and on that promontory, called Acidale, Venus herself was said sometimes to seek repose.

When Calidore came upon it, he heard the sound of a merry shepherd's pipe, and saw on that hill a hundred nude damsels moving in a graceful circular dance. Within their circle were three more maidens, also nude and beautiful beyond compare, themselves circling round a damsel who was the most beautiful of all. The three sang to her and strewed flowers and fragrances about her, while the shepherd played his sweet music for love of her.

180

The Three Graces, painted by Rubens. The maiden around whom the Graces dance, in Book VI, may be the shepherdess Rosalind, Colin Clout's beloved in the Shepheardes Calendar—*but her presence may also be a graceful compliment to Spenser's own wife Elizabeth, to whom he addressed many poems.*

But as Calidore, enraptured, drew closer, the entire throng of damsels vanished entirely from sight. And the shepherd, furious with disappointment, flung down his pipe with such force that it broke in two. Calidore at once made every courteous apology for his intrusion, placating the shepherd, and then asked who and what the lovely damsels were.

The shepherd, who was Colin Clout, told him that they were all the handmaidens of Venus, and that the three in the centre were the Three Graces, daughters of Jove, whose names were Euphrosyne, Aglaia, and Thalia. "They are the givers to men," said Colin, "of all that makes us comely and well-favoured to others—the gifts of courtesy, the skills that we call civility."

So, he added, they are always smiling and mild, and always naked because without guile or dissemblance. And the fourth maiden in the centre of the ring was Colin's own true love, a mortal damsel of such beauty and gentle virtue that she had been brought by the Graces to be herself another Grace.

Then Calidore regretted even more that he had disturbed the beautiful scene, and stayed awhile with Colin to enjoy both his company and the glories of that place. But eventually the demands of his love for Pastorella drew him back to her side.

There, as before, the jealous Coridon stayed near to them, striving always to supplant Calidore in the maiden's affection. But one day, while the three of them were gathering berries in the woods, a fierce tiger sprang out of hiding and charged at Pastorella. Coridon was struck with fear and took to his heels—but Calidore, though carrying only a shepherd's crook, halted the beast's attack and felled it with a tremendous blow, then hewed off its head and presented it at Pastorella's feet.

From then on her love for him was without limits, and they were joined together in felicity and deep fulfilment. But after a time, on a day when Calidore was away hunting in the woods, a band of lawless brigands descended on the shepherd settlement—looting, destroying and slaying, and leading the survivors away as captives. And among those whom the brigands took back to their hideout, dark caves and tunnels beneath a hidden island, were Coridon, Meliboe, and Pastorella.

The brigands took captives to sell them into slavery; but the brigand chief, fired to lust by Pastorella's beauty, decided to keep her for himself. By many crude blandishments he sought to win her affections—and though the maiden repulsed him for many days, in the end she deemed it wiser and safer, since she was so wholly in his brutal power, to pretend that she was being swayed by his attentions. But when he grew even more determined, she feigned illness in order to keep him from her.

Then the hideaway was visited by the merchants who came to buy the captives, as slaves. The thieves brought out Coridon and Meliboe and the rest, but then clamoured that their chief should produce Pastorella, who would claim a vast price. The chief declared that she was not to be sold, since her illness had wasted her and made her worthless. But the merchants went to her bedside to see for themselves, and even in that gloomy prison Pastorella's loveliness shone like a diamond. So the merchants insisted that if they could not have her they would not buy any of the captives.

The other brigands, seeing the promise of wealth slipping away, demanded that she be sold. The chief drew his sword, asserting that she would remain his—and like a pack of dogs fighting over carrion, the brigands began a wild, murderous brawl.

Many were slain in that tumult, including most of the prisoners, who were killed so they would not rise against their captors. Old Meliboe was one of those who fell, but Coridon craftily took his opportunity to creep away in the darkness and so made his way to freedom.

The brigand chief fought furiously, but in the end he was overwhelmed and slain, and his corpse toppled across Pastorella. By then the maiden too had been wounded by a sword-slash, but other corpses were heaped above her where she lay and kept her from further harm. Then at last the brigands halted their savage slaughter, and began searching through the heaped bodies for any who lived. They came upon the maiden, weak and fainting from loss of blood; but they revived her, putting her in the charge of one of the cruellest of their number, who gave her neither food nor treatment for her wound.

Meanwhile Calidore had returned to the settlement and found the destruction and horror that the brigands had left. Grieving and raging, he began a vengeful search, but found no indication in woods or fields or plain of where the villains, and his Pastorella, might be.

Then one day he came upon a ragged figure who seemed to be in flight from some danger, and the knight recognized his former rival, Coridon. When he demanded of the shepherd where Pastorella and the others were, Coridon through tears and great sighs told him of their captivity, the brawl in the brigands' caves, and how most of the prisoners had been slain—no doubt, he added, Pastorella among them.

Calidore was so stricken that he grew near to killing himself. However, his mourning soon changed to fury, and he vowed to avenge his beloved's death or to die, and join her, in the attempt. Guided by Coridon, he made his way to the brigands' hideout, but now he wore his armour beneath his shepherd's garb. On their way they came upon substantial flocks of sheep, which Coridon recognized as those from his own settlement, stolen by the brigands. Calidore approached the brigand herdsmen guarding the flocks, pretending that he was merely a wandering swain, so hoping to gain news of Pastorella. And during their conversation Calidore learned what he most hoped to hear—that while the other captives were dead, Pastorella still lived.

That night, Calidore slipped away from the others and made his way to the brigands' caves—alone, for the fearful Coridon stayed behind. The cave door was fastened solidly, but Calidore's determined power smashed it aside. And when the brigand guarding

The entry by Calidore into the brigands' caves follows the theme of the "descent to the underworld" in many hero myths, especially that of Orpheus. In this 16th-century illustration from a French edition of Ovid's Metamorphoses, *Orpheus pleads with the god of the underworld for the return of Eurydice, his wife.*

Pastorella rushed out at the noise, Calidore slew him effortlessly; then he entered the chamber and gathered his joyful shepherdess into his arms.

But the other brigands had also been alerted, and the entire throng mustered to attack the intruder. Calidore met them in the doorway, so that only a few could come at him at once, and wielded his sword with such fury that soon the door was heaped and clogged with corpses, so that no others might enter. Behind that barrier Calidore rested, until daybreak—then burst through the wall of bodies and fell upon the remaining brigands.

He raged into their midst like a lion in a herd of deer, his sword hewing and striking on every side until another heap of corpses was piled up on the cavern floor, and the few remaining brigands took to their heels to save their lives. Then Calidore brought Pastorella out into the light of day, and afterwards brought out all the looted treasure hidden in the caves. The finest of this he gave to Pastorella, and the stolen sheep he gave into the care of Coridon, before carrying his beloved away.

*   *   *

He took his shepherdess to the castle of a great lord, Bellamour, who in his youth had been among the most famed knights of the land. At that time Bellamour had loved the fair Claribell, daughter of the Lord of Many Islands, who had promised her to the Prince of Pictland. But she too loved Bellamour, and eventually they contrived to marry in secret.

When Claribell's father learned of the marriage, in his rage he threw them into a dungeon, in separate cells. But Bellamour bribed a jailer so that he might see his bride—and over the months she became pregnant, and gave birth to a girl-child. Fearing that her father might kill the child, Claribell gave it to a handmaid, Melissa, ordering her to place the baby somewhere so that it could be nurtured by others in safety.

Melissa took the baby to the fields and, while adjusting its coverings before leaving it there, noticed a small birthmark on the baby's breast, like a tiny rose. Then she laid the baby down, and watched from hiding as a shepherd, drawn by the infant's wails, came and took it up, carrying it home where it was raised by the shepherd's wife as if it were her own.

Some time afterwards Claribell's father died, and she and Bella-mour were freed from the dungeon and able to live in proper state. So they had spent many years of happiness and love together—and in the same way they made Calidore and Pastorella welcome, and Claribell gladly tended the shepherdess's wound and made her comfortable. Then Calidore, seeing that his beloved would be well looked after, recalled to himself the task put upon him by the Faery Queen, which he had forsaken for so long.

In his absence Pastorella was sad and forlorn, but soon her health returned, under the careful tending of Claribell's old handmaid, Melissa. And one day while the maid was helping Pastorella to dress, she noticed a strange mark on the shepherdess's breast—a birthmark, shaped like a tiny rose.

At once Melissa recognized it, and hastened to Claribell. And when that lady herself had seen the mark, she too knew that Pastorella was her own child, whom she had so long ago been forced to abandon. With tearful gladness she embraced Pastorella, and made known to the maiden her true parentage. Then all the castle rejoiced that Bellamour and Claribell had regained their daughter.

In that time Calidore had relentlessly resumed his search for the Blatant Beast. He sought it throughout the land, everywhere finding the destructive signs of where it had been. And that trail of outrage and havoc led him at last to a monastery where the Beast was even then engaged in its monstrous work. Hating all goodness, it had

The Blatant Beast's desecration of a holy place reflects the destructive anti-church feelings of some groups in Spenser's time, including the more extremist Puritans. Illustration from a book, printed in 1587, on heresy.

broken into the monastery, driving the monks into flight, scattering its ordure and filth, throwing down the sacred objects, ruining and despoiling everything in its path.

But when it saw Calidore advancing upon it, the Beast fled, knowing the danger that he presented to it. Calidore pursued with all his speed, and soon overtook the monster, forcing it to turn at bay. Then it charged at him, its vast mouth gaping with its iron fangs and all of its thousand tongues: some the tongues of cruel and noisy beasts, some the poisoned tongues of serpents, some the lying tongues of men.

Calidore struck at the Beast with furious might, and drove it back. But it reared up, the poison of its spite and rage foaming round its jaws, slashing at him with deadly claws. Calidore blocked that attack with his shield, and his heroic strength flung the Beast over on to its back. Then Calidore sprang on it, pinning it to the ground, and grimly maintaining that mighty grip no matter how the Beast foamed and bit and clawed as it struggled to break free. The poison that it spat had no effect on the knight—nor did the foul, lying outcries that it made against his honour with all its evil tongues.

186

At last the Beast began to weaken in the knight's unflagging grasp. And Calidore took a great muzzle forged of sturdy iron and fastened it round that hellish mouth so that its vile and slanderous lies were silenced. Then he took a great chain of iron and bound it round the Beast. Never before had its power been so restrained; cowed and trembling, it followed obediently like a fearful dog as Calidore led it away.

Throughout the land of Faery it followed the knight, and all the people thronged wherever Calidore went to see the monster now chained and silenced. And it remained silenced for a long time after, until, whether by ill fortune or the fault of man, it broke those bonds and escaped. From then on it could never be overcome again, though many a brave knight attempted the task. And so it roams free to this day, pouring out its vile calumnies, sparing no one from its venomous assaults—whether great nobles or fair ladies, or learned scholars, or even poets. Nor may the author of this tale hope to escape its wicked spite.

Portrait of Spenser, an engraving from an edition of the Faerie Queene *published after his death.*

NOTES ON THE ILLUSTRATIONS

Figures in **bold** refer to illustrations in colour
JACKET *Garden of Delight*, from a medieval miniature. *Robert Harding*
FRONTISPIECE *Elizabeth going in procession*—attributed to Robert Peake (d.1619). *Simon Wingfield Digby, Esq., Sherborne Castle*

GLOSSARY/INDEX

The following list includes capsule explanations of the characters' allegorical roles and, where necessary, their names, as well as definitions of some of the less familiar terms that have been retained. Page numbers in *italics* refer to captions.

Acrasia: from Greek, 'uncontrolled'; allegory of sexuality taken to destructive extremes 51, 54, 55, 61, 77–81, 84

Acrates: from Greek, 'uncontrolled'; a 'deity' apparently invented by Spenser 59

adamantine: mythical crystalline stone, impervious and unbreakable 80, 130

Adonis, Garden of: from myth of Venus's love for the youth Adonis; earthly paradise, allegory of fertility 74, 95, 105

Aemylia: *see* Amyas 120–3

Aladine: from Latin, 'nourishing'; allegory of love in conflict with social conventions 164

Albion: archaic name for Britain: 73, 102

Aldus: derivation uncertain; *see* Aladine 164

Alma: from Italian, 'soul'; allegorical ruler of the body, represented by her house 51, 71–6, 72, 84

Amavia: from Latin, 'lover of life' 53–5, 54

Amazons: warrior women of Greek myth allegory of 'improper', overturned social order 129, 138–41, 139, 144

Amendment: i.e. 'correction', personified 41

Amidas: from Latin, 'loving'—of property 137–8

Amoret: from Italian, 'little love'; allegory of chaste married love and its enemies, especially sexual 83, 95, 105, 106–9, 116, 118, 119–20, 119, 122–3, 125, 126

Amyas: from Latin, 'friend'; the 'squire of low degree', allegory of true friendship 120–3, 122

angel: symbol of God's grace conferred on Guyon 67

Angela: Saxon warrior-queen invented by Spenser 90

Antiquity of Faeryland: chronicle-history invented by Spenser 73

Archimago: i.e. 'supreme master of the image'; allegorical figure of deceit, also representing religious hypocrisy, Catholicism, the Pope 13, 17–18, 17, 22, 30, 49, 51–2, 56, 64–5, 67–70

Argante: allegory of sexual perversion 98, 105

Ariosto, Ludovico: Italian poet (1474–1533), author of the heroic romance *Orlando Furioso* 59, 85

Artegall: i.e. 'equal to Arthur'; knight of Justice and specific allegory of Lord Grey de Wilton 83, 90–1, 115, 116, 117–18, 129, 130–50, 130, 132, 140, 154–7, 155, 160

Arthur, Prince: representing 'magnificence' and the perfection of all knightly virtues; some details are borrowed from Malory's, *Morte d'Arthur* (printed 1485), others are Spenser's invention 13, 32–8, 34, 37, 51, 56, 68–76, 68, 83, 84, 92–3, 95, 121–3, 129, 145–54, 149, 150, 159, 169–74, 176–7

Astraea: Roman goddess of justice 130, 130

Ate: Greek goddess of discord 108, 109–10, 114, 116, 123, 149

Atin: name derived from Ate; allegory of malicious wrath 59–60, 61, 63, 64–5, 67–70

Avarice: one of Seven Deadly Sins 23, 24

Bacchante: from Italian, 'revelling'; one of seven brothers representing stages in a sexual relationship, or a seduction 87

bailiff: high-ranking servant, usually an overseer on an estate 174

Basciante: from Italian, 'kissing'; *see* Bacchante 87

beads: Catholic rosary, used to 'tell off' a sequence of prayers 21

beast man: allegory of animal lust; *see also* wild men 119–20, 119

Belge, Lady: allegory of the Netherlands, oppressed by Spain 129, 149, 149, 150–4

Bellamour: from French, 'beautiful love'; the story of Pastorella's rediscovered parentage is a common plot in romance 185

Belphoebe: from Italian, 'beautiful', with 'Phoebe', alternative name for Diana; allegory of celibate chastity, and a representation of Elizabeth 57, 83, 94–5, 94, 120–1, 139, 169

bill-hook: long-handled cutting tool, often adapted for battle 94

Bladud: ancient British monarch 73, 91

Blandamour: from Latin, 'flattering', with French, 'love'; allegory of shallow love and unreliable friendship 109–11, 114–15, 116, 123, 148

Blandina: from Latin, 'flattering', 'blandishment' 167, 172–3

Blatant Beast: from a form of 'bleating', i.e. 'noisy'; allegory of malicious slander 157, 159, 160, 165, 165, 168, 169, 171, 171, 172, 177, 185–7, 186

blazon: heraldic emblem on knight's shield 13, 80, 91, 100, 110, 125

boar-spear: sturdy javelin used in hunting wild boar 57, 94, 162

Bower of Bliss: derived from the convention in romance of a garden-paradise, transformed by Spenser into an allegory of corrupting sensual excess 51, 51, 54, 61, 77–81, 79, 81

Bracidas: from Greek, 'loss of property'; *see* Amidas 137–8

Braggadochio: Italianate term for 'boastfulness'; a conventional comic figure in Renaissance writings 56–8, 94, 100, 110, 114, 116, 123, 136–7, 137

Briana: derivation uncertain; *see* Crudor: 160–61

British Monuments: history based by Spenser on actual medieval chronicles of ancient Britain 73–4

Britomart: name from a poem by Virgil about a chaste maiden, but also a blend of 'Britain' and 'martial'; knight of Chastity and another representation of Elizabeth 83, 84–91, 84, 85, 102, 105–10, 115–16, 117–19, 123, 126, 129, 131, 141–5, 144, 159

Bruin: story from Irish legend of heroes descended from a bear 168

Burbon: royal house of Bourbon; allegory of Henry of Navarre, who abandoned Protestantism in 1593 to gain French throne 154–5

Busirane: from name of Egyptian king; allegory of illicit sexual passion 105, 107

buskins: calf-length boots 139

caduceus: staff of Roman god Mercury, winged with two entwined serpents 77

Calepine: 'alter ego' for Calidore, but also an allegory of Courtesy as 'mildness' 159, 165–9, 166, 173, 177

Calidore: from Greek, 'beauty'; knight of Courtesy, identified with Sir Philip Sidney 159, 160–5, 166, 177–87, 184

Cambell: story borrowed from Chaucer; allegory of true friendship and harmonious 'concord' 83, 111–15, 111

Cambina: *see* Cambell 111, 114, 116

Canacee: *see* Cambell 111, 112, 116

Castle Joyous: allegory of sexual licence *see* Malecasta 86–9

Celia: from Italian, 'sky' or 'heaven'; her home is the house of God on earth 13, 40, 41, 43

charger: battle-trained war horse of armoured knight 23, 46, 52, 54, 56, 58, 60, 75, 85, 91, 117, 130, 152

Charissa: the virtue of Charity, sister to Faith and Hope 40, 41, 42

Chaucer, Geoffrey: 1340–1400; author of the *Canterbury Tales*, admired by Elizabethans as the first and greatest English poet 59, 111, 111

chivalry: code of gentlemanly conduct and idealized (romanticized) framework for the life of a knight, involving prowess in battle, high-principled devotion to a lady, concepts of Christian duty, and a questing for both personal glory and spiritual fulfilment 56, 68, 84, 89, 108, 109, 140, 144, 159, 162

Chrysaor: from Greek, 'gold sword'; wielded by the god Zeus in Homer's *Iliad* 130, 132, 156

Chrysogone: from Greek, 'golden-born'; based on many 'spontaneous pregnancies' in Greek myth 94

city of God: the heavenly New Jerusalem, ultimate goal of God's chosen; echoing St John's vision in the Book of Revelations 43, 44

Claribell: from French, 'bright beauty'; the knight with this name, oddly, is a figure of false love; the lady who bears it is more deserving of it (*see* Bellamour) 123, 185

Clarin: based on Dido's handmaiden in Virgil's *Aeneid* 139, 140–1

Cleopolis: from Greek, 'city of glory'; Gloriana's capital 43, 74

Clout, Colin: name for a shepherd first used by poet John Skelton (1460–1529) 159, 179, 180, 181, 181–2

Concord: personified; allegory of the role of harmony in the universe and human relationships 125

Corflambo: from French, 'heart-flame'; allegory of destructive sexuality 122

Coridon: name of a shepherd in Virgil's pastoral *Eclogues* 178–9, 182–3

coup-de-grâce: death blow struck by victorious knight on fallen opponent 70, 70, 140, 161

courtier: nobleman in attendance at royal court 24, 25, 47, 159, 159

courtly love 109

Crudor: from Latin, 'crude' or 'cruel'; allegory of overbearing discourtesy 160–1

189